W9-BKF-848

# THE
# LINES
# WE
# CROSS

## ALSO BY RANDA ABDEL-FATTAH

Does My Head Look Big In This?

Ten Things I Hate About Me

Where the Streets Had a Name

# THE
# LINES
# WE
# CROSS

Randa Abdel-Fattah

Scholastic Inc.

If you purchased this book without a cover, you should be aware that this book is stolen property. It was reported as "unsold and destroyed" to the publisher, and neither the author nor the publisher has received any payment for this "stripped book."

Copyright © 2017 by Randa Abdel-Fattah

First published in 2016 in Australia as *When Michael Met Mina* by Pan Macmillan Australia Pty Ltd 1 Market Street, Sydney, New South Wales, Australia, 2000

This book was originally published in hardcover by Scholastic Press in 2017.

All rights reserved. Published by Scholastic Inc., *Publishers since 1920*. SCHOLASTIC and associated logos are trademarks and/or registered trademarks of Scholastic Inc.

The publisher does not have any control over and does not assume any responsibility for author or third-party websites or their content.

No part of this publication may be reproduced, stored in a retrieval system, or transmitted in any form or by any means, electronic, mechanical, photocopying, recording, or otherwise, without written permission of the publisher. For information regarding permission, write to Scholastic Inc., Attention: Permissions Department, 557 Broadway, New York, NY 10012.

This book is a work of fiction. Names, characters, places, and incidents are either the product of the author's imagination or are used fictitiously, and any resemblance to actual persons, living or dead, business establishments, events, or locales is entirely coincidental.

ISBN 978-1-338-28205-4

10 9 8 7 6 5                                        20 21 22

Printed in the U.S.A.  40
This edition first printing 2018

Book design by Maeve Norton

To Deyana, Noor, Adam,
and the little one on the way.

# MICHAEL

I know two things for a fact.

My parents are good people.

And ever since I can remember, they've been angry about almost everything.

---

I scan the area and see my dad, draped in the Australian flag, talking to Li Chee, who's wearing a flag top hat and holding up a *Turn Back the Boats* banner. I negotiate my way through the crowd of people and flags on our side, ignoring the boos and taunts coming from the counterprotest.

"Hey, Michael!" Dad pats me on the back. His forehead is glistening with sweat. "Really happy you made it."

"It could be your big moment. I don't want to miss it."

"Appreciate it, mate." He takes a deep breath, wipes his forehead with the back of his hand, and looks around nervously. "Geez, it's hot under this. What do you think? Reckon the media will come?"

It's hard to tell. The numbers on our side of the protest are growing but they're still small compared to the other mob. It's also hot. Really hot. One of those days where the heat is so oppressive you feel like meat being chargrilled on a hot plate. But then Kahn and Andrew arrive, and Dad's mood lifts.

Kahn's carrying a spade in one hand and a sign in the other: *Start Calling a Spade a Spade: Islam = Terror.* Andrew's dressed as a Spartan guard, carrying a shield and sign that says: *Democracy Started in Greece: Protect Our Democracy.*

Dad's thrilled. Personally, he's not one for stunts, but he has an instinct for what will grab the media's attention. If somebody else is willing to wear spandex for the cause, he's not going to say no.

Andrew asks me to take photos so he can tweet them to news outlets. Kahn, Andrew, and some of the others pose for the shots, and then Andrew works his social media magic.

Dad and I are taking a selfie to send to Mum and Nathan, who are in Melbourne for an air show, when a guy with a grotesquely muscled body bulldozes his way through our crowd and steps up close to us. He's carrying a couple of signs in one hand, snapping photos of the crowd with his smartphone with the other. I haven't seen him before. He's not so much steroid-pumped nightclub bouncer as ex-commando-who-visits-war-zones-in-his-spare-time kind of guy.

"Hey, Alan," he says sternly, nodding at Dad.

The testosterone force field around this guy is so strong I feel like I might grow a full-length beard just taking in his vibes.

"G'day, John," Dad says. "Thanks for coming, mate."

"Wouldn't miss it," he barks, then snaps a photo of Dad for his Facebook page. John looks me up and down. "Where's your sign?" He doesn't give me a chance to reply but instead hands me one of his (No to Sharia Law), raises his eyebrow (there's only one), and looks grimly at the opposing crowd.

"Fucking bleeding-heart terrorist-loving freedom-hating traitors."

"Does that come in a bumper sticker?" Dad asks with a laugh. He discreetly nudges my foot with his shoe and I struggle not to laugh.

"It's not a joke," John says gruffly. "You should know that, Alan."

"I know, mate," Dad says good-naturedly, patting him on the back. "I'm just pulling your leg."

"They should shut the hell up and respect the fact they have free speech in this country."

"No one's saying they shouldn't protest," Dad says. "That's the beauty of this great country of ours, John. That they can be here, same as we can. The irony is that they don't appreciate that we're fighting to make sure this democracy of ours doesn't change."

John flashes a look of contempt at the mob of counterprotesters. They've escalated the shouts of abuse. John walks off to join some of the more vocal ones on our side and starts chanting at the top of his lungs.

I give Dad a look. "He's a bit . . . deranged?"

"Nah. He just looks tougher than he is. He's Andrew's good mate." Suddenly Dad's face breaks out into a grin. "Michael! Look!"

I glance in the direction he's motioning and, noticing a reporter and cameraman, smile.

"Your mum's press release must have worked." He runs his fingers through his thinning hair and readjusts the flag. "How do I look?"

"Like the leader of a new political organization," I say proudly. "Who's sweltering under that thing. Don't forget it's all about the sound bites. *Aussie Values aims to represent the silent majority* blah blah. The kind of thing you and Mum were practicing last night."

"We have about fifty members," Dad says with a smile. "In a population of twenty-three million, I wouldn't say that really constitutes a majority." He leans in close to me and winks conspiratorially. "But nobody needs to know that, hey, mate?"

The chants of the other protestors are getting louder. Rick, from our side, starts up a chant in reply. Game on. The atmosphere is electric, and people are fired up on both sides. I can see Dad across the crowd, a camera in his face as he talks to a journalist. He glances at me and I grin.

And then I see her.

Her eyes. I've never seen eyes like hers before. What color are they? Hazel and green and flecks of autumn and bits of emerald and I'm standing holding my sign and there she is, standing steps away, near the cop, holding hers (*It's Not Illegal to Seek Asylum*), and all I can think about is how the hell I'm going to take my eyes off her.

Her hair is jet-black, hanging loose down her back, and I think hair that gorgeous has no business being on *someone like her*. She's wearing jeans and a plain white T-shirt. She's the most beautiful girl I've ever seen and it stupidly, inexplicably, throws me.

There's a girl standing next to her, shouting at the top of her lungs, waving her sign in the air with all the energy of a kid flying her first kite. She elbows the beauty, prompting her to laugh and raise her sign higher.

On my side I can hear people's chants rising: "*Stop the Boats!*" "*No to Queue Jumpers!*" "*Islam is Fascism!*" But my voice isn't working.

Suddenly John's beside me. He nudges me in the side and scoffs, "They're a disgrace, aren't they?"

I manage a grunt. John grimaces and motions to my sign,

which I've inadvertently lowered. I quickly hold it up, smile meekly at him, and wonder what the girl's name is.

———————————

"So it was a success?" I ask Dad on our way home.

Dad smacks the steering wheel with both hands and lets out a cheer. "Michael, it was *brilliant*! I'll be on the news tonight—well, *maybe*, they said they couldn't guarantee, and only for half a minute, but it's still something . . ."

"It would help your organization out if it runs. Did you tell Mum?"

"She couldn't talk. She texted though."

"They having fun?"

Dad chuckles. "You kidding? They've sent about fifty photos already. Nathan's in heaven."

He turns to face me as we stop at a traffic light. "Hungry?"

"Ravenous."

"Joe's shop at the Village closes tomorrow. You up for some fish and chips? A chiko roll?"

"Sounds good."

He changes lanes, makes the yellow light, and turns left.

"Could be the last chiko roll this area ever sees, Michael. The way the place is going, some trendy café will open serving free-range organic duck on a bed of foraged mushrooms."

I chuckle. "Dad. Wow. That was kind of meme-worthy. I'm impressed."

"Your mum and I were over at Joe's the other night. Twenty years he's been there, Michael. Poor guy's taking it badly."

"Where's he going to go?"

"*Go?* That's it, Michael. He has to retire now. People like Joe don't start over. He's priced out of the area now. He'll take his fiberglass shark that's been up on that wall since the seventies, hang it in his lounge room at home, and get a subscription to Netflix."

We turn into the parking lot behind the local shops and Dad parks the car. He turns off the ignition, faces me, and looks me in the eye. "That's why we're fighting, Michael. For people like Joe."

"Let's go get our last chiko roll then."

"For Joe," Dad says.

# MINA

This will be the last time I wake up here. I keep my eyes closed, savor my final moments lying in bed listening to the cacophony of morning sounds from nearby Auburn Road. If I concentrate hard enough I can bring the place alive: the fishmonger's van rumbling around the corner and over the uneven asphalt of the alley behind the mall adjacent to our house. The pungent scent of fish wafting out of the fish shop at the entrance to the mall. The fruit and vegetable store teeming with early morning shoppers, nobody queuing up, everybody somehow managing to buy their stuff without any fuss. The group of Sudanese men sitting at the corner coffee shop, smoking, sipping coffee, and talking. Big W next to a discount shop, a cheap lingerie stall, and a hijabi/anything-goes fashion house fronted by mannequins dressed in jeggings, long shapeless abayas, or sequined minidresses. Mehmet will be starting on the salads at the corner Adana shop, while Ferhat mounts the doner kebabs onto the sticks. There's something for everyone here, and I'm leaving this corner of my world, the only world I've known since arriving in Australia from Afghanistan ten years ago, to move to the lower North Shore of Sydney.

My mum knocks on my door. "Come on, Mina!" she says, her voice strained. She opens the door and sticks her head in.

"Ten more minutes," I groan.

"Nine," she counters, and goes downstairs.

I throw the duvet over my head and plug in my earphones. Eventually Mum forces me out of bed and we spend the morning packing the last loose items and wiping down walls, doors, and cupboards. We fall into a rhythm. We work hard, every mark on the wall taunting us: *You'll have to wipe harder if you want the deposit back.* By the time we're done, I'm exhausted. I collapse onto a chair.

"Wasn't Baba due with the van half an hour ago?"

"Flat tire." Mum carefully ties her hair into a bun at the nape of her neck. "I told him to book that local company but you know him. He likes to do things himself. Unplug the earphones, Mina. I've told you a million times. You'll be deaf before you turn twenty listening to that rubbish."

My mum hates my taste in music. She thinks it'll make me want to pierce my entire body, chop off my hair to look like "the lesbians," and elope with a tattooist.

"Baba better not scratch my chair. Make sure he doesn't, Mum." I'm not optimistic. My stepfather likes to think of himself as a jack-of-all-trades. He's a chef, and moving furniture is not his strong point.

My mum fixes her eyes on me. "You're still insisting on taking that old thing with you?"

I give her a defiant look. "I'm not backing down."

She looks like she has a whole lot more to say but then a slight smile ruffles her composure.

I smile, probably smugly.

"Fine," she says.

Mum had me when she was very young. She's thirty-three now and our battles can sometimes feel like sibling rivalry. She's not a yeller, never has been. Her emotions are tucked deep inside her body, but she doesn't need to scream and shout for me to know how she feels.

I found the chair in an antique store in Leura on a day trip to the Blue Mountains last year. It reminded me of the chair in my father's study in our house in Afghanistan. Quilt padded, floral greens and mauves, a high curved back. I have nothing left of my life in Afghanistan except faded memories. The Taliban destroyed most of my life. What wasn't destroyed, we left behind, including my father in his grave.

I continue working but I'm hungry now. I can feel my stomach muscles tighten.

"I'll go get us some lunch," I say, grabbing my handbag from the corner of the now empty family room.

Her face lights up. "That would be nice actually."

"Our last chance to get the best food within walking distance of home before we move to Pretentiousville, where you pay triple the price for Kabuli palaw."

Mum chuckles softly. "In some areas, the more expensive, the more exotic."

Twenty minutes later I'm back with fresh bread, chicken sheesh, dips, hot chips, tabouli, and cold drinks. We sit on the tiles and use a suitcase as a table.

Mum eats slowly, calmly. I'm scarfing my food down, but it's more than hunger. I suddenly feel a heightened awareness of everything, the aroma of garlic and mixed spice in the foods, the sound of traffic outside. Eating this food here, now, in our empty duplex, a surge of emotion charges through me.

"Tell me again," I say, "how big is the apartment we're moving to?"

Mum looks at me, chewing her bread slowly. Finally, she replies, "It would probably fit into the downstairs space here."

"I can't see why we have to move. I could just catch public transport to Victoria College. We belong *here*."

She takes a long sip of water, then wipes her mouth with a tissue.

"I don't want you spending hours on public transport. You need to be focused on your studies. Getting a scholarship is one thing. Keeping it is another."

"The stakes aren't high enough already, Mum?"

Mum tilts her head to the side and looks at me fondly. "A

scholarship for eleventh grade at one of the top schools? You know I'm proud of you, Mina. Anyway, you won't be the only one under pressure. We're opening the new restaurant there too. It's a big change for us all." She sighs. "Double the rent for the restaurant over there though. The supplies will cost a lot too. It used to be a fish and chip shop."

"So you've got a lot of work ahead of you, hey?"

She shrugs. "That's for Baba and Irfan to deal with. I've got other plans."

Surprised, I quiz her. "Such as?"

But she just shrugs again and moves the food around on her plate. "Just plans." She fixes her eyes on me again and, as an afterthought, adds, "Plans that involve making sure you get the scholarship for twelfth grade too."

The scholarship had been the idea of my teachers at Auburn Grove Girls High. My parents immediately embraced it, even though the logistics of living in Auburn and going to school in the lower North Shore would be complicated, to say the least. But they had big dreams for me. They wanted me to have the best education and the best future. Moving out of Western Sydney hadn't been part of the plan though. Baba had a successful restaurant here. Mum did all kinds of creative outreach classes at the community center, and worked at the after-school care at one of the local grade schools. Auburn has been home ever since Mum and I were released from Villawood detention center, ten years ago.

But then I passed the scholarship exam. And we discovered the transport situation would be two hours minimum on either side of the school day. Then my parents heard that the Lane Cove shops could do with some "exotic" food. One thing led to another, and now here we are sitting among boxes about to relocate. I feel like border control will demand to see our visas when the moving van ventures beyond Parramatta Road.

A silence settles between us as we finish our meal. Then suddenly, without warning, Mum says, "By the way, did you go to the protest with Maha yesterday?"

I reassure her that I had Baba's permission and just went along with Maha because Aysha bailed on her. She doesn't need to know I was curious too. She doesn't want me getting involved in political stuff. Not with my scholarship.

She's up now, pacing back and forth in front of the line of boxes, checking they're sealed and labeled. "You've got enough to worry about without going to protest marches." She stops and, with a sigh, corrects herself. "*We've* got enough to worry about, Mina. We've made a new life for ourselves here. Let's be grateful for that rather than drawing attention to ourselves. All I want is for you to get the best grades possible. Be a doctor or a lawyer. And to do that you need to *focus*."

"You know, that kind of pressure doesn't help, Mum. I'm about to start a terrifying chapter in my life ..." I stand in

front of her, swigging down the last of my drink. "You do realize that, don't you?"

"Of course I do. But you were also smuggled out of a war
zone, lived in a refugee camp, traveled here on a leaky boat,
and were locked in detention for months. By all means be
scared." And then, without a hint of irony, she adds, "But just
remember, I'm expecting you to be top of your class."

She's done it. She's actually pulled out *that* card. I've got
nothing to trump that.

# MICHAEL

Terrence and I are shooting hoops at the local court. It's been our thing since I met him during lunchtime detention in seventh grade. We don't have much in common (except when it comes to basketball) but have somehow stayed close mates since.

Terrence is filling me in on a game he played last night.

"He got a foul against me, man," Terrence says. "Dare me to get it from here?"

"Go on."

He takes the shot, scores, yells out, "Yeah, baby!" and then does a little dance.

The ball rebounds and I lunge forward, catch it, and dribble it between my legs. "All so I could get stuck with a pressure-packed free throw," he continues.

"Did you score?"

"Missed by a fraction." He takes possession of the ball and starts slowly dribbling around me, a big grin on his face. "Zara was there."

"No shit?"

"Yeah. Looking Victoria's Secret as ever."

Given our breakup was ugly, the image does nothing for me.

I shake my head and let out a small laugh. "Too bad about the psycho jealousy."

"I would have put up with it for that body . . . And he scores! In your face!"

I steal the ball from him and dribble to the three-point line. "No, you wouldn't. She thought I had a thing for Tessa just because I had to spend one freaking study period with her finishing a joint math project. All hell broke loose. Don't make me relive it." I bend my knees, take aim, and shoot the ball.

Terrence asks me what I did yesterday and I tell him about the protest. He groans.

"I've yet to meet somebody who supports mining and also happens to be a sex siren. Why would you bother?"

"Mining?" I laugh. "This one was about boat people. And unlike you, I don't plan my weekend activities based on the probability of hooking up with a girl." I grin at him. "Loser, we spent all of ninth grade doing that, remember?"

He shakes his head at me in dismay. "Those protests are usually all dreadlock hippies, wannabe hipsters, or hairy feminists."

"Wow. You're a really good listener, you know?" I shoot the ball and miss. "There was a girl there, by the way. And she was a stunner. Happy?"

"But *at a protest*," he says in a duh tone. "Girls talk enough already without getting all political on a guy too."

I stop and stare at him. "Do you have any idea how well you pull off sexist pig? I mean, I'm a guy and that offended *me*."

Terrence grins. "That's because you're all New Age and metrosexual and shit."

I roll my eyes at him. "I don't exfoliate my face."

"Moisturize?"

"No. But isn't it kind of sad that your masculinity test is based on moisturizer usage?"

We spend the rest of the hour ribbing each other and then split ways to go home, arranging to go online to play *FIFA* tonight.

I crash through the house, starving. "Mum, what's for dinner?" I yell, kicking off my shoes.

Dad's setting the table and Mum's dressing a salad. My ten-year-old brother, Nathan, is sitting at the kitchen bench, hunched over his iPad. Hearing me come in, he looks up and grins. I high-five him.

"How are you, champ? We missed you! How was the air show?"

He cocks his head to the side. "It was the best weekend of my entire life. Ever."

Mum beams and I grin at her. "You're feeling like you need a Mother of the Year award now, hey, Mum?" I tease.

She giggles. "Nah. I got all the reward I want. Nathan loved every minute of it."

"Except for the security screening in the airport," Nathan says. "They made me take off my belt. And shoes. I didn't like that."

"I'm always afraid I'm wearing mismatched socks," Dad says.

"KLM is the world's oldest airline." Nathan goes back to playing on his iPad.

"Really?" I sit down next to him, stealing a slice of cucumber from the salad bowl. Mum hits my hand. "How old?"

"Established in 1919." His gaze is still fixed on the screen.

"Wow. Fascinating, champ."

"Darling, tell Michael about the weekend," Mum coaxes. "Here," she says, passing me the salad bowl, "put this on the table."

Nathan is silent, absorbed in his game.

"Nathan," Mum says. "Go on, tell him."

Mum dishes up and we sit down to eat, patiently listening to Nathan, who finds summaries difficult because of his need to share the finest details. When he's finally finished, Dad grins at us all.

"I have good news. SBS TV called to confirm—drumroll, please!—I'm going on the show."

Mum squeals.

"Wow. Serious, Dad? You're going to be on TV?"

"Yep. It's called *Don't Jump the Queue*. Four weeks trailing the route of a boat person. Iraq to Indonesia to Australia."

"You'll be famous," I say. My mind wanders as I think of the possibilities. Would this mean we'd get to go to the Logie TV Awards? Mix with all those stars on the red carpet? Then again, it is SBS. Hardly the big-time. In fact the only person I know who watches it is Jason Starke, and he only watches it because his parents refuse to let him have the Internet because of its "corrupting influence."

Dad puts down his knife and fork and leans back in his chair. "They've been following reports about me in the media, and the interviews at the protest helped boost my profile. Maybe people are starting to realize we're onto something important here."

"It's fabulous!" Mum exclaims as she cuts up Nathan's chicken. Nathan's still fixed on the iPad, frowning in concentration as he studies a model of a plane engine. "Eat up, Nathan. I'm just surprised they have the courage to put someone like you on the show, Alan. I guess they know you won't be peddling all that politically correct *let's open the borders and flood our country into a disaster* nonsense."

"It's basically free national advertising for your organization," I say. "You'll probably attract more members."

Dad's chewing slowly, his mind elsewhere.

"You contemplating your best side for the cameras?" I ask.

He chuckles. "Just thinking. It's a big responsibility. I've got to do this right, make sure I can convey the organization's message effectively."

"You'll be great, Alan," Mum says, placing her hand on his arm.

"They want to interview all of us to get a sense of our family life, our values," Dad says.

"Really? Well, that'll be interesting." Mum leans her head back against the chair and heaves an exhausted sigh. "What a day. I got called in for two extra lectures this morning because one of the part-timers was off sick."

"UNSW?" Dad asks.

"Nope." She scrunches up her face. "UWS. Milperra campus."

Dad lets out a whistle. "You haven't lectured there for years."

"They're good students. First years. Always so eager at the start. So many young girls in hijab though," she adds. "And some of them don't even wear it modestly. Honestly, I think it's just to make a statement: *Look at me, I'm different.*"

"I suppose it's understandable in the Middle East," Dad says. "They all cover up. But here it *attracts* attention. They want to flaunt their difference."

Mum lets out an exasperated sigh. "That's half the problem though, isn't it? When my parents came here they got called poms, so they made sure us kids fit in." She raises her eyes to the ceiling. "You can't wear the hijab, get a negative reaction, and then complain. You have to take responsibility for yourself and think: *How are people going to treat me? Am I inviting trouble?*" She shakes her head sadly.

Dad smiles. "Maybe you should go on the show instead of me, Mary. You articulate it much better than I do."

Mum lets out a short laugh. "Oh no, thanks. I'd never get academic work again. It's hard enough getting part-time work without people labeling me a racist."

"Well, at least I know you'll be able to talk about what we stand for when the cameras roll for the family interview," Dad says.

"Why would anybody roll a camera?" Nathan asks incredulously. "It'll just break."

"One of those figures of speech we talked about, darling," Mum says distractedly.

"Actually it's got a technical explanation too, Mum."

She flashes me one of her dagger looks, daring me to provoke her in her exhausted state.

"Really?" Nathan's all ears now.

She looks at me, a signal that this one is on me. I turn to Nathan and give him a crash course in predigital cinematography, and she gives me a grateful smile. When I'm done, Mum and Dad are still deep in discussion. I leave them at the table for some one-on-one time and take Nathan upstairs to help him with his homework. When we're done, and Nathan's in his bed reading a book, I go to my room.

I open the UTS Design School website and feel the same flurry of excitement I did when I discovered it last month. I've crossed a threshold and I don't know how I'm going to tell my parents. Tell them that I no longer want to follow in Dad's footsteps and study architecture. That all the drawing and sketching and time spent on digital art programs all these years has made me realize that I have a different plan for my future. What I really want to do is graphic design.

Dad's talked about me becoming an architect ever since I was a kid. His dream is that I'll join him in his practice one day. How do you smash your parents' dreams and still live with yourself?

# MINA

Victoria College takes the art of topiary seriously. In an enormous garden bed in the center of the circular driveway leading to the main office, the hedges have been shaped into perfect geometric letters to form the name of the school. With every step I take into the school grounds I feel as though I'm about to hand myself over to be clipped, trimmed, and sheared into the shape of a good private-schoolgirl.

The grounds are all vast lawns and ovals, manicured hedges and color-coordinated flower beds with a combination of grand, romantic heritage buildings and ugly modern clichés. I follow the signs and eventually find the office. It's in a majestic building: high stained-glass bay windows, shining timber floors, black-and-white photos of past school years lining the walls. The receptionist looks like she belongs in a corporate office with harbor views. Her hair is slicked back into a low ponytail, not a wisp out of place. The color description is probably honey malt with a hint of butternut, rather than blonde. Her lipstick is bright red, a masterpiece of outlining. She beams at me, her White Glo teeth flashing, and cheerfully tells me to take a seat and wait for the principal, Mrs. Robinson.

It feels like déjà vu, only at my first meeting, after I'd passed the scholarship exam, my parents had been here too. Mum had worn the charcoal two-piece suit she wore to Tahmina's wedding, and a mauve hijab she'd loosely draped over her head, flicking the ends over her shoulders. Her dyed bangs had been blow-dried straight and swept to the side. She'd clutched her prized fake Chanel bag that Baba got her from the markets in Malaysia on their vacation there last year. Baba had worn gray pants, a new short-sleeved blue shirt, and tan shoes freshly polished. I was mortified, especially when Mrs. Robinson had emerged, dressed in an immaculate *genuine* designer outfit.

The meeting had gone well enough. My parents had listened attentively to Mrs. Robinson, nodding at the right time, too intimidated to ask any questions of real significance. I'd known they were desperate to ask about the *incidental* expenses, the stuff the scholarship wouldn't cover, but they held back. Mrs. Robinson had been very impressed with my exam results, and excited about offering me a place at Victoria College, a school that produces "global citizens."

At that point my mum's back stiffened and she quickly said, "We have the citizenship."

Mrs. Robinson had looked momentarily flustered, and rushed

to apologize if her meaning wasn't clear. She explained that Victoria College was "not just about the academics" but about being "a well-rounded and cultured student of the world."

Mum had nodded as if she understood, and Baba had sat there, looking solemn and serious.

"They are the future leaders of this nation," Mrs. Robinson had said, "and we are determined that they have a sense that the world is bigger than they are. For example, in junior high school years, the students go to language camps overseas. In tenth grade we send them to a third-world country to give them the opportunity to immerse themselves in a different culture. The experience is life-changing for them."

I'd stolen a glance at my parents at that point. They'd looked slightly bewildered.

"Any more trips?" Baba asked hesitantly. I'd guessed he had been doing the sums in his head and was panicking.

"No, in grades eleven and twelve the students have already enjoyed those experiences and are hunkering down with their studies."

Relief washed over Baba's face.

The meeting had ended with Mum boasting that I'd been top of my class at Auburn Grove Girls High and had a short story published in the *Auburn Gazette*. I'd flinched as I wondered what Mrs. Robinson would think about a local paper when Victoria College had produced internationally acclaimed authors and playwrights. Yet Mrs. Robinson was genuinely pleased to hear I'd been published and congratulated me warmly.

It's all still fresh in my mind as I wait for Mrs. Robinson on my first day of school. I'm staring at the class photos lining the walls of the foyer when she emerges. She is smiling as she greets me.

"Hi, Mina! Excited about your first day?"

I nod and smile back at her, trying to ignore the fluttering sensation in my gut.

She recites another encouraging spiel and then wishes me luck for the first day. I'm to wait for the eleventh-grade coordinator to collect me. She turns to leave but then turns back on her heels to face me.

"Oh, I almost forgot! The first issue of the school's quarterly magazine will be out in a month. Would you like to be on the front cover? It would be a wonderful opportunity to showcase Victoria College's commitment to diversity and multiculturalism."

"Um, sure. Okay."

She beams at me.

As I wait for the coordinator, I take out my phone and text Maha. I imagine her at our old school. She's probably with the other girls, gossiping and laughing before the first bell. I feel a pang of nostalgia.

I have two more years of being Victoria College's cultural diversity mascot.

She responds almost instantly.

> You have a swimming pool in your school. The a/c in our homeroom isn't working. PS Any Ryan Gosling look-alikes? Love ya.

The eleventh-grade coordinator, Ms. Ham, arrives to escort me to my homeroom class. She has the typical flustered energy of a teacher, although she's all smiles and easy chitchat. We walk quickly through noisy halls and corridors. Having been at a girls' school, I feel like I've been dropped onto another planet. There are boys everywhere. And yes, I'd gathered this would occur at a coed school, but actually being so close to adolescent boys is a lot to take in, beginning with the overreliance on cheap aftershave. Pimply, short, tall, huge, scrawny. They're loud and boisterous and it terrifies me. Ms. Ham is too busy multitasking—chatting to me, directing kids, telling others off with the eyes in the back of her head—to notice.

She opens a classroom door and I follow her in. All eyes are on me.

"Here we go, Mr. Morello. Mina's the new girl. All the way from Afghanistan!"

"Auburn, actually," I say, quickly adding a smile so she doesn't interpret my correction as insolence.

Ms. Ham is in too much of a rush to register and leaves.

"Auburn?" I hear a voice call out, followed by a snicker. The voice is attached to a guy with an ash-blond crew cut and pale blue eyes framed by long eyelashes.

I pretend I don't hear. Mr. Morello smiles at me and scans the room.

"There's an empty seat next to Jane," he says, pointing to a girl who's sitting at the back, braiding her hair. I pass a guy who's staring up at the ceiling fan, balancing a pen on his upper lip. There's a girl doodling in the margins of a book, another boy swinging on his chair, his large body spilling over the edges.

Jane gives me a half smile as I sit down next to her.

Mr. Morello starts reading aloud student notices: reminders about school rules, IT policies, uniforms. He has to tell the guy who spoke out before to settle down. Terrence is his name, and he clearly enjoys being the center of attention.

A guy sitting next to Terrence turns around to look at me. His gaze lingers for a moment and then he turns to face the front.

"So where are you from?" Jane asks after the bell has rung and we're walking to first period, English.

"Auburn Grove Girls High."

"I'd hate to start a new school in eleventh grade. It would be awful."

I smile. "I feel so much better now."

She laughs guiltily. "Sorry. So where are you from?"

"I told you. Auburn."

"I mean *originally*."

"Afghanistan."

"Oh yeah, Ms. Ham said that. Wow, you're Afghanistanian. That's so cool."

"*Afghani*. And why *cool*?" I ask, a little dumbfounded.

"It's different," she says with a shrug. "Different's cool. Are you a refugee?"

I never know how to answer that question. Do you ever stop being a refugee? Even if at some point in your life the place of refuge becomes home?

She leads me through a labyrinth of corridors and stairwells. Finally we arrive at our classroom.

"Come and meet my best friend, Leica. She's got Childs for homeroom but we have English together. You'll hit it off."

"Okay," I say hesitantly, mildly curious as to the basis upon which she's made this assessment given we've barely exchanged thirty words.

"She's half Asian," she adds by way of explanation.

I have no idea what to make of this, so I decide silence is the best option.

I'm introduced to Leica, who takes one look at me and says, in a wry tone, "Excellent. We need more pepper in this place."

I like her instantly.

"Mina's from Afghanistan," Jane explains. "She escaped Saddam Hussein's Taliban regime."

My mouth hangs open. Jane hits me playfully on the arm and bursts out laughing.

"I'm messing with you."

At least she can do political jokes. But she thinks "Asian" is an ethnic descriptor. I'm exhausted already.

We sit in the second row waiting for the teacher, who is in an intense conversation with a student just outside the classroom.

Terrence from homeroom walks in with staring guy and, as they pass our table, says, really casually: "Your hair looks good like that, Jane."

Jane stammers, "Thanks." The poor thing's cheeks look like somebody's marked her with red paint. Combine this with the way she's absentmindedly caressing her braid and I'm guessing she's into Terrence. Bad.

The teacher enters and starts setting up the Smart Board. Leica and Jane are now huddled close, lost in hushed whispers, reminding me that I've been their friend for all of two seconds. I take out my diary and study my timetable.

Most grade levels have one: the kid people don't feel guilty picking on. It's always just for a laugh, nothing to take seriously. *It's not bullying or anything. Relax, we're just kidding. Lighten up.* Paula Watson's definitely that girl. In homeroom she didn't look up from her book. I watch her in English and then, later, in math. I don't think she has any friends, but she doesn't seem to be too bothered about it. I saw her speak to Jane and Leica, but it was in passing. While we wait for the teacher to arrive she sits and reads, has no interest in trying to squeeze her way into conversations to avoid being seen as a loner. But she's not quiet, withdrawn. Her hand's usually one of the first up; she's always offering her opinion, has this weird habit of quoting Oscar Wilde whenever she gets a chance. The others groan but I like her spunk. She's smart and not afraid to show it. I want to get to know her but I'm not sure how to approach her.

---

Last period. Society and Culture.

"What's culture?" Mr. Morello asks.

Silence. It's last period on the first day of school. I admire the man's optimism.

"Anybody?"

I see some of the class looking at Paula, gesturing for her to save the hour and answer.

Paula proceeds to give a definition of culture that would put Hermione Granger to shame. Mr. Morello is full of praise, and Paula sits there and beams, ignoring some of the boys who mutter "nerd" and other such intelligent comments at her.

"Anybody else? Okay, how about this?" Mr. Morello paces the front of the room. "Is culture static? Does it always stay the same?"

He looks around. Still nobody speaks up. I'm not about to

volunteer. It's my first Society and Culture class and I don't want to make a fool of myself.

Mr. Morello snaps his fingers in front of Terrence, who's sitting next to staring guy, who I catch stealing another glance at me—and not the kind of look that might flatter a girl. It's almost as though he's puzzled by my presence. What's his problem?

Terrence is slumped in his seat, legs out, looking down at his lap. Dead giveaway.

"Terrence? Care to answer?"

Terrence looks up quickly. "What's the question?"

Mr. Morello puts his hand out. "Pass it here," he says calmly.

"Pass what?" He grins, like somebody who knows he's been caught out but is still cocky enough to feign innocence.

Mr. Morello keeps his arm extended and waits one, two, three . . . Terrence rolls his eyes and hands over the phone.

"Now, Terrence, enlighten us, please. Do cultures evolve over time?"

"Depends." Terrence shrugs.

"Come on, Terrence. Try harder."

"Some cultures are, like, stuck in the Middle Ages."

A couple of other students speak up, and pretty soon the class is in a heated debate that veers off into stonings and beheadings. Lovely.

"What do you think, Michael?"

So that's staring guy's name.

"I think it's religion that's the problem," he says casually. "Like Islam claims to be about peace but all we hear about is violence."

I want so badly to raise my hand. But every instinct in my first-day-at-school body is warning me not to. I sit in silent agony, fighting with myself.

Mr. Morello is looking like he's having a this-is-why-I-became-a-teacher moment as the rest of the class goes back and forth with their arguments. Then Paula surprises me and, bristling with indignation, says to Michael, "I really, *really* hate it when people in the West take the moral high ground. *Really.*"

Terrence groans. "Paula, is there anything you *don't* have an opinion about?"

"I'm sixteen, Terrence," she says coolly. "It's a bit early to tell."

Michael considers her for a moment and then, his tone careful, says: "But, Paula, it's on the news all the time. It's just differences in values. My dad says it's not a personal clash between people. It's more a clash of civilizations."

Paula huffs with indignation. "So Hiroshima, Nagasaki, Guantánamo Bay, Abu Ghraib, bombs on Afghan weddings and parties, CIA torture, drones, white phosphorous—all wonderful examples of *civilized* behavior, right?"

"You can't compare," Michael says. "It's the war on terror."

I roll my eyes and doodle in the margins of my textbook.

"Are you saying stonings and cutting off hands are okay?" Terrence asks Paula.

"Obviously not," she snaps.

Mr. Morello reads out a section from the textbook and throws questions back to the class for discussion. At one point Terrence, who I suspect has been marinating in testosterone for some years now, snorts loudly. "In Saudi Arabia, does downloading movies count as stealing? I mean, could you get your hands cut off for downloading the next season of *Game of Thrones*?"

In terms of the Muslims-are-barbaric joke theme, I'd give Terrence points for originality. It's the general contempt that goes with the joke that leaves a sour taste in my mouth.

A guy called Fred, sitting beside Terrence, high-fives him.

"Oi, how do they high-five in Muslim countries?" Terrence continues, grinning. "It'd be wrist to wrist!"

That sends Fred and Terrence into another fit of giggles.

"One more inappropriate comment and I'll see you in detention at lunchtime, Terrence," Mr. Morello says coolly.

"I'm just saying," Michael says, "that people have values in the West."

The words escape my mouth before I even know what's happening: "Try telling that to the people locked up and abused in detention because they were naive enough to think Australia would care about their lives."

All eyes are on me. What a way to announce myself. I think trapdoors and invisibility cloaks.

A couple of the boys, led by Terrence, do the "Oooh, fight" stirring thing.

"Look, it's not ideal, what they're going through. But Australia has the right to protect its borders," Michael says.

"Oh, because women, children, and men fleeing persecution are *such* a threat, hey?"

Michael frowns. "I didn't say that. I meant, if you come by boat, you've jumped the queue."

The bell rings and the din of noise rises as everybody starts packing their things and Mr. Morello tells us our weekend homework.

"There's no *queue*," I tell Michael as I slam my books into my bag. "I would know. I came here by boat."

"Well, you have nothing to complain about then, do you?" Michael replies calmly.

Oh no. He didn't just go there.

# MICHAEL

I can't believe that the girl from the protest—Mina is her name—has started at my school. *In my grade.*

She's sitting quietly, observing everybody with those eyes that are driving me crazy. Terrence is having fun working the class up because giving people a hard time is pretty much his standard MO. The third wheel in our trio is Fred, and he's finding our political posturing amusing. We usually save zealous for our race to see who can get the Easter egg first in *COD* zombie mode.

Fred's generally a lie-low kind of guy. His real name is Minh Nguyen. It took all of twenty seconds for us to rename him Fred on his first day at school in seventh grade. Because, well, non-Anglo names with too many consonants and vowels can sometimes freak out my people.

One would think, from the way I'm acting in my Society and Culture class, that I've inherited my parents' passion for politics. But the thing is, I wear my politics like hand-me-down clothes: Some bits feel like they don't fit properly, but I expect I'll grow into them, trusting that because they're from my parents they've come from a good source.

Mina takes me by surprise when she finally speaks up. I manage to insult her before I've even had a chance to get to know her. I wish I had my parents' way with words. When they talk, they sound smart and convincing. I feel kind of bad that it gets personal. So when the bell rings and everybody's making their way to the front gate, I rush to catch up with her. She's walking alone and I come up close beside her. She throws me a sideways look and continues walking.

"Hey," I say, trying to sound casual.

She slows down. "Yeah?" she says impatiently.

I do what I consider is a reasonable attempt at a conciliatory smile. "I didn't mean to come across so harsh."

Eyebrows raised, she scans my face. "I can handle harsh. Offensive is another matter."

"Yeah, well, sorry. I didn't mean anything personal. It sounded personal, but it wasn't. You know what I mean?"

She stares at me. "So. Queue jumper. *Nothing to complain about.* Not personal?"

"Well, look . . ." I pace myself, try to find the right words. "I didn't specifically mean you. It was more general facts."

"*Facts?*"

"Yeah. My dad's done a lot of research. I'm not judging you. I was talking more about the people who say they're fleeing persecution when they're really just economic refugees."

Her eyes widen. I soldier on.

"It's cheating. What about all the people who have been waiting in refugee camps and can't afford to buy their way up the queue? And then there's the fact that if you can afford to pay a people smuggler all that money, how bad a situation are you really in? That's what I was trying to say, but it came out all wrong."

I shrug and give her a satisfied smile.

"You can't be serious?" She stares at me incredulously. "Those arguments are getting old."

I look at her, puzzled. "Is that your idea of accepting an apology?"

"Was that your idea of an apology?"

"Well, yeah."

She raises her eyebrows.

"I didn't have to track you down and apologize," I say curtly. "I just wanted to put things right."

"Thanks. That's really *magnanimous* of you."

I'm baffled by her hostility. "What's your problem?"

She rolls her eyes. "I'm not going to do the refugee myth-busting thing with you. If you're still running those slogans, you're the one with work to do, not me."

And with that she storms off.

# MINA

"How was your first day?" Mum asks on our way home.

"Great. I fit right in."

"That's good."

Groaning, I recline the front seat all the way back and stare up at the car ceiling. "You're not doing irony today, hey?"

She regards me with wry amusement. "It will get easier."

"You are the queen of pep talks, Mum," I say dryly.

We pass the restaurant on our way home. To the left is an alley that leads to the back parking lot, and to the right is a pizza shop. The sign at the front of our place says *Joe's Fish 'n Chips 1979* in faded black writing. The restaurant is still a mess of renovations. Baba and Irfan are inside with some workers who are knocking down a wall and the front counter. Baba sees us and his face lights up.

"We'll get there soon," he says cheerfully, wiping white dust off his face.

"*Assalamu alaikum*, Mina!" Irfan cries out happily. "You look so fancy in that posh uniform!"

"Be careful with your uniform, Mina," Mum says as Baba and Irfan show us around.

When I can no longer feign enthusiasm over floor plans and color schemes, I ask about dinner and Baba sends me next door to get some pizza. Mum comes along too.

We step into the Pizza Hub. There are two small families dining in, and a young guy ordering at the counter. The heat wraps around me like a friendly hug. The scent of melting cheese and rising dough makes my stomach cramp.

Mum and I wait our turn. It takes me a minute to realize that a woman sitting down is staring at Mum, looking her up and down. I take in Mum's floral scarf, striped harem pants, and two-toned long cardigan. I wince. Without a hijab, the clash of patterns and colors would ooze hipster chic. With a hijab, she just looks like an "ethnic." I take a step closer to Mum and, in Farsi, caution her not to ask if the meat is halal.

When it's our turn I order a vegetarian pizza and a seafood pizza. Mum is watching the guy (Tim, according to the pizza-shaped name tag on his T-shirt) behind the counter closely. I can tell Mum is getting anxious as Tim dips into and between the toppings. The seafood is close to the ham, and my mum watches him intently.

"Please, can you wear different gloves?" she asks.

"Different gloves?"

Tim has no idea what Mum is talking about. I start to explain but Mum cuts me off. "We don't eat ham. You need to please wear new gloves so that ham does not come on our pizza."

Tim looks confused but shrugs in agreement. "Okay."

"Thank you. You have a very nice shop."

"Thanks."

"We are opening next door soon. Kabul Kitchen. Afghan food."

"Really? Next door? That's yours?"

Mum nods.

Tim smiles briefly. "Joe's was popular. Guess it'll be nice to get some diversity into the place."

"You are welcome anytime."

Tim smiles again but, thankfully, doesn't say anything. The woman staring at Mum is packing her things to leave. She seems half puzzled, half contemptuous of Mum's presence. It's been a long day. I don't want to have to deal with her saying something to Mum. We've only just moved to this neighborhood and I don't want any trouble.

————————

The school café makes a great latte. They get the extra hot right too. It's neither a second-degree tongue burn nor an I-might-as-well-gulp-a-cordial drinking experience.

I've arrived at school early today and sit in one of the gardens (what school has gardens, *plural*?) to read our English text, *Emma*. My iPod's on, earphones in, music on low in the background.

"Hey."

I look up. Paula is standing over me, balancing her school-bag, a pile of books, and a coffee. I can't help but smile. I remove my earplugs and turn off the iPod. She motions to my book and I hold up the cover for her to see.

"Cool. So you're doing extension English too?"

I nod and she plants herself down next to me. "Ms. Parkinson is awesome. *We are all in the gutter, but some of us are looking at the stars.* I read that this morning. Beautiful, huh?" She pats the jacket of one of her books. I lean close to read the title. *Lady Windermere's Fan.*

"Read it?" she asks.

"No."

"Oscar Wilde. My favorite writer of all time. It's kind of pretentious to quote books in regular conversation, but he's worth the reputation."

I laugh. "I love reading too. Quote away."

"You will regret that, my friend. *I'm quite illiterate, but I read a lot.* Who said that?"

"Holden Caulfield." I grin. "I studied *Catcher in the Rye* last year."

"And so our friendship begins." She leans back against the tree and stretches out her legs, crossing one ankle over the other. "Nobody writes like that now."

"Like Holden Caulfield?"

"No, like Oscar Wilde. Mediocrity reigns. A world without poetry."

"Do you always talk like this?"

She fixes her eyes intently on me. "Yes. Is that a problem?"

"No. A relief."

We burst out laughing.

"You were brilliant last week by the way," I say.

"You're going to have to be more specific, as it tends to happen more than once each day."

I grin back at her. "Society and Culture."

"Ah, yes." She takes a sip of her coffee. "Terrence is part dumb jock, part class clown, part vicious bully. Be warned."

"And Michael?"

She pauses, thinking for a moment. "I think even he's surprised that he's lasted this long as Terrence's friend. It was the first time I heard him talk like that, to be honest. He's usually a pretty easygoing guy. I mean, as vanilla as they come, but hey, look around you. It's Victoria College. We do vanilla seriously well here."

"You think?" I raise one eyebrow, and she flashes me a sympathetic look.

"I see you met my cousin," she says after a pause.

"Did I? Who's your cousin?"

"Jane."

"Oh. I had no idea. She never mentioned it. Well, not that the topic came up."

"We're not that close. Jane's way too self-conscious to cope with me. Anyway, what do you think of Morello?"

"Morello? He's cool. Why? Are you related to him too?"

She sighs dramatically. "If only. I'd have to kill off his wife first and then hope he'd return my undying love."

"Are you kidding? He's a teacher!"

"He's only thirty. That's a fourteen-year age gap. It's nothing, especially when you consider I'm mature for my age." She grins. "Relax, I'm not a home-wrecker. Plus I saw Morello and his wife in the parking lot one morning and they are obviously and disgustingly very much in love."

"So it's unrequited love then?"

"Yep," she says, standing up, dusting off her uniform, and extending her hand to pull me up. "Unrequited love is better than returned love that fails. This way I can dream. Oops!" She stumbles and coffee spills all over her skirt.

"Oh no!" I cry, lunging at her with tissues and frantically trying to wipe the coffee off. Mum's warning from last night is still ringing in my ear: *You have one set of the uniform so keep it clean.*

Paula looks at me, baffled. "What's wrong? Relax."

I take a step back. "Sorry." I motion to her skirt. "Your uniform."

She shrugs. "I've got three."

I can't help but blush and quickly change the subject as we head to class.

"So, um, does Morello know?"

It's her turn to look mortified. "No way. I'm completely discreet. It would be beyond embarrassing if he found out. So tell me, do you like animals? Because I'm an animal lover. I own a Labrador named K4, two cockatiels named Kryss and Sunday (because we found him on a Sunday), one budgie named Green (because he's blue), a bearded dragon named Forseti after the Norse god of justice, and two turtles named Magneto and Xavier. K4's been part of the family since before I was even born. Nancy got him for her birthday. K4's the closest thing to me at home. Do you have any pets?"

"Mum's not really an animal person. Plus we're in an apartment."

"Come on, the bell's going to ring in ten and I need another coffee now that my skirt's had a caffeine hit. We've got math now and Ms. Hamish is only worth facing with extra caffeine in the system."

We walk to class together. I think maybe Victoria College might just turn out all right after all.

---

Mum and Baba are at the restaurant finishing the last touches of the decor in preparation for opening next week. The real estate agent they're leasing the shop through put them onto an interior decorator, and he's out there with them tonight giving them some last-minute advice.

I'm in my bedroom, surrounded by study reinforcements (junk food), with music cranked up to a volume that would antagonize my mother but not the neighbors. Maha texts me while I'm doing a character profile of Mr. Knightley for my English homework.

> Jasmine got caught cyber-stalking Jasper so Paul dumped her & Jasmine's gone all I have an eating disorder my world has ended but we know it's just an act because we busted her gorging on veg toast and claiming she hasn't eaten in days.

It's random, frivolous, and gossipy but the familiarity of that voice sends a pang through me.

We send each other texts back and forth. Maha makes me ache with a longing to return to Auburn Grove Girls High, which was a kaleidoscope of cultures and ethnicities. Somewhere where I'm not the ethnic supporting character.

> **Maha:**
> Relax. You'll fit in soon.

> **Me:**
> I'm NOT using that whitening cream.

**Maha:**

Calm down. Nothing wrong with cosmetically changing your race to fit in.

**Me:**

You worry me.

**Maha:**

Nina just brought back a batch from India & swears by it but Pretti tried it and it burned her skin ☹

**Me:**

OMG. Where?

**Maha:**

Left butt cheek. She thought it best to try it in an inconspicuous spot first.

**Me:**

God I miss you.

**Maha:**

Chillax. You moved suburbs not countries.

When I feel I've written just as much as I can about Mr. Knightley, my phone beeps again. I glance at the text and see that it's Paula.

I don't want to get too romantic but I can definitely see we have a future together.

I grin and instantly text her back.

You had me at *hey*.

# MICHAEL

I go to Terrence's house on Saturday night. His older brother, Mason, and some of his friends are there too, drinking in the backyard.

"Your parents home?" I ask as I grab a beer from the cooler beside the outdoor table.

"Nope. We're prefueling under Mason's supervision," he laughs.

"They trust Mason?" I chuckle.

We hang out with Mason and his friends for an hour, have several rounds. They're okay, in their first and second years at university. They make us laugh, especially Mason, who's even more of a goofball than Terrence.

One of Mason's friends lights up a joint and passes it around. Terrence takes a few deep drags but I pass. Drugs have never interested me. I've tried dope before. I didn't really get high, just a little buzzed. It burned the hell out of the back of my throat, gave me bad cottonmouth. Life can fog up enough by itself without me giving it a hand.

"Let's go into the Cross," one of them suggests at around ten-thirty.

"What time do you have to be home, Michael?" Mason asks me.

"I could push it to two. Was hoping to play some *GTA* though."

"Nah, let's go out. Hey, Terrence, reckon you're up to it?"

Terrence looks a little spaced out. He takes a sip of his beer and bursts out laughing. "Sure. I'll be Robin and Michael can be Batman. He'll look after me, won't you?"

Mason hesitates for a moment. "*Batman?* Christ. Didn't take you long to get stoned."

"Thought you said Brittney's meeting you at Heat?" Liam asks Mason.

"Yeah . . ." He thinks for a minute, eyes fixed on Terrence.

"*And* her friends," Noah adds, grinning at Liam. "Come on, man, she's hot for you."

It takes about five seconds for Mason to cave. We order a taxi and pretty soon we're at the Golden Mile. It's a typical night. We've arrived right about when things start to get going. Mason and his mates are going to meet the girls at the club. Terrence and I have no chance of getting in underage. We agree they'll go in for an hour while we walk the streets, check out the scene.

"You'll look after him, won't you?" Mason asks me, a worried look on his face.

Terrence is full-on stoned and is acting like a bit of a douchebag, laughing uncontrollably, saying stupid things. I've drunk quite a bit but I'm not hammered or anything. I can think of better ways to spend a Saturday night than babysitting a stoned Terrence in the Cross, but we're here now so I figure we might as well make the most of it. I reassure Mason that I have Terrence's back and they leave us.

"I'm STARVING," Terrence immediately wails. After giggling uncontrollably for a little bit, he suddenly raises his arms with his palms facing out and says, "These are *my* hands!"

"Oh, boy," I say. "Yeah, those are your hands, you moron. Come on, let's get some food."

We walk up William Street. Terrence can't resist commenting on every girl he sees—at the top of his lungs. "You're gorgeous!" "You're hot!" "Go easy on the junk food, sweetheart!" "Check out those boobs!"

"Yeah? Enjoy the view, asshole," one of the girls shouts back.

We make it to a fast-food place. It's packed with other mostly underage rejects like us, locked in nightlife limbo until we turn eighteen. I get us some vein-clogging burgers and chips and we sit down near the window.

Terrence has mellowed and is concentrating on scoffing down his food. When we're done, Terrence announces he wants to go for a walk. The street is crawling with people now. We're due to meet Mason anyway so we squeeze ourselves through the crowds toward Heat. At least Terrence's new nobody-loves-me mood means he isn't shouting out ratings for every girl who walks past us.

It's almost twelve-thirty when we meet up with Mason and his friends. They're standing outside the club, with some giggling girls who are clearly wasted.

We all walk together to a taxi stand. The queue is insane. Terrence is just standing, staring at the ground. Liam and Noah are all over the girls.

It all happens so suddenly. I hear shouting from behind us: "What you fucking looking at my girlfriend for?"

Then I hear Mason yell out, "It's a free country. Anyway, who says I was looking at her, you dickhead!"

Then the guy yells, "Can't handle an Aboriginal guy with a white chick, huh? You dumb racist fuck!"

"What are you on about? I didn't say you were Aboriginal!" Mason yells back. "You're fucking white!"

Things have suddenly graduated to weird.

The next thing I know, the guy lunges at Mason and takes a swipe at him. Then a couple of other guys join in and start laying into Mason too. Liam and I immediately jump in. I get some good kicks to my ribs but I give some too. The fight doesn't last long. Security from outside the nearest club sweeps down on us pretty quickly and breaks it up. And it's just our luck—there are some cops nearby and they're on us in a flash too. You can't throw a stone without it hitting a cop in the Cross.

The cops have a bit of trouble restraining Mason and the guy who threw the first punch, seeing as they're both drunk. Liam and I don't bother resisting. Despite the cops holding them down, the guy and Mason are still mouthing off at each other. We get hauled off to the nearest station.

I'm underage so I have to call a parent to be with me when they question me. Dad comes.

"Are you okay, Michael?" Dad cries as soon as he sees me.

The cop, obviously experienced in dealing with hysterical parents, manages to calm Dad down. I feel awful.

Dad folds his arms across his chest and sits tight-lipped, nervously jiggling his leg up and down.

"I only joined the fight because Mason was outnumbered," I explain to the cop. "The other guy threw the first punch. Mason was just defending himself."

"My son would never start a fight," Dad says. The cop raises his hand to silence him.

"What was the fight about?" the cop asks me.

"The guy just flipped out. He thought Mason was looking at his girlfriend, then all of a sudden they're in a scream-ing match about him being Aboriginal. He called Mason a racist—"

Dad is suddenly animated. "Is that what the other guy is

saying? That this was about *racism*?" He sighs. "Everybody loves a racism story, don't they? My son told you. The other guy *started* the fight."

"Sir! I need you to stop interrupting."

Dad, bristling, nods and sits quietly. The cop writes down some more notes and steps outside to speak to the cop questioning Mason.

In the end nobody is charged. It's a first-time offense for us all, and nobody has been seriously hurt.

I have no idea at this point that Liam and the girls have filmed the fight on their phones and that later that night Noah will post the video on YouTube with the tagline *Reverse Racism*. I have no idea that someone from Aussie Values picks it up and tweets it: *They call US racists? Look what this "Aboriginal" guy did to Mason and his friends.* I also have no idea that the current affairs programs pick it up from there.

I go home oblivious to the furor to come.

# MINA

Paula texts me on her way to school on Monday morning.

> Good morning, Mina. This is a public service announcement from Bus Route 419. Heard on the train just now:

> Student 1 finds permanent marker in student 2's bag.

> Student 1: What's this for? Are you in a gang?

> Expect updates on further Millennial embarrassments in the future.

> PS I know we're Millennials too but these sorts are a liability.

> PPS Meet me at the café in ten.

At Auburn Grove Girls High I was always top of my class. My blazer was covered in badges. I was by no means the smartest girl, but I am a perfectionist and competitive and that helped. Mum's expectations that I take the title for the Afghan community's Best Academic Performer in New South Wales might have had something to do with it as well.

I feel a different breed of pressure at Victoria College. There's a competitive spirit among a lot of the students here that's both exhilarating and utterly terrifying. Some of the teachers have an *It's the journey not the destination* kind of philosophy. For some of the others, there's a little too much talk about exams and grades.

Everybody warned us about the jump from tenth grade to eleventh grade, but I truly never expected the pile of work to grow so high so fast, or the pool of competitors to be so big. These are kids who live and breathe success. I misunderstand a girl called Joy when she refers to her father working at Woolworths. My mind goes *things in common* and I casually mention that her father might know a family friend called Kamal who works in admin at the head office. Turns out Joy's father might indeed. Given he's Woolworths' CFO.

Here, ambition isn't even a prerequisite. At Auburn Grove Girls High, ambition was a word you'd see in Comic Sans MS font on a poster stuck to the library door. But anybody with half a brain knew a brother or sister or friend who had the grades but not the contacts. Had the résumé with the wrong address and zip code. Had a cousin who was Raj at home and Ray at work.

I know I've got to work twice as hard as everybody else because I've got twice the distance to run just to catch up.

So today when Paula's in band practice (she plays the cello), I'm in the library at lunchtime, getting a head start on a major history essay due next week. Two girls from my history class, Zoe and Clara, are sitting at a nearby table, working on their laptops. From the titles, I can tell they're working on the same essay.

I know that these early days are critical. Mum and Baba have spent all week drumming it into me: *Lay a good strong foundation from the start.* They just don't think this applies equally to the social part of school.

I muster up the courage to pack my things and walk over to them. We haven't yet spoken, and Paula's not in history with me, so until now I've been sitting alone. From the classes we've had so far, I can tell these two girls are smart and driven in a slightly scary, if admirable, way. They remind me of the kind of girls you come across in a gym class: highly coordinated, perfect form, big energy, no sweat or frizz. The ones everybody else follows as they pant and trip their way through Zumba moves. That's okay though. I like the competition.

"You're doing the Treaty of Versailles essay too, huh?" I say brightly.

Zoe offers a fake half smile. "Yep," she says. She continues typing, eyes glued to the screen.

"We're in the same class," I say, looking at Clara.

"Yeah, I know," Clara says. She's friendly enough, but there's none of Paula's warmth about her. "You got a scholarship here, right?"

I nod. "Yeah."

"Where were you before?"

"Auburn Grove Girls High."

Zoe raises an eyebrow. "Congratulations," she says, facing me. "You must be really smart to get a scholarship."

Clara doesn't give me a chance to respond. "You know, I've never been out to that part of Sydney."

"Watch out, Clara," Zoe adds. "We've got serious competition now." She laughs to herself, but there's no cheer in her.

There's an awkward silence. Zoe goes back to typing and Clara picks up her book. I hover for a second, embarrassed, wondering what the most dignified exit strategy is, when I'm saved by Paula, who comes rushing toward me with her laptop open.

"Did you hear what happened?"

Zoe and Clara look up. "What?"

"Don't you have band?" I ask her.

"We finished early. Mr. Moreland's taking the eighth graders on a field trip."

Paula places the laptop on the desk, closer to me. "Here, check out Facebook." She scrolls down the page.

"Your profile picture is a cat," Zoe says flatly. "I'm a dog person."

"Oh, me too!"

"You can't be a cat *and* dog person." Zoe rolls her eyes.

One of Paula's friends has tagged her in a post of a video clip. The video clip has the caption: *My friends getting beaten up: but you won't hear about that in the media because they're white.*

"Okay, girls, check this out!" Paula clicks play.

A bunch of guys are yelling abuse at each other. One of them yells out something about racism, then takes a swing. A fight breaks out. And then suddenly there's Michael, in the middle of it all. I just make out Terrence's terrified face as he stands to the side, watching.

"Seriously?" I shake my head in disbelief.

"Yep," Paula says, nodding. "The Terrence connection I can understand. But *Michael?*"

"I hate seeing people fighting," I say in disgust.

"Morons," Zoe pronounces. She takes a closer look at the screen. "I'm surprised Michael's in on it. Just shows there's a dumb caveman in all guys."

Clara clucks her tongue. "I can't believe Jane has the hots for Terrence. Sure, he's okay-looking, popular, blah, blah, but where's her self-respect?"

"She's never aimed high in anything, so I'm not surprised."

Paula flashes an angry look at Zoe. "That's low, Zoe."

Zoe pretends to look surprised. "*Sorry.* I get she's your cousin, but come on, even you can tell Jane's always been happy playing it safe and bare minimum."

I want to laugh in her face. Bare minimum? Jane got fifteen out of twenty on a test and practically imploded.

"When I said that's low, Zoe, I didn't expect you'd sink lower," Paula says quietly.

Zoe looks momentarily ashamed but then quickly regains her composure. "I'm not going to apologize for having high expectations." She looks at me directly now. "Being top of the class is not something I intend to give up."

Paula's no longer interested and starts packing her laptop. Zoe's words float in the air and she seems suddenly uncomfortable. She sits up straight.

"Look, is it too much to ask that Clara and I can do our work without being harassed with gossip and idle chatter?"

*Idle chatter?* Who talks like that?

"Sure, sure," Paula says dryly, and we move to another table.

"What's her problem?" I ask Paula. "I mean with me specifically?"

"Zoe's been the top of our class since forever. That's her role, that's who she is. Then along you come from gangland Sydney with a scholarship that puts you in the same league as a girl who's had tutors and study plans since she was a toddler. You haven't seen anything yet. Hold steady."

I raise an eyebrow. "Don't worry. I can handle competition. In fact, I love it. As far as I'm concerned, bring it on."

---

One of the current affairs programs picks up the fight in a story that manages to mix several hot topics at once. First it's "youth street violence," then it's "binge drinking," then it's "bystander racism." They show the YouTube clip but the images of Michael and Terrence are blurred, I guess because they're underage. Then they interview some experts and finally a guy called Mason, who was at the center of it all.

*"So he accused you of racism? Just out of the blue like that?"* the reporter asks him.

*"Yeah. I wasn't even staring at his girlfriend. It was obvious he was looking to start a fight. I had no idea he was Aboriginal. He doesn't look like one. He's got light skin. I mean, he's probably not even really Aboriginal. They claim it sometimes so they can get benefits and stuff. For some reason he'd decided I had a problem with him and his girlfriend."*

*"And he swung the first punch?"*

The reporter then interviews a guy from some new lame organization called Aussie Values.

*"There's no excuse for alcohol-induced violence. We certainly don't condone that kind of behavior. But what this footage clearly*

*shows are the double standards in our community. It's reverse racism."*

*"By Aboriginal Australians you mean?"*

*"Yes, although whether that thug who punched the young man really is Aboriginal is another question altogether."*

*"Could you elaborate?"*

*"There's a lot that can be said about the identifying-as-Aboriginal industry in this country and I'll just leave it at that."*

*"What do you mean—"*

My bile production escalates and I switch channels, lose a few brain cells watching the latest season of The Bachelor, and eat a block of chocolate.

———————————

I'm on my way to my locker the next day when I pass Michael in the corridor. He's got a cut on the side of his face, a bit of a swollen eye.

We haven't so much as spoken a word to each other since our argument after Society and Culture. But seeing his face, and knowing he's friends with that idiot on TV, makes it too hard to resist. A strange confidence comes over me.

"Wow. That's pretty bad," I say, feigning sympathy.

He seems surprised and then pleased. He touches his face. "Oh, it's nothing," he says bravely, squaring his shoulders. "Just a small fight."

"Yeah, I saw," I say. "With a *so-called* Aborigine, correct?"

He peers at me as if he's trying to figure me out. He's suddenly defensive. "That's got nothing to do with me."

I smirk. "So is that Mason guy your friend?"

"He's Terrence's brother."

"Oh!" I say knowingly. "Well, that explains a lot, I guess."

"Terrence's not that bad," he says. "He doesn't mean half of what he says."

A small growl escapes my mouth. "Words. And meaning. You can't own one and not the other."

He holds his hands up in surrender. "Woke-up-on-the-wrong-side-of-the-bed kind of day?"

"*That's* your rebuttal point? And they said you're one of the smarter of the male species in our class."

"Who said?" His grin indicates that what was meant as an insult has been interpreted as a compliment. He flicks back his dark tousled hair. *He's quite attractive up close*, I catch myself thinking. Light brown eyes, good skin, height—

Wait a second. Why am I checking him out?

"Anyway, I'll leave you to bask in your masculine glory."

"Mason didn't start it, you know," he explains. "And I only jumped in to help him out. He was outnumbered."

"Very heroic."

"You're full of compliments today."

I hold his eye for a moment. "Can I give you and your friends some advice?"

"Do I even have a choice?"

I lean in conspiratorially. "Being an Indigenous Australian has nothing to do with skin color."

Surprised, he frowns for a moment. "Yeah, I know *that*," he stammers defensively.

I raise an eyebrow skeptically. "You might want to pick up a history book sometime. I mean, I'm just a boat person from Afghanistan and even I figured that out." I flash him a big smile. "Anyway, see you!"

I quickly walk away, unable to wipe the grin off my face.

# MICHAEL

An angry journalist in Brisbane picks up on the story and spins it into an op-ed on people passing themselves off as Aboriginals to get benefits. Then some shock jocks in Sydney and Queensland go on about it on the radio for a couple of days. Facebook and Twitter typically start frothing, either casting Mason and Kahn, who spoke to the media for Aussie Values, as heroes (down with political correctness!) or neo-Nazis (racist scum!). Thankfully, the spotlight is off me. I warn Mason to keep me out of any media. As for Aussie Values, Dad wants the organization to focus on the "issue," not my involvement in the fight. Then the best thing happens: A state MP gets accused of using government funds for escort services, and our story dies while the media works itself into a frenzy over that scandal. Thank God for government corruption.

I keep thinking about Mina. She's the one person I would least expect to have anything in common with. But our encounters have left me intrigued. One minute she's quiet, the next minute she's fiery and passionate. I can't figure her out.

I'm playing basketball with the guys at lunchtime when I notice Mina and Paula talking to Mr. Morello and then leaving him to sit courtside. It messes with my mind for a moment. I wonder if she's here to watch us play, but then I remember that I'm probably the last person she wants to speak to. Still, knowing she's there makes me feel all funny. I start showing off, flicking the ball between my knees, doing fancy tricks with my dribbling and shots. I steal a glance her way to check if she's watching. What a waste of time. She's deep in conversation with Paula.

Fred takes a shot from the half-court line and misses. The ball rolls in Mina's direction and, without even thinking, I run over to grab it. It lands close to her feet and she kicks it over to me.

"Thanks," I say, pausing for a moment, hoping she's noticed me flexing my muscles as I've been playing.

But she ignores me.

Paula acknowledges me with a slight tilt of her head, and then goes back to eating her lunch. I grab the ball and start to walk off, turning the ball on one finger, hoping Mina's watching me.

When the bell rings for the end of lunch I hear my name, and Terrence's, called out on the loudspeaker, asking us to report to the principal's office. My stomach sinks.

"Relax, nothing will come of it," Terrence reassures me as we wait in reception. "We'll get a slap on the wrist, at most."

Mrs. Robinson soon appears and ushers us into her office. Ever since I've been here, she's had the same inspirational quotes from famous dead people pinned to her bulletin board.

"I'm disappointed in you both," she says after a long lecture about responsible alcohol consumption.

I'm tempted to alert her to one of her proverbs. Disappointed in us? Why, Mrs. Robinson, *Nine-tenths of education is encouragement.*

"It's not just that your behavior reflects poorly on the school's reputation. Videos like that never go away. They will follow you to job interviews. And both of you have promising futures. With your grades and support networks at home, the sky is the limit."

On and on she goes. Thankfully, after years of fine-tuning, I have perfected the ability to look at a teacher and give her the impression that I am listening and absorbing her every word. My mind wanders and I start imagining hidden augmented-reality devices with programs that would let me remove Mrs. Robinson with one click, or replace her head with a giant Post-it Note.

---

The last class of my day is one of my favorites, Design and Technology. Our teacher, Mr. Riley, is wearing one of his Star Wars T-shirts (he has a big range) under a navy blazer, tan pants, and suede shoes. Rumor has it that he has a Boba Fett tattoo on his back.

"The chair you're sitting on, the shoes you're wearing, the icons on your devices, the graphic interface on your favorite games: Don't forget that everything made by humans that you see and use every day started off as a design idea."

I hang on Riley's every word. He announces that the DAT department has purchased a new augmented-reality design program and I shout out in excitement and swing back on my chair, grinning wildly.

"Yes, I was expecting that reaction from you, Michael," Mr. Riley says. He tells me to settle down, but I can tell by the gleam in his eyes that he's taken my enthusiastic outburst as a compliment.

We're assigned the task of designing a greeting card, uploading it to the program, and then creating a personalized AR experience for the recipient.

"Bring your card to life!" he encourages us. "How can you enhance it as an interactive digital experience? Do you want to include a video message? A music clip? An interactive photo slideshow? The possibilities are endless."

———————

The presenter, Joe, is wearing designer jeans and a designer shirt. He has TV-presenter hair and makeup but a genuine smile. The camera crew spends half an hour setting up, trying to get the lighting right, the equipment in order. We're going to sit side by side on a couch in front of the bay window. Mum fusses over Dad, Nathan, and me, adjusting our clothes, reminding us to check our teeth.

"Can I talk to him about planes?" Nathan asks.

"Sure you can," I say.

"*Michael,*" Mum hisses.

I grin at her. "Just trying to spice things up."

Dad gives me a pleading look. "Michael, no spice! It's the last thing we need."

"Okay," I say, raising my hands in surrender. I turn to Nathan. "Nathan, you just stick to answering Joe's questions," I say. "Nothing *whatsoever* to do with planes, okay?"

Nathan nods. "Yep."

"Is that clear, mate?" Dad asks gently.

"Yep."

"Good on you, champ." Dad ruffles Nathan's hair, much to Mum's annoyance. She leaps over, takes out the brush, and fixes his hair again.

Joe is relaxed and friendly. TV sleaze factor is less than I expect. We barely notice when the cameras eventually start rolling. Joe asks Dad what he hopes to gain from the journey.

Dad starts off slightly nervous and self-conscious. Joe tells him to take his time. "It's just a conversation between us. Forget about the cameras." Joe's a natural at this and eases us in by getting us to talk about where we've traveled, what we like doing as a family. Then he asks us how we'll feel about Dad being away from home for the month.

"It'll be very hard," Mum says. "We'll miss him."

"What about you, Michael? Will you miss your dad?"

"Nah," I joke. "He hogs the TV remote and always eats the last Tim Tam."

We all laugh.

"Luckily I don't like Tim Tams," Nathan says. "I find that they melt too quickly and I don't like gooey chocolate."

"I have to agree with you there," Joe says. "So, Alan," he continues, turning to face Dad, "what do you hope to get out of this experience?"

"I consider myself an open-minded person," Dad says. "I've never denied that many of the people who come here by boat have suffered. If I learn a little more about their plight that would be a good thing."

"Do you think Australia should be accepting more refugees?"

"No. I think we're meeting our obligations. I know this is an emotional issue and people get very worked up about it. I understand that. But policies should not be based on emotion."

"And what about you, Mary? Do you agree with locking people in detention?"

Mum's articulate, pleasant, and firm. She's against people

coming via the wrong channels. She doesn't want us to lay out a red carpet for them. Turning back the boats and offshore detention are good deterrents.

"We have the sovereign right to protect our borders," she says in conclusion.

Joe turns to me next. I feel my insides go all funny. I feel like a phony. There's no way I can match my parents' passion and eloquence.

"It's like my parents said," I start, clearing my throat, trying to remember what we rehearsed last night. "Just because we want to protect our borders doesn't mean we're heartless. There are wars all over the world. More and more refugees. There has to be a limit, or we'll be flooded . . ."

I smile, but I'm sure it comes out a little constipated. Dad is beaming proudly at me so I must have gotten something right.

Joe turns to Nathan next. I can feel Mum tense up beside me. She's warned Joe about what to ask Nathan.

"So, Nathan, your dad flies out tomorrow. How do you feel?"

Nathan freezes, staring blankly at Joe.

"Nathan?"

"I can't speak about planes. Not allowed."

Joe is confused and throws a look of appeal to my parents.

Mum laughs nervously. "It's okay, Nathan. You can answer."

"It's okay?" Nathan asks.

"Sure, honey."

Nathan turns to face Joe. "What kind of plane is my dad catching? Is it a jet? Or an A380?"

Joe, bewildered, says, "Um, I'm not exactly sure, Nathan."

Dad jumps in. "Nathan, champ, are you going to miss me?"

"When you subtract the eight hours you're at work and six hours you're asleep, it only amounts to an absence of about three hundred and ten hours over thirty-one days."

I freeze. Mum takes a long, calming breath. Dad looks uneasy. None of us wants Nathan to be ridiculed or pitied on national TV. I'm eyeing Joe like a hawk, ready to pounce if he exploits the situation.

But Joe has obviously picked up on the sudden shift in our mood. He smiles brightly at Nathan and then turns to Dad.

"It's okay, we can edit it if necessary," he reassures him.

Nathan, bored now, sits back, stares up at the ceiling, and kicks his legs against the back of the couch.

"How do you feel about going to Iraq?" Joe asks Dad. "Given how dangerous it can be there, are you scared?"

Nathan suddenly sits up and dives in with a response before any of us has a chance to stop him.

"Dad says Muslims are violent. So of course he should be scared. But you know, our bird was run over by a car in our street last year. Death is everywhere, not just in Iraq."

# MINA

"You wouldn't believe it used to be a fish and chip shop!" I walk through the restaurant on opening night, marveling at the transformation. "I can't believe how quickly you guys finished."

Baba, looking thrilled, is eager for me to see every last inch of the place. He leads me around, pointing out all the trinkets and decor. The place is like a postcard from an Orientalist fantasy: part ethnic fetishism, part kitsch.

"It looks completely different from the one in Auburn," I muse.

"The interior designer, he said, the more the better," Baba explains. "People want it to feel *authentic.*"

There are decorations on every last inch of the restaurant walls: large stitched fabrics decorated with dangling swords as tassels; a huge Afghan rug depicting some of the sultans from the Ottoman Empire; a wooden cabinet filled with silver or wooden camels, tea and coffee sets, daggers and prayer beads. The centerpiece is a large golden throne with deep crimson upholstery. There is a huge sign behind it, *Kabul Kitchen*, in shiny gold calligraphy.

"And we are putting up a sign to encourage people to take a photo sitting on the throne and then post it on Facebook and Instagram," Baba says triumphantly.

I look at him, gobsmacked.

"The interior designer advised us," he hastily explains.

I grin at him. "Will there be a belly dancer? I can handle gold calligraphy, but please, no belly dancer."

"That was the one thing we said no to."

Who would have thought? A silver lining among all the kitsch gold.

———

Within two hours of opening, we've got enough customers to keep the kitchen busy. I'm helping behind the counter and Mum is in the kitchen with Baba and Irfan. I've just taken a photo for a couple sitting on the throne when Baba approaches me and asks me to check on Mum in the bathroom. He looks worried and I rush to the ladies'. I find her bent over a toilet bowl, vomiting.

"What's wrong?"

I wet some paper towels and help her clean herself up. She washes her face, wets the crown of her head, and pulls her beautiful thick hair into a ponytail.

She stands in front of me, panting slightly.

"I feel old," she says wearily.

"Mum," I scold. "You're thirty-three, you just threw your guts up, and you still look beautiful. Give it up."

"I'm having a baby." She stands there, grinning at me.

"*What?*" I lunge at her and give her a massive hug. I'm thrilled and feel like doing cartwheels around the restaurant. I'm surprised too. I'd given up on the idea of a baby a while back. Within the first few years of Mum and Baba marrying, I'd hoped for a brother or sister. Mum and Baba had their hopes high too. As time went on, and they murmured to each other about God's will, I resigned myself to being an only child. So the news that it's going to happen, after all this time, brings tears of joy to my eyes.

Mum hugs me tightly and then gently pushes me away. "Sorry. I smell like vomit. I need to go home and shower." She giggles. "Oh, Mina, I'm sorry I had to tell you here, in a bathroom. I told Baba not to send for you. But he panics. Some nausea because I smelled the meat and he wants to send for an ambulance."

I laugh. "How many weeks are you?"

"Almost three months." She puts her hijab back on, adjusts it around her head. "Come on, we can talk about it at home later, in more dignified surroundings."

Baba is pacing outside the bathroom door. "Are you okay?" he asks anxiously when we emerge.

He looks at Mum with such tenderness and concern that my insides go all funny. There was a time when all Mum and I wanted was a safe place to live. We didn't dare to hope we could find happiness. It had been hard for a long time. Everything was different. Mum used to tell me, *Being in a new country is like learning to walk with a prosthetic. It takes time for the body and mind to adjust.* I caught her crying alone often enough to wonder how much time it would take. Things got better when she started taking some courses at the local community center and making friends. That's how she met Baba, through one of the Afghan women doing the same sewing class. I was nine when Baba came into our lives and I wanted so badly to hate him. But it was impossible. He never tried to replace my father. He would sit and watch cartoons with me for hours. He rarely asked me to change the channel, and seemed happy just watching with me, laughing along sometimes too. I didn't know then what had happened to him back home.

I can't believe I'm going to be a big sister again. It seems a lifetime ago when I was in the camp in Pakistan, rocking my three-month-old baby brother, Hasan, to sleep, trying to find him powdered milk and clean bottles because my mother's milk had dried up. The water was dirty; there was never enough formula. He cried a lot. We all did. Except my mum. She was possessed of something I didn't understand. A strength that both comforted and terrified me.

Hasan died quietly. Just slipped away in his sleep one afternoon, a couple of months before we found the boat that brought us to Australia. It's hard to admit even to myself, but I can't remember what his face looked like. The realization of that cuts me to the bone. Sometimes if I concentrate hard enough I can just make out a nose or mouth, but the image is always blurred.

# MICHAEL

Nathan's sprawled on my bed, playing on his iPad and telling me about his latest *Minecraft* creation while I do my homework. After an hour, Dad knocks on my door.

"Hey, Michael, are you busy?" He hovers in my doorway.

"You're home early."

"I have the AGM tonight. Any chance you can come along? Take the minutes?"

"What's in it for me?"

He cocks his head to the side. "Thai food and doughnuts?"

"Sold!"

"You come cheap," he says with a laugh.

"I want jam doughnuts," Nathan calls out.

"Already ordered them," Dad says.

"Hey, did you dye your hair?" I take a closer look at him.

"Yes. I've got a public persona now. Media can be brutal.

Everything counts." He raises his hand to his head, self-conscious. "Too dark?"

I try not to laugh at him but he's grinning at me anyway.

---

The meeting is at the local veterans' club. I recognize some familiar faces, people my parents are particularly close to.

There's Li Chee, born in China, migrated to Australia in the late sixties. Totally against increased migration and boat people. Dad tells me that Li has been useful for spreading the organization's message in the local Chinese newspapers. Margaret and Jeremy Thompson live on the Central Coast and knew my grandfather there. Jeremy's retired now, and they spend a lot of their time volunteering in community clubs. There's Kahn Chatha, born in India. He worked in Saudi Arabia for two years before immigrating to Australia and therefore has street cred and assumes the role of resident expert on all things Islam. Carolina and Andrew Jameson have known Dad the longest. Andrew and Dad went to university together and boarded in the same college. Carolina is a librarian at one of the top boys' private schools in North Sydney. Andrew works as the manager of the IT support team at a big city marketing firm. He's big on conspiracy theories, and probably the most hardcore of Dad's friends. He also has a disturbingly enormous black birthmark on his right cheek, with one protruding long hair. Encounters are fraught with where-do-I-look anxiety.

"So, you're Alan's son?" a guy called Laurie asks me as I sit at a desk waiting for the meeting to start.

"Yep. That would be me. The firstborn."

"Pleasure to meet you." He shakes my hand enthusiastically. "Here, let me give you my card. It's got the website for my blog on it. Read my latest post. It's all about how Obama's a Muslim and really the love child of Malcolm X."

"Um. Okay."

"I'm currently working on a piece on the Muslim boy in One Direction. He was sending subliminal conversion messages to young girls whenever he tweeted. Had to quit before he got caught."

I stare at him, wondering if he's pulling my leg. The look on his face tells me he's dead serious. I make up a story, excuse myself, and track down Mum.

"Who is that Laurie guy? He's nuts!"

Mum half smiles. "He's more on the fringe. You'll come across people like that. But we don't want to turn anybody away. It's a free country."

"One Direction as a sharia plot? That's pretty funny."

She smiles again. "He's not ideal, I know. But, well, it takes all sorts to spread our message."

We're interrupted with an announcement that the meeting

is about to start. There are about sixty people here. Dad's fan base has increased.

Dad's on fire tonight. The audience cheers him on when he speaks about potential terrorists hiding among boat people. They clap when he warns about the Islamization of Australia with halal food labels on jars of Vegemite. He talks about how the economy can't sustain further immigration. He demands that moderate Muslims stop their silence about radicals.

A round of applause, enthusiastic nodding of heads. I'm recording the minutes, "One Thing" playing on repeat in my head thanks to blog man.

"Most of us here are old enough to remember a different Australia," my dad says when the crowd has quieted down. "An Australia where it was safe for kids to play on the streets, where neighbors looked out for each other, said g'*day* and *Merry Christmas* without fear of offending. An Australia where Judeo-Christian values were the norm. When there was no threat of a clash of civilizations."

He ends with a call for people who come to this country to "assimilate," and there's thunderous applause. Mum grins at him with adoration. Nathan's in his own world, engrossed in a Tom Clancy thriller. I'm typing furiously.

When it's time to mingle, Dad pulls me aside and introduces me to Kyle Hudson, director of a boutique architecture firm in the city.

"Kyle's pretty much promised me that once you start university you can work part-time at his firm."

I do everything in my power to muster a grateful smile.

"Most of the big law firms hire me in hearings as an expert witness in their property insurance cases," Kyle says. "So we do a lot of expert reports. Big money in that. It's a good, solid career, and from what your dad has told me, you're more than up to the challenge."

I thank them.

Profusely.

Exaggerate my enthusiasm.

Pretend to be excited by the bright future they see ahead of me.

Ignore the sick feeling in the pit of my stomach.

# MINA

Paula texts me as I arrive at school.

> Public service announcement from Route 419 Bus:

> Student: "Man, I can't believe it's 2015. 2010 was six years ago!"

> PS Round the corner now. Meet me in the café?

Today Ms. Parkinson instructs us to get into groups for a shared task. I'm with Jane, Leica, Paula, Cameron, and Adrian. We're supposed to be discussing a passage from *Emma* but Jane's distracted. Apparently at recess she was at the counter at the café buying a juice but was short on money. Terrence was standing behind her in the queue and gave her the shortfall. Then, on the way to class now, he passed her in the hallway and made a point to smile at her.

"He smiled with his eyes," she whispers. "It wasn't just, like, some facial twitch. He meant it."

Adrian is chewing on the end of his pen, a bewildered expression on his face. "I don't get it."

Cameron, who's busy looking through the book trying to find quotes to answer the questions, says in a deadpan tone: "Jane's doing that let's-overanalyze-things that girls do."

Leica makes a face at Cameron. "Don't be mean."

"You know it's true," he says, not looking up from the book.

"One day he smiles at me, the next day he ignores me," Jane says softly, in case anyone overhears. "Can I help it if I'm trying to read into it?"

Adrian shakes his head. "It must be exhausting being a girl."

"Yeah, using your brain can be a workout," Leica jokes.

"Guys use their brains," Adrian says. "We just don't have deep and meaningfuls about whether giving somebody fifty cents so they don't miss out on buying a juice is a love declaration."

"Can we get back to Emma and Mr. Knightley?" Cameron says. Cameron's got absolutely no problem embracing his inner nerd.

We're discussing whether Emma was right to interfere in Robert Martin's marriage proposal to Harriet when Terrence gets up to throw something in the trash (well, actually, he threw it from across the room and missed and Ms. Parkinson yelled at him). He winks at Jane on his way back.

Jane tries to play it cool but I'm guessing there's some serious cardiac activity going on at this moment.

"See," she says to us through clenched teeth. "Still think I'm making it up?"

Adrian shrugs. "Isn't it just easier to not think about it until he actually asks you out? What's the point?"

Cameron lets out a laugh. "Yeah right."

"Or how about you just forget about him altogether?" Paula tells Jane when the bell rings and we're packing away our books.

"Why would I do that?" Jane says. "I like him."

I can't help myself. "For his *personality*?" I say incredulously.

Jane rolls her eyes. "I know he picks on you both sometimes. And he's been totally out of line with you, Mina."

"Wow. But not with me?" Paula says, eyes flashing.

Jane thinks for a moment, searching for the right words. "Maybe if you just, you know, tone it down a little."

"Sure. I can do that," Paula says. "I'll stop being myself to make it easier for Terrence to resist acting like an asshole."

"I didn't mean it *that* way."

"Why do people always say that?" I murmur.

"Huh?"

"Never mind."

"It's fine," Paula says. "Really. Congratulations on your taste in guys."

Jane, wounded, walks off slowly by herself.

It comes as a complete shock when Mr. Morello pairs Michael and me for an assignment. We have to interview five strangers about how they define Australian culture.

"At least he's cute," Paula whispers to me.

"Dark brooding eyes and a dimple can only get a person so far."

"What? You've been keeping an inventory of his looks? That doesn't sound like indifference to me."

I hit her playfully on the shoulder. "Morello's leaning against his chair again. There's muscle flexing. Lap it up."

Michael walks up to me after class. "So. Morello can do irony, hey?"

"Looks like it. So when do you want to do it?"

"Hey, Mina, steady now. You move fast!" Terrence bursts out laughing.

My face reddens.

Michael growls at Terrence to shut up.

"Sorry, sorry," Terrence says, not maliciously, but insincerely. I'm still trying to figure him out. He's part malevolent douchebag, part class clown.

He walks off with Fred, still laughing.

I'm too embarrassed and angry to hang around to talk to Michael about the assignment. I turn on my heel and walk out of the classroom.

# MICHAEL

I find myself stealing glances Mina's way in English, watching her laugh and chat with Paula or Cameron. I try to concentrate but my feelings are clumsy, like untied shoelaces I keep tripping over.

I walk into the library and find her sitting near the window reading, her legs propped up on a chair in front of her. I approach her, nervous for some stupid reason. But not for a second am I going to show it.

I slide into the seat across from her and put my bag down on the desk.

"Hey."

She eyes me warily.

"Sorry," I say.

"For what?" she snaps.

I don't get her. I feel like giving her a *Dummies' Guide to Teenage Boys* and informing her that:

Boys don't apologize easily.

Girls are usually impressed when a boy apologizes.

Ergo, be impressed with me.

She's staring at me, waiting for me to respond.

"Well, I'm sorry for what I said in our first class, but you've already rejected that apology. And I guess I'm sorry for the fight . . . but I'm not sure why really, seeing as you had nothing to do with it. But still you're making me feel guilty for some strange reason, so that's another apology you can reject. And I'm sorry for Terrence, which you have also managed to throw back in my face."

"I don't get you" is her response.

"Huh?"

"One minute you're *reject the refugees!* The next minute you're *oh but I still feel sorry for them.* Then you're defending a guy who refers to Indigenous Australians as Abos and in *quote marks.* Terrence may be a smug idiot, but at least he knows it and owns it."

I'm slightly annoyed now. "Look, can we not do the personality analysis thing?"

She raises her eyebrows at me but doesn't respond.

I take it as a cue to change the subject. "So how about we do the interviews in the Village? That's the main hub."

"Fine, fine. So what day are you free to meet?"

"How about Sunday morning?"

"Yeah, I can do that."

"Do you know the area well? You're new here, aren't you? You've moved here from Auburn, right?"

"Yep." I pick up a hint of defiance in her tone. It's as though she's challenging me to say something. "Been there before? Or are you a strictly North Shore kind of guy?"

"I've been to Parramatta."

"You brave boy, you. Did you wear a bulletproof vest?"

I can't help but laugh. "You know, you have a deceptively laid-back vibe about you until you open your mouth."

"So I'm completely out of line in making that assumption?"

"Totally," I lie.

God help me if she knows what my parents and their mates say about southwestern Sydney. *Ethnic ghettos. No-go lands. People stick to their own kind.*

The bell rings.

"So interview the public on Aussie culture." She rolls her eyes. "Morello, with his sense of humor, paired us together because we clearly have *so* much in common."

"Clearly," I say, grinning.

The beginnings of a smile stir on the edges of her mouth as she busies herself with her bag.

We are worlds apart in every sense and I want to know everything there is to know about her.

So that smile she gives me? It's a first step—in my mind anyway.

On Saturday we say good-bye to Dad. He makes me promise to look after the family, and then Joe ushers him away, reassuring us he's in good hands. I feel queasy just thinking about him in war zones. It sounded exciting at first. Now it seems like a stupid thing for him to have agreed to do.

Seeing my mum cry is tough. She's a strong woman and it takes a lot for her to break. I give her a big bear hug. She's short and plump and her head comes to my chest. She looks up at me, wiping the tears from her eyes.

"When did you get so tall?" she says sentimentally, taking a step back and blowing her nose.

Nathan is taking it all in stride. "Why are you sad, Mum?" he asks.

"Because I'll miss your dad."

Nathan proceeds to recite statistics on road accidents in Australia, and how we should be more worried about people falling off ladders and dying than being killed in a terrorist act.

"Hmm" is Mum's simple response.

Nathan is not satisfied he's convinced her. "Mum, we have a bigger chance of dying in an accident on our way home than Dad has of being shot in Iraq," he says matter-of-factly. "Be more worried about us getting in our car now than Dad going to Baghdad."

"Oh, Nathan," Mum says, and blows her nose.

I spend Saturday night at Terrence's place. Fred is there too. We interrupt a game of *COD* to surf the net to trace

Dad's route and find out as much as we can about Iraq and Indonesia.

"It's bloody information overload," Terrence mutters.

"Your dad could get killed, you know," Fred says.

"Gee, thanks, man. That's just what I needed to hear. Although, Nathan would challenge you on that."

Fred pulls a face. "Yeah, sorry. Just telling it as I see it."

"Don't worry. I'm stressed. Happy? This won't be *MasterChef.* Undercook a roast and you're kicked out. The program's going to try to get the ratings."

"Yep," Terrence says. "The more drama and danger, the better. They'll push them all to their limits. Imagine if they make them watch a beheading."

"He won't crack," I say, but I'm terrified about how he's going to cope. How do you go from North Shore Sydney to a war zone? How can you go in and out and still be the same person?

# MINA

"*This* lady. White shirt, jeans, coffee."

"Okay."

"Quick!"

"*Okay*."

"Now."

"Okay!"

"What happened?"

Michael scrunches up his face. "I really hate this. I mean, why should they stop to talk to us? I'd be annoyed if I was them. Maybe you should do the interviews. I'll do the editing."

"We have to do it together," I say. "Morello warned us all, remember? The trick is eye contact. Find someone who isn't looking down at their phone."

"So we're left with old people."

"That is *so* ageist, Michael."

"It was a joke."

"Ha. Ha." I roll my eyes. "Come on. Let's get this over with.

If we get a no, we move on to the next person. Your ego will survive. It's not as though you're asking people out on a date."

Michael's eyes flash cheekily. "What makes you think I've experienced rejection in that department?"

"My God, judging from this assignment you'd be an emotional mess if you did. Okay, pass the recorder to me. I'll do the next one. And then it's your turn, no ifs or buts."

We somehow manage to find five people who will talk to us, and then we go to a café to debrief.

"Barbecues, beer, the beach, and the bush," I say, and smile. "We hit cliché central."

"I mean, really, the *bush*?" Michael says, and we both laugh.

He surveys the café and snorts. "I nearly laughed in that woman's face. She's going on about the bush and then gets into her BMW convertible." He rolls his eyes.

I sip my iced coffee. I want to tell him that when we were in the camps waiting for a boat we spoke about what we imagined Australia would be like. Kangaroos, koalas, wide-open spaces. Then, when we arrived, we were locked up, and the images we had shrank smaller and smaller until Australia became tiny patches of sky beyond the barbed wire.

I want to tell him this and more. But I don't.

"So are you a beach person?" Michael asks. His eyes are fixed on me again. There's an intensity in the way he stares at me sometimes, as though he's trying to read my mind, figure me out.

"Not really."

Just then my phone vibrates. I look down. Mum's left me a voice mail message. That's when I realize there's a missed call from her too. I listen to the message. She tells me to come home early from the library (my cover for today) because they need me at the restaurant. I text her back and put my phone away. I can sense Michael's eyes following me as I take a sip of my drink.

"So what do you want to do when you finish school?" I ask him.

He sighs. "Architecture. UNSW. My dad's old university. Part-time job at a boutique firm while I study. A prestigious career, following in my father's footsteps. Nothing left to chance."

"You don't sound very enthusiastic about it."

His voice drops a few tones, but his eyes are lively, his face mobile. "Yeah. It's kind of complicated."

"Why?"

"Because it's actually the last thing I want to do."

"Hmm. That *is* complicated."

"Told you."

"So what do you want to do?"

Now, a torrent of words. His eyes light up as he talks to me about wanting to go to UTS Design School. About wanting to do graphic design, but not traditional graphic design, the cutting-edge stuff: augmented reality. Virtual reality. A completely different way of thinking about branding, marketing, gaming.

"Let me guess," I say when he takes a breath. "Your dad's against it?"

"Worse. He has no idea." He looks at me helplessly and then exhales. "So *anyway*, what are your plans?"

"I have absolutely no idea. I just need to get the best grades so that my parents don't die of disappointment."

"No pressure or anything for you either, hey?"

I smile. "I'm at Victoria College on a scholarship. We've moved to the other side of Sydney to make the next two years possible for me. Moved from the one place in Sydney where my parents felt completely at home. If that wasn't enough, they've invested in a partnership to open an Afghan restaurant, when the restaurant they were running in Auburn was doing really well. They've turned their lives upside down for me. So getting average grades is not an option."

"Yep. That's pressure."

"Will your parents melt into puddles of abject depression if you don't do architecture?"

Leaning his chin on his hand, he thinks for a moment. "Yep. I think that just about summarizes my current situation."

"Welcome to the parents-overly-invested-in-our-future club."

He suddenly bursts into laughter.

"What's so funny?"

There's a look of triumph in his eyes. "Looks like we have something in common after all."

———————————————

I send a text message to Paula.

**Me:**
So. It seems Michael might not be so bad after all.

**Paula:**
The Terrence friendship thing though?

**Me:**
Still confused about that.

**Paula:**
All hope lies with u now Mina.

**Me:**
What do u mean?

**Paula:**
Rehabilitation.

**Me:**
LOL. Reckon I can get him delivering food packs with me to Villawood?

**Paula:**

Keep batting those criminally long eyelashes of yours & u just might.

**Me:**

Gee it's nice to know I'm worth respecting for my mind.

# MICHAEL

I need a new job. Last year I worked part-time at a local juice bar but my shifts were cut and I couldn't find anything else over summer vacation. My MacBook Pro is on its last legs, and I want to preorder the Oculus Rift and HoloLens, because you can never have enough virtual reality headsets. My parents could easily fund my addiction to gadgets with big fat weekly direct deposits to my bank account, like Terrence gets. But they pride themselves on old-fashioned "stand-on-your-own-two-feet" values. That means no silver platter. We might be upper middle class, they constantly tell me, but things are tough in the real world and you need to be prepared.

Tough is relative I guess. They've basically lined up a job for me at the end of university thanks to Dad's friend Kyle (a job I have no intention of taking). Then there's the fact that I already have my own car, a Jeep Wrangler. It came as a surprise, not a birthday present like some kids at school. When my granddad passed away last year he left Nathan and me each a chunk of money in his will so that we could buy a car when we got our licenses. The only thing I'd ever won before was a Mother's Day raffle in third grade, which consisted of a tacky basket with plastic flowers and floral soap that ended up giving Mum a rash. So when Dad told me about the will I kind of fell apart—in a good way, and still respecting my alpha male credentials (no, I didn't cry). I'd been close to my grand-dad and he'd only had us because my grandma had passed away when I was a kid and Dad was an only child. Mum had wanted to delay me getting the car until I finished school, but Dad and I convinced her in the end. It made life easier for them if I could get myself to school and basketball games. The rule was I had to stick to local.

On Sunday, Terrence, Fred, and I go to Chatswood so that I can submit my résumé to different shops. It feels positively Jurassic having to hand in a hard copy, but I've had no luck with my online applications.

When we're done, we go to the food court for lunch.

"I told you I can lend you money," Terrence says. "What's the point of being friends with a spoiled rich kid if you don't use me?"

I laugh. "Nah, man, I'm good. Thanks anyway."

"He's got too much pride," Fred says. "Me? I've got none. Can you get a guy another burrito?"

Terrence throws Fred a ten and Fred kisses the note, laughs, and gets up to buy round two.

"I'm serious," Terrence continues. "I know you're into all that geeky hardware stuff. I can get it for you."

"Quit it, you bastard. You're getting soppy."

He grins.

Fred comes back with a burrito and hot chips.

"Keep the change," he says, throwing ten cents on the table. We all laugh.

"So did you meet up with Mina for that dumb assignment?" Terrence asks.

"Yeah," I say, suddenly feeling uncomfortable. I don't want to talk about Mina with him.

"She's smart," he says. "Good-looking too. But a stuck-up cow."

"Nah, she's all right actually."

"It was fun stirring her up like that," Terrence laughs.

"So did you meet up with Jane?" I ask, trying to change the topic. "Morello paired you together, didn't he? Has that guy got no clue about the torture he's putting her through, assigning the two of you together?"

Terrence is too busy chewing to bother responding.

"She's got the hots for you bad," Fred says.

Terrence swallows and then grins. "Yeah, I know."

"You're messing with her, aren't you?" I say, frowning. "Don't do that, man."

"That kind of attitude is the reason you've had girlfriends and I've had fun."

Fred bursts out laughing.

"You guys are such Neanderthals," I say, rolling my eyes at them.

Terrence shrugs, taking my comment as a compliment. "Just because you've always been a sensitive New Age geek doesn't mean we have to be as well."

I shoot Fred a look. "I don't know why you're laughing, you moron. The one and only time you've kissed a girl was when the lifeguard gave you CPR at Coogee." Terrence roars with laughter. Fred is easygoing and in no denial about his abysmal record with girls, so he laughs along too.

# MINA

Mum's on her phone, checking out Facebook.

"What's so funny?"

"I'm just looking at the photos of the kids at Jolly's After-School Care." She smiles. "I miss them."

"Why don't you apply to work at an after-school-care center around here? You're a natural."

Mum eyes me. "I have been applying," she says slowly.

I grin at her, impressed. "Really?"

"I sent my résumé to fifteen places in the area. I got one response. When she heard me speak she was surprised. Said she expected me to speak English fluently." Mum gives me a reproachful look. "Didn't I warn you that polishing my résumé too much would create false expectations?"

I shrug my shoulders. "I just fixed the spelling and grammar."

"Well, I don't know what to do. Someone with my name

and background isn't going to find work here, whether I can structure a sentence or not."

"So it's not my fault then," I say, trying to distract her so that neither of us has to contemplate the weight of her words.

I just manage to dodge the cushion she throws at me.

"I miss Auburn," she says.

"Yep. I hear you." I pause. "But, Mum? Don't give up."

She shrugs, and it's as though she's flicking my comment onto the ground. "Sometimes the apartments here feel like graves," she says. "They're not places where people come out and speak to each other."

I smile coyly. "You really want creepy bifocals with staring problem in number twenty-five to socialize with you?"

She waves her hand in my direction and shushes me. But I'm just getting started.

"You don't even like the couple next door because they have a dog."

She pulls a face. "That's not why I don't like them. Stand in the elevator with them one day. It's as though any eye contact will kill them. I'm lucky if they grunt hello. People here are just cold."

She throws her phone to the side and stretches her arms above.

"Better than people being in everyone's business."

"But at least people care about each other."

"Excuse me, but Aunty Tashima didn't care about anybody but herself when she busted me for skipping school in seventh grade and had to tell everybody. The news probably reached Kabul."

"Oh, you are a drama queen, Mina." Mum lets out a faint chuckle. "That was years ago. Anyway, being a nosy gossip is different. I want people to talk to me, not gossip."

"What kind of elevator small talk are you so desperate for anyway?"

"I want big talk. I want to know people and for them to know me. But it's all on the surface here. Nothing personal. I stick to *good morning* and, maybe if they smile long enough, the weather. But we're strangers and that's how people want it."

"Shake things up and talk then."

She rolls her eyes at me. "Ten years in Auburn and I felt finally that I could just *be*. Here, I have to try to learn to be all over again. Who I am in Auburn cannot exist here."

Her words ring true, but I worry that agreeing with her will only exacerbate her feelings.

"Just be yourself and things will sort themselves out," I try.

"Your advice is terrible, Mina," she says, practically wincing. "Just terrible."

I have to admit she has a point.

She shakes her head at me and we grin at each other. "Please just fix me a cup of tea, will you?"

"How many weeks pregnant again?" I ask, getting up.

"Enough to be pampered day and night."

"Does the self-pity routine get worse?"

"Oh yes, definitely. That, and hemorrhoids."

"Ew!" I splutter. "Too much information."

"See. Nothing *personal*. I've lost you to them already."

I laugh and make her tea.

"Sorry, Mum."

"For what?"

"For making you leave Auburn."

"Oh, don't be ridiculous, Mina," she scoffs. "All I care about is securing the best future for you. And we have the restaurant here too. So it's a move for us as a family."

"But you sound so upset."

She waves my words away like a pesky fly. "Ignore my silly whining. We don't have the luxury to do grass is greener. We've got to make this work. And we will. I don't want you to worry about anything except your grades. Every now and then I might carry on, but just ignore me. Who wants to try to get kids to do arts and crafts when all they want to do is run around after a long day of school anyway?"

---

It's Thursday and we're busy tonight. Baba and Irfan are out back running the kitchen. We're a couple of staff down, so I've stepped in to help, along with Mum, who's steering clear of the meat.

I'm behind the front counter chatting with a couple as they settle the bill, when the restaurant door is flung wide open and a man with a huge birthmark on his face walks purposefully toward me. He stops and waits, eyes darting around the restaurant as I finalize the bill. I sense a nervous energy about him. He's tapping one leg impatiently; his arms are folded tightly over his chest. When the couple leaves, I turn my attention to him.

"Can I help you?"

"Yeah. Yeah, you can."

I stand tall, waiting for him to continue.

"Yes?" I press him.

"Is your meat halal?"

I look at him, dumbfounded. His question takes me completely by surprise.

"I said is your meat halal?"

"Yes." I wonder if he's been hired to check certification and point to the halal certificate behind the counter. "We're certified, as you can see."

"Pretty obscure place to put the certificate, isn't it? The customers can't see it there."

I study his face closely, trying to make sense of what's happening. "It's right behind me in plain view."

"It doesn't say where the money's going."

I don't know who he is or what he wants, so I hold my tongue, not daring to provoke him until I know more.

"And who are you?" I ask. "Sorry, I didn't catch your name."

"I didn't offer it." He looks around the restaurant again and then whips out a phone and scrolls through the screen. He looks up at me. "Is the manager here?"

"Yes. Both of them. Why?"

"I just need to talk to them."

"Well, they're in the kitchen now and we're low on staff tonight. So unless you're ordering, I'll have to ask you to leave, please."

He takes a long breath and lets it out. He looks like he has a whole lot more to say but must think twice because he barks that he'll be back soon, turns swiftly on his heel, and marches out the door.

It gets manically busy after that and by the time we close up I've forgotten all about him.

———————————

The best part about eleventh grade is the free study periods. The worst part is that Paula's don't coincide with mine.

I'm in the library with Jane, Leica, and Cameron. Leica and Cameron are nestled up close to each other doing work, but not close enough for the librarian to give them a hands-off warning. Jane's giving me a brain freeze, sparing me no details about her hour with Terrence for their assignment. I can think of better things to do than try to decode Terrence's feelings for her. Things like, say, pouring salt into an infected blister.

That Jane's not getting the message that I'm bored has me seriously doubting her credibility when it comes to interpreting Terrence's mixed signals.

I'm saved when Sienna, from history, comes up to the table and invites us to her birthday party.

I panic inside. Parties are nightmare territory for me. I'll have to spin a story to my mum about studying at a friend's place. But even if that works, because of my early curfew, I'll probably have to leave before most people have even arrived.

My head isn't coping with trying to summarize the chronology of World War I while listening to Jane go on and on about Terrence. So I close Word, knowing this means a late night tonight, and open the website of one of my favorite bands, The xx.

Not long to go for their album to drop. I'm counting down.

The bell rings, to my relief, and I'm left alone.

Then I notice Zoe and Clara enter the library. They can see that there's plenty of space next to me and, given we're in the same class, avoiding my table isn't a neutral decision. They make eye contact with me, then sit down at another table, close enough to me to make the point. A short while later Zoe gets up and makes a beeline to a bookshelf near me. On her return, balancing a pile of books in her arms, she stops to talk to me.

"How'd you go with the essay?" Her tone is off balance.

Here is a girl who's trying desperately hard to suppress her anxiety about coming second. I feel a wave of pity for her.

"I got an A."

Her face crumbles for a split second. She quickly regains her composure. "Do you have a tutor?"

"No," I snap, irritated. "Why would you ask that?"

"It's just a question." I have to hand it to her. She seems to think I'm the impolite one.

I throw the question back at her. "Do *you* have a tutor?"

Now it's her turn to be indignant. "I don't need one!"

"So what did you get—"

She doesn't give me a chance and quickly turns on her heel.

Weary of her antics, I plug my earphones into my ears.

Bliss.

I'm in the moment but outside of it. The people and things around me don't exist. It's just me and the music and a swell of joy and sorrow and memory courses through my veins. It was Christy Bonnaci from ninth grade who first put me onto indie music. She took me aside after a particularly vigorous free-dance class in drama and said, very seriously, very sage-like, "There's nothing wrong with liking the playlist of a *Just Dance* Wii game, but I think you can do better than that." One recess with a pair of earplugs and I was converted.

I should be studying but Zoe's put me right off. I just feel like chilling out, except that word is all wrong because the music doesn't cool me down—it warms me.

But then somebody plonks a bag on the table and sits down opposite me.

"You like The xx?" A bewildered tone. I force an eye open to check who the voice belongs to.

Michael stares at me, a look of surprise on his face.

I slowly raise my head. "Yeah. I do."

He smiles.

"How'd you know?" I ask.

He points to my laptop screen, open on the band's website page.

"Oh. So are you a fan too?"

"Love them," he says.

"Album drop soon."

"I *know*. I can't wait." A pause. "They're not mainstream." He looks at me like he's trying to figure me out.

I raise an eyebrow. "Are you wondering how somebody who lives in *Western Sydney* could be into indie pop?"

He tries to backpedal but it's crash and fall.

And then, as a sudden afterthought, he says: "Lived."

"Huh?"

"You said *lives* in Western Sydney."

"Oh. Okay . . . lived."

"You say that word almost mournfully. Do you miss the place?"

"Every day."

"What do you miss?"

"Tacky clothing shops, cops chasing cars with defects, the smell of Adana kebabs, the zillion different accents and languages and, best of all, wog warmth."

"*Wog warmth?*"

"Yeah." I smile.

"What does that even mean?"

"Everyone's *darling*, up in people's business, ready to help and talk and get in your face with their opinions and overdosed aftershave and loud voices. It's quiet here. Stiff. People are ironed crisp and unruffled."

"Aren't you generalizing?"

"Shamelessly."

"Anyway, I thought *wog* was a derogatory word."

"Yeah, it is. If *you* use it."

He raises an eyebrow.

"So . . ." He drums his fingers on the table. "The xx . . ." I've impressed him.

"Well, if we're talking preconceived notions, I would have had you down as a Bieber fan myself."

He makes a gesture of a knife stabbing his heart.

I chuckle. "Any other assumptions about me you need to sort out, here's your chance."

He shakes his head. "Nah, it's okay."

"Come on. I'm curious. I promise I won't take offense."

"You think I'm falling for that line?" He laughs, and I feel an unexpected wave of attraction to him. I look away, focusing my attention on my laptop screen.

"I take my promises seriously."

"Maybe. Probably. But the promise part isn't the problem. It's how you define offense."

I can't help but laugh.

He fixes his eyes on me. "Okay, fine. We'll start easy. Favorite food?"

I lean back in my chair and raise an eyebrow at him. "Oh, is this one of those lame twenty questions?"

"Yeah. Why not."

"Okay. That's easy. Pizza."

"Pet peeve?"

I think for a moment. "Well, you know what I find annoying? When you're at the movies, gorging on popcorn, and there's that one couple who aren't eating anything. Who does that?"

"Weird people."

"Exactly! It's just common courtesy to join in. Because when everybody else is shoving the popcorn in, I feel safe to munch on mine. But that couple sucks all the joy out of it because I'm sitting there thinking, *Can they hear me? Are they annoyed? Have I just ruined that scene because they can hear me cracking a corn kernel?*"

"Wow. I was expecting maybe something along the lines of close talkers, or people who take a sip of their drink while there's still food in their mouth. But that was about as thorough and considered a reply as I've ever gotten."

"I take my movie experiences seriously. So what's your pet peeve then?"

"People on public transport clipping nails, or eating something smelly. Or worse, putting their bags on seats."

"And then they give you a filthy look if you ask them to move their bag so you can sit down."

"Just sit on the bag. Works every time. So, favorite movie?"

"The *Lord of the Rings* trilogy."

"You're a Tolkien geek?" He grins.

"Yep. I'm holding out for a *Lord of the Rings/Hobbit* movie marathon one day. I've got it all figured out too. Everybody dresses up—you know, just to increase the geek factor—and we rent out a community hall or some such place from the morning. Everyone brings a beanbag, cushions, junk food."

"And you march people out and subject them to some form of public humiliation if their phone rings or they take selfies mid-movie."

We keep on talking and when the bell rings it takes us by surprise. Michael leaves, and I pack my bag. As I stand up, I notice Zoe and Clara staring at me, slight smirks on their faces. It irks me, and before I have a chance to even think twice I walk up to them, stop, and say, "Better luck next time on the essay, Zoe," and saunter off, head high.

# MICHAEL

Mum is slipping into paranoid fantasies about Dad being killed by a suicide bomber, or else appearing in a scratchy YouTube video with an unruly beard and a gun pointed at his temple as he's forced to read out demands for the withdrawal of infidels from Muslim lands.

There's no contact allowed. When the phone rings, she panics, thinking we're going to be sucked into a hostage crisis. We get daily calls from an SBS producer reassuring us that everyone is fine. But Mum ends up wondering if she's in fact been speaking to a terrorist putting on a good Aussie accent.

She's convinced Dad's politics might have landed him on some international terrorist hit list.

"How could we have agreed?" she wails over dinner one night.

"Mum, I hate to break it to you," I joke, "but it's highly unlikely that Dad has a political profile that's actually extended beyond the lower North Shore of Sydney."

"Well, thank God for that," she says to herself.

"You know, Mum," Nathan says, taking a noisy slurp of his juice. "If Dad *is* killed, the organization will become even more popular."

"Do you want Dad to die?" Mum suddenly snaps, but then her face is awash with guilt and she quickly apologizes.

She sometimes has moments when she forgets to self-censor around Nathan. They're usually entertaining (well, in hindsight anyway), but if they go too far the consequences can be disastrous (like the time Nathan was seven and she'd had enough in the shops and told him to just get out of her way and so he did. For an hour. Westfield security was very supportive).

"Everybody dies," Nathan helpfully offers. "I don't want Dad to die. Or you. Or Michael. Or me, although I'd rather you die first because you've lived longer and it's only fair. But you will die, you know. You could kiss me good night tonight and die in your sleep and Dad could be alive and okay in Baghdad as bombs detonate around him." He shrugs as though Mum is an idiot for not working out something so logical.

"Thank you, Nathan," Mum says wearily.

"Any time, Mum. Can I have more juice, please?"

# MINA

Paula's coming over for dinner tonight. I've been buzzing all day, like a kid waiting for her birthday party to start. The house is sparkling and smells of lemon bleach, frangipani, and lamb biryani. Mum and I have been cleaning and cooking for hours because according to my mum's logic, adolescent friendships are made or broken by the orderliness of one's linen closet.

I'm putting the last touches to the table for two that I've set on the veranda, and Mum is checking the stove.

"So her parents are both lawyers?" Mum asks.

"Yep."

"And they go on vacation overseas every year?"

"That's what I've picked up from our conversations."

"And she has a car?"

"Well, not exactly. She's only sixteen, Mum, I told you that."

"But you mentioned she has a car."

"It's her sister's car. But she's overseas so she's left her car here and Paula's taking driving lessons in the car."

"And the car is a Saab?"

"Mum, quit it, will you? I know what you're thinking and she's not like that, and no, she's not going to judge us because we're living in a shoe box."

Mum pauses, then draws a breath. "I just want to make a good impression. For your sake."

Mercifully, the front buzzer rings. I leap from the couch and run to answer and let Paula in. Within seconds she's at the front door. She sees Mum and launches at her, giving her a big hug and a lopsided, utterly endearing grin.

It doesn't take long for Paula to be inducted into the Hall of Acceptable Friends.

Mum insists on leaving the two of us alone to eat dinner and hang out. Because the apartment is so small, she retreats to her bedroom with a cup of tea, bowl of salted pumpkin seeds, and the second half of a Bollywood movie.

"I've always wanted to watch a Bollywood movie," Paula says as we eat dinner.

"If you ever end up watching one, just expect to watch it over a few days, because who has three straight hours free?"

After we've eaten and washed up, we balance a junk food stash between us and go to my room. We settle onto my bed, spread the food around us, take out my laptop, and start watching funny YouTube clips of models tripping on runways, people falling off bikes, and other Fail compilations that send us into fits of hysteria.

"So you think my *Lord of the Rings* movie marathon is a good idea?" I ask Paula after we finally catch our breath.

"Definitely! Morello's a big fan, by the way. So, you know, we have Middle-earth in common. Bet you his wife doesn't even know the difference between an orc and troll."

"Easy. Just think of the difference between Terrence and Fred."

She laughs.

"So where will we hold the marathon?" I ask. "If we get enough people we could all chip in and rent the community hall here."

"How about we do it at my place? We've got a cinema room."

"A *cinema* room?"

Paula looks momentarily embarrassed. "Yeah, yeah. I know."

Despite my misgivings, Paula insists that her parents won't mind an invasion of teenagers.

She waves a hand dismissively. "It's called emotional blackmail. Let me demonstrate." She sits up, grins at me. "Pay attention," she tells me. "Unleashing my finest acting skills here.

"*Mum, can my friends and I have the house all day and can you supply all the food and drink and make sure you're out until the last person's gone?*"

She clears her throat, then puts on a breezy voice. "*Make*

*sure we're out of the house? Why, Paula, we had no intention of being home in the first place. We'll be in the office that weekend.*

*"But you don't know which weekend yet.*

*"Minor detail, darling. Here's my credit card. Buy as much food and drink as you need. Have a wonderful time!"*

Paula bows, lets out a bitter laugh, and then falls back onto the pillow. "So in other words, venue and sustenance are taken care of. We just need to figure out who to invite."

"So they work long hours?"

"Yep."

"My stepfather does too."

"Does your mum?"

"She's in and out of the restaurant."

"I'm a feminist; I don't care which of them cuts back their hours, I only wish one of them would. Meanwhile, my sister, Nancy, abandoned me and is spending her gap year in the States. So I'm basically an orphan with a one-email-a-week sibling." She shakes her head. "So hopefully I've made you feel sorry for me now, which is why you have to get into slam poetry with me!"

"Slam poetry?"

She grabs the laptop and goes back to YouTube.

"Check this channel out: *Def Poetry Jam.* It's an old HBO show. I've died and gone to heaven. It features all these spoken word artists. Prepare to lose your breath."

It's like nothing I've seen or heard before. The words pierce me. The beat, the intensity, the rhythm. Some performers' voices are soft melodies, lulling you into a false sense of security until wham, they've pulled the ground from under your feet. Others puncture your heart with every word.

"Wow."

"I want to perform one day. I've been going to a poetry slam event in the city. I've made some friends there, but I don't have the courage to get up on stage yet. Would you come with me to the next one? I might have worked up the courage by then."

"Sure! I'd love to."

She grabs my hand dramatically. "Thank you! Okay, let's do a Facebook invite for our movie marathon!"

> *One does not simply receive a LOTR movie marathon/ costume party invitation and decline. Dress up as your favorite LOTR character.*

We decide to send the invite to Adrian (because he's smart and laid-back), Jane (because Paula will feel guilty if she doesn't), Leica and Cameron (because they're joined at the hip). Paula's going to ask a couple of friends from her slam poetry group too. I tell Paula about Maha and a couple of my other friends from Auburn Grove Girls High and ask her if I can invite them too.

"Of course!"

"You'll love Maha," I tell her with a laugh. "Or not . . . It could go either way."

"Hey, I have an uncanny knack for memorizing book and film quotes and a crush on a dead gay writer *and* a teacher. I'm not one to judge."

---

Paula's text comes through as I enter the school gates.

> **Public service announcement from Bus Route 419:**

> **I don't think I could survive an apocalypse. Canned food. No poached eggs on sourdough with mushrooms in balsamic. Pass.**

> **See you soon, Mina Colada.**

---

We file into the school hall for a special assembly. The entire campus of Auburn Grove Girls High would fit inside this hall. Ms. Ham stands in front of the podium on a stage I'm sure rivals anything on Broadway. She announces that the tenth graders have put on a Global Citizen Photography Reflections Exhibition following their two-week trip to Ghana. She encourages us—well, *orders* us would be more accurate—to visit the Middle School Atrium to have a look before the exhibition moves to the foyer of the local council building.

"I am so proud of our tenth-grade students, who have demonstrated a real commitment to understanding the responsibilities that come with their privileges. You are all this country's future leaders and that is both an immense privilege and a burden."

As I listen to Ms. Ham drone on and on about how Victoria College graduates will run the country one day, two thoughts dawn on me. The first is that all the teachers here just assume that the guys and girls sitting around me have the world at their fingertips. And the second is that despite wearing the same uniform as everybody else, I feel like an imposter. Like I'm in the wrong manufacturing plant, only seconds away from a tap on the shoulder and a gentle but firm, *You belong in the people-who-will-be-led production line, not this one.*

At Auburn Grove Girls High, when teachers stood up to address us in assemblies, it was to urge us to study hard, stay focused, remain resilient, set goals, seek support. If there was a "leader," she was the exception, not the norm.

Listening to Ms. Ham, I wonder if things would be different if we spent thirteen years being told that we were born to lead, and that the only thing that would ever hold us back would be a limited imagination.

I'm starting to realize that being born into this social world is a little like being born into clean air. You take it in as soon as you breathe, and pretty soon you don't even realize that while you can walk around with clear lungs, other people are wearing oxygen masks just to survive.

———————————

Mr. Morello decides to hold our Society and Culture class in the Middle School Atrium so we can see the tenth grade photography exhibition.

The photos have been blown up and mounted on canvases. There are shots of Victoria College students posing with young children. Photos of Ghanaian kids staring into the camera lens. Or just sitting. Or standing.

Zoe and Clara are standing near us, and I hear them gushing to each other about how *beautiful* the children are. "Oh my God, they're just gorgeous!"

Something about the whole exhibition unsettles me, but I'm struggling to put it into words, even to myself.

I stand in front of a photograph of a young Ghanaian kid. Barefoot, in an undershirt and faded oversized jeans, he has a solemn expression on his face. There's something almost rehearsed in his pose and demeanor. A tenth-grade girl named Sandra is crouched down on her knees, one arm around him, grinning at the camera. The whole photograph feels staged, as if he's just playing out a role for her benefit, like some kind of third-world kid mascot helping people from the first world find themselves. I don't know why it disturbs me, because it's a good thing that they're helping these kids, isn't it? But still, there's a queasy feeling in the pit of my stomach.

"These photos are so much better than the ones we took when we went to Botswana for our trip," Paula says, as we stop and look at a photo of a group of the tenth-grade students digging a veggie patch.

"It's all a bit too *National Geographic* for me," I say.

"What do you mean?"

"Hard to explain," I murmur.

There are some things so deeply sedimented that the slightest excavation and the walls will start to fall in on themselves.

"Do all the tenth graders go on these trips?" I ask Paula.

"Yeah, pretty much most of them."

"How much does it cost?"

"Hmm, several grand I think. I'm not sure exactly."

We keep moving, and then there's Michael, standing in our path.

"They're good photos, hey?" he says cheerfully.

"Mina doesn't think so," Paula says with a smile and shrug.

"Have you gone on one of these trips?" I ask him.

"Yeah, with Paula too, in tenth grade. We went to Botswana. It was amazing. We trekked through the Kalahari Desert—"

"I liked it when we tracked rhinos in the Khama Rhino Sanctuary," Paula says excitedly.

"Yeah, that was brilliant. We fixed up run-down buildings and built a sports field at an orphanage too."

"That's nice," I tell them.

Michael gives me a quizzical look. "What's wrong?"

I shrug. "The world's one big wide adventure playground for some people, I guess."

Paula and Michael both look at me but choose not to reply.

———————————

Michael appears at the library during second period of my double free period.

He says hi, throws his bag down, and takes out his MacBook. He starts working, no fuss. I don't comment. Maybe all his friends are in class and he's a bit of a loner for this period too. But then, why me?

We settle into a quiet rhythm, each of us doing our own thing. I've got my iPod hooked up to my earphones, as does he.

"Are you always so cynical?" he suddenly asks.

"Pardon?"

"Cynical. I thought rich kids going to poor countries would be the last thing to feel offended by." He quickly raises the palm of his hand. "Wait, I'm not trying to provoke you. I'm genuinely interested in why that exhibition annoyed you."

"It didn't annoy me," I say hesitantly.

"Yeah. It did. I could tell."

"Things can be more complicated than just being annoyed. Anyway, let's just leave it, hey?"

He shrugs. "Suit yourself. Do you know Grouplove?"

I smile and hold up my screen so he can see my favorite albums playlist. He scans it and grins.

"I have 'Tongue Tied' on repeat so much even my mum can practically sing it," I say. "She hates it of course."

"Every respectable teenager should love the kind of music their parents hate."

"Definitely."

Smiling his approval, he adds, "Impressive playlist."

"Yeah, the Taliban gave me a solid education in indie music."

He laughs uncertainly.

"It's okay," I reassure him. "You *can* laugh."

"Hard to tell when every joke manages to offend somebody."

"Oh, give me a break. People only pretend they don't know the difference between being a dumbass racist jerk and, yeah, er, not being one."

"You better polish that one before using it as your next Facebook status."

I make a face at him and he gives me a mischievous smile.

"Wait a second." He feigns a look of offense. "So are you saying I'm a dumbass racist jerk?"

"Not necessarily." I snort.

"Wow, thanks."

"I'd say we'd pretty much disagree with each other on most things—"

"—except music and the pitfalls of public transport and movies."

"You keeping tabs?" There's more grinning.

"Anyway, you don't know anything else about me. And I don't know anything else about you."

That just sits in the air as I contemplate a response. Have we upgraded from classroom screaming match, to Sunday coffee for an assignment, to needing to get to know more about each other?

Saved by the phone. It's Baba. He never calls me during school hours. Worried, I answer. He tells me a man came into the restaurant throwing around accusations about halal food funding terrorism. Baba is upset and I apologize to him, tell him that the man came in last week but things got so busy it slipped my mind. I calm him down, tell him it's probably just some stupid prank. He's going to call the police if the man shows up again.

"Is that Farsi you were speaking?"

"Yeah," I say, distracted. Who is that man and what does he want?

He cocks his head to the side and grins at me. "Talking about the brilliant company you keep?"

"Don't flatter yourself," I say, but I can't help but laugh.

# MICHAEL

I get a job at a call center. I'm working two afternoon shifts a week and the money's not bad.

I go through training first. How to answer calls, how long to speak, clocking in and out, monitored toilet breaks (what the?), how to deal with complaints (otherwise known as Don't Say the F-Word).

Then Anh, the manager, plants me down at a cubicle, hands me my headset, and says: "Don't screw this up."

My first day's charity is the Salvation Army. I open up the document with the list of people I have to contact in my shift. I have a target to meet. It seems easy enough. Everybody loves the Salvos.

I dial the first number. A man answers. He sounds groggy, like I've woken him up.

"Um, hi, sir, my name is Michael and I'm calling on behalf of the Salvation Army—"

"Are you a telemarketer?"

"Um, no, sir." I read out the script, trying to sound natural. "With winter approaching, more and more people at risk are finding it difficult to make ends—"

"Then they should bloody get a job like the rest of us and maybe I'll be able to do mine properly if I get some sleep before my shift starts. Don't call again!"

He hangs up on me. The rejection is hard.

But I get over it. Fast.

Twenty calls later I've been called a dick and a nuisance and a liar. When people agree to donate, they spend most of the call yakking on about their personal lives. I know I have to cut the calls short because there are strict time limits. I try to tell one woman that I don't have the time to hear her out about her husband's affair with the next-door neighbor and she gives me the wrong credit card number as punishment. Every time I hang up, convinced I've spoken to the rudest person on the planet, the next call proves me wrong.

I make twenty dollars in total.

My target was one thousand.

Anh shakes his head at me. "You're not here to play counselor. Get the money, cut back on the small talk, and move on to the next call."

"Okay. Sorry."

"Next charity will be guide dogs. If you can't get money for guide dogs, do yourself a favor and get a job selling Big Macs."

Such an encouraging mentor, Anh is.

I'm ravenous. I charge through the front door and straight to the fridge. Nothing appeals to me and I call out in desperation to Mum. She emerges from the family room.

"I'm starving," I moan.

"Let's order pizza."

Half an hour later, Nathan, Mum, and I are stuffing our faces with pizza and garlic bread and watching a couple who are planning to turn an old wool mill into a modern mansion on *Grand Designs*. Mum's in multitask mode, watching as she works on her laptop.

"Grading essays?" I ask her.

"Nope. Editing our *Who We Are* page on the website."

Ten minutes into *Grand Designs*, Nathan airily blurts out: "Why are we watching this show? Dad's not here, and Michael doesn't want to be an architect anymore."

I stiffen, slowly swallow the piece of pizza that's threatening to lodge in my throat.

Mum looks up sharply from her laptop. The woman misses nothing. "What was that?"

Nathan jumps up on the couch and lands on his knees. "Why are we watching this show? Dad's not—"

"Yes, I heard you, Nathan," Mum says, her voice strained. She turns to face me, dabbing a bit of sauce on the corner of her mouth with a tissue. "What's Nathan talking about?"

There's a long pause. Caught off guard, I have no game plan

for this discussion. I haven't rehearsed my lines and I certainly would have preferred the chance to break it to her gently.

"Well?" she presses me.

"Jesus, Nathan," I mutter. "How'd *you* know?"

"I heard you talking to Terrence."

Mum stares at me, confused. I heave an exhausted sigh.

"I want to go to UTS Design School."

She sucks in her breath. "What do you mean? *Instead* of architecture or *alongside* architecture?"

"Instead."

She purses her lips. She's silent. Half a minute passes.

"Obviously it's your life, Michael," she finally says, so slowly and carefully I can practically picture her selecting each word with the attention and care you would apply to the task of picking apples at the grocer's. "But you've always wanted to do architecture. You have everything it takes and all the support you need to make a promising career of it. It's a prestigious profession, Michael."

"Prestige is overrated, Mum."

She scoffs. "Don't be silly. Is it anxiety? Are you worried your test results won't be high enough? Your last report card was excellent. Why would you begin to doubt yourself now?"

"I'm not doubting myself." I shift uncomfortably in my seat. "But I want to do graphic design. I want to create things, be part of something that's changing all the time. I mean, who knows what designs will be possible by the time I go to university? Do you know that medical students can use AR to examine cross sections of human anatomy?"

"AR?"

I give her a mini lesson on augmented reality. But I can tell by the look in her eyes that she thinks I'm proposing to go on welfare and play *Minecraft* for the rest of my life.

"Architecture is solid and reliable," she says. "Life isn't all about sitting in front of a computer, Michael. Gaming doesn't pay bills. Art doesn't even pay bills. Those aren't careers. They're hobbies you pursue on the side of a career."

"It's my life. I'm sorry, but I don't want what you and Dad want for me."

We go back and forth. Mum wants me to understand how lucky I am. She pleads with me to not decide on anything yet. To just get the highest test scores I can and then make a decision.

We fight. I'm bringing this up at the wrong time. I'm being impetuous and ungrateful for an opportunity other people could only dream about. Dad has enough on his plate with Aussie Values and this would seriously demoralize him.

I hear enough and storm upstairs to my room.

# MINA

The restaurant doors swing open and the guy who questioned me about halal food the other night walks in. He strides up to the counter and asks Baba if he can talk to him privately, suggesting they step outside.

"Why?" I say, standing close to Baba.

"We can do this in front of all your customers," the man says, "or outside. Your pick."

"What's this about?" Baba asks.

"We don't have to speak to you," I say. "Get out of here or I'm calling the police."

The man smirks, and then turns around and walks out.

---

Baba's feeling stressed and I insist he go home early and leave me and the other staff to handle things tonight. He's stubborn but no match for me. Finally he relents, puts his jacket on, lists a string of instructions, and leaves. But just as soon as he's closed the door behind him he's back, calling me outside. The restaurant is full so nobody's really paying attention. But I can see the panic in his face. I rush outside.

There's a guy in a suit, a man with a handheld camera with a *News Tonight* insignia, standing with the man I'd kicked out earlier. Baba is yelling at them to step away from the restaurant, but the sidewalk is a public area and the reporter's not about to leave.

"With reports of halal food funding terrorism overseas, can you confirm whether you know where the money you spend on halal food is actually going?"

Baba looks utterly stricken. I run over to him, blocking him from the camera.

"You have no right," I cry. "We don't have to answer your questions."

"If you've got nothing to hide then why won't you talk to us?" the reporter says.

"I'm calling the police," I say.

"We're well within our rights here," the reporter says.

The doors to Pizza Hub open and a couple steps out. They take in the scene and raise their eyebrows at us. Tim steps out behind them.

"Piss off with your trashy program," he shouts at the reporter.

"Do you have any concerns about where halal funds go?"

"Mate, you're scaring customers away. Piss off or I'll call the cops on you."

Tim meets Baba's eye and Baba mouths a thank-you to him. I grab Baba's hand and quickly lead him back into the restaurant, out to the back.

We're both shaking. I call the police. They arrive in half an hour and take a report. But there's nothing they can do because it all happened off our premises.

---

It airs that night. With the editing job they've done, it just sounds like we have something to hide. The report ends with the reporter outside a mosque, telling the audience about some people's fears of "creeping sharia." There's a shot of the man who harassed us in the restaurant. He's a member of a new organization that wants to stop the "Islamization of Australia." There's a shot of the founder, Alan Blainey. Then there's some file footage of a group of people at an anti-asylum-seeker rally.

*"But is all this just fear-mongering?"* the journalist asks in the end.

A bit too late for that.

I feel like vomiting.

---

It's Hasan's tenth birthday and it's time to cut the cake. I've been looking for him all afternoon but he's been too busy running around with his friends and only offered me a wave whenever I called his name. I'm grinning as I chase him now. He's laughing so hard that he has to stop to catch his breath. I grab him from behind. "Got you!" I cry, and spin him around. I stumble back in horror. His face is featureless. Its anonymity taunts me: the sister who survived; the sister who cannot even remember what her own brother looked like. Guilt plagues me even in sleep.

# MICHAEL

Mum's standing at the kitchen bench swigging down her morning cup of coffee as she makes Nathan's lunch and tests him on his spelling words. I go to the pantry, take out a box of cornflakes, and pour some straight into my mouth.

"Michael!" Mum yells. "Use a bowl."

My mouth full, I shake my head and point to my watch. I grab a banana from the fruit bowl, wave to them both, and head to the front door. Mum rushes after me.

"Wait," she calls out.

I turn to face her, wiping my mouth with the back of my hand.

"Is your decision really final? I mean, don't you want to at least wait until you finish high school and receive your grades?"

"It's final, Mum. Pretty much the one thing I'm certain of in my life is that I want to do graphic design. I'm going to break it to Dad when he gets back and finally I can stop pretending."

Mum's eyes widen. "At least wait."

"Mum!"

"I don't want him to return and have to deal with the disappointment straight up. Let's give him time to settle in and then you can tell him."

I exhale loudly. "Okay, fine."

---

I'm playing with Nathan on the Xbox in the early evening. Mum is in the next room watching an inane current affairs program. She suddenly calls out to me.

I ignore her at first. *FIFA*, or segment on neighborhood feud/restaurant health scare/exploding breast implants? Hardly a difficult choice.

"It's about Aussie Values! Quick! It's coming on after the commercials!"

Nathan and I jump up and run to the family room.

It's like watching a car crash in slow motion. I'm glued to the spot, a wave of nausea rushing through me as I see Mina on the screen, her face racked with panic.

"What's it about?"

"I'm not sure." She looks slightly disturbed. "Nobody should be doing media without your father's authorization. Oh!" Her tone is now one of relief. "It's Andrew!"

Andrew's ranting to a reporter. "*How do we know halal certification money isn't being used to fund terrorism? People don't have a choice. Halal is taking over. The new Afghan restaurant in the neighborhood has forced out an old fish and chip shop, a fixture among locals for years."*

Mum beams. "Good work, Andrew! We got some national coverage."

All I can think about is Mina's face. Weren't there other ways to draw attention to halal scams without dragging her into it?

The report continues and I do a quick Google search. To my surprise, a federal government inquiry found no links between halal certification and funding terrorism. I ask Mum if she knows about it.

"Obviously they won't find any evidence," she scoffs. "That just proves how deep the funding scheme is."

I frown. "So no evidence is evidence?"

Mum, distracted by the TV, nods absentmindedly.

I feel the urge to be outside, alone. "Mum, can I go for a drive?"

Mum now looks tormented. Her standard response since I got my license three months ago.

"If you didn't want me to be seventeen at the end of tenth grade, you shouldn't have held me back at school," I say.

She gives me a death stare but gives in.

"Stick to the speed limit. And no phone."

"Thanks, Mum."

I go into the hall, grab my car keys, yell out that I'll be back in an hour, and leave. I hear the front door open and slam shut behind me, Nathan on my heels.

"I'm coming too!" he says. "Mum said it'll force you to drive more carefully. Because you love me more than yourself."

"She needs a meme generator of her own," I say with a groan. "I was kind of hoping to be alone . . ."

"Okay!" he cries back cheerfully, opening the passenger door and climbing in.

I sigh and get in.

"Why do you want to be alone?"

"To contemplate life."

I stop at a McDonald's on the way, pick up some meals for us, and then head to the national park. I pump the music loud the whole way, ignoring the frowning faces of people in the cars at traffic lights.

"Does this music help you contemplate life?"

"Yes."

My phone vibrates. Nathan grabs it first.

"You shouldn't use a cell phone when driving. We might have an accident and you could kill me and then you would deprive Mum of the pleasure of grounding you for life. So I'll read it to you?"

"Okay."

"It's from Fred. *Saw your dad's organization on TV. And Mina from school. Looks like her dad's into some dodgy shit big-time.* How do you want me to reply?"

"I don't know," I say distractedly, thinking about a response.

After several tries I settle on: *Who knows what the full story is?* The response is excruciatingly lame. I dictate to Nathan, feeling piss weak and slightly confused. Why should I even care?

"Okay, sent," Nathan announces. "You can contemplate life now. I'm going to play *Minecraft*."

My mind is in overdrive, wondering if Mina will connect my last name to Dad's. And then Aussie Values to me.

# MINA

Baba drops me off early at school this morning. I'm drinking a coffee at my usual spot under one of the large fig trees on the school grounds. I see Mrs. Robinson in the near distance, carrying an expensive-looking briefcase, ambling up the path as if she might be trying to delay the beginning of another day.

My stomach plunges. Will Mrs. Robinson mention the program? Will this be the moment I'm going to be tapped on the shoulder and told I'm in the wrong production line?

She's close now and notices me as she approaches.

She stops and makes small talk with me and it's soon clear that she hasn't seen the program. I try not to do a fist pump.

"How's school, Mina?" "How are you fitting in?" "What's your favorite part of Victoria College?" "Yes, I think the student café is a great idea too. Fabulous for building math skills." She goes on in this vein for a few minutes, and then asks, "So you like this tree too, hey?"

I nod. "It's pretty spectacular."

"When I got the job as principal here, I gave up the water views from the North Sydney school I was teaching at for the leafy North Shore. I love the tree change." She smiles warmly at me. "This tree's been a sentry over generations of graduates."

"Full of secrets," I say. "And history. That's why I like it."

---

Paula rushes up to me fifteen minutes before the first bell is due to ring. She throws her bag on the ground, sits down to face me, legs crossed, and stares intently into my eyes.

"Oscar Wilde wants you to know that *there is only one thing in life worse than being talked about, and that is not being talked about.*"

"Oscar Wilde could say that. He had excellent taste in clothes."

"Nobody with even half a brain takes that show seriously. They'll be back to real estate crooks and crazy fad diets tomorrow. I say we have fun with this. I'm thinking a halal kebab van outside the café. A huge banner: *One Bite and You're Converted.* What do you think?"

She grins at me.

I grin back at her. "I love you. The end."

She seems genuinely touched.

"Okay. Cheesy, sentimental moments quota for the week reached," I joke.

"Totally." She laughs.

"You know what the trick is?" she says when we hear the bell ring and reluctantly rise and make our way to homeroom. "Learning that it can't always be about them. Sometimes, maybe even most times, you fight back. But sometimes you can end up dignifying their arguments when you defend yourself. And even if you're in the right, it's exhausting to live your life in constant resistance. You have to keep a space to yourself, Mina, a space where they don't exist. And doing that will piss them off more, anyway."

"How?"

She shrugs. "I think some people just can't handle people who go about their life genuinely not caring about what other people think."

"This is from personal experience?"

"I've had years of practice." She grins at me. "After all, you've only known me in my Wilde days."

———————

Homeroom is quiet.

Recess, not so much.

A lot of people are really sweet and sympathetic and it gives me the confidence to decide I'm not going to bother defending myself.

*Hey, was that you on TV last night?*

No, I've got a twin.

*What's going on with your dad?*

Ringworm.

*But why'd they single your dad out? They must have had a reason.*

The producer has a thing for Afghan men.

*Why do you serve halal in Lane Cove anyway? There aren't many Muslims here, are there?*

Not yet. The breeding program's in progress and we'll be able to take over soon.

———————————

My name is called on the loudspeaker. Trying to mask my trepidation, I get up from my desk and go to the office.

Mrs. Robinson has been informed about the program. "Did you watch it?" she asks.

"No, I didn't," I reply.

She smiles. "Some of the teachers were chatting about it at morning tea and were quite concerned for you and your family."

She gives me a pep talk, advising me to ignore the tabloid media.

"Instead of bullying and harassing people like you, we should be welcoming you to our country," she says, shaking her head in dismay. "Your parents are hardworking, decent, moderate people who have clearly made extraordinary sacrifices for you to have this opportunity."

There's a reason why I'm drawn to the tree in the school yard most mornings. The roots spread wide, twisted and coiled. The trunk is enormous, rough and crusty. Can you be jealous of a tree? Of its roots that dig deep into soil, staking their claim? I smile to myself as Mrs. Robinson reassures me that I should always feel welcome here.

I'm like an Afghan sapling that grew a little, only to be snatched out of the ground and planted somewhere else.

Everybody's pruned and shaped somehow, I guess. But not everybody has to fight to stop from being torn out of the ground.

———————

A backpack on his shoulder, Mr. Morello takes us outside for Society and Culture. He instructs us to assemble side by side to form a straight line. Then he divides the class into two.

"Everybody on the right of Zoe is able-bodied," he says. "Team Kyle. Everybody on the left of Zoe, including you, Zoe, has a physical disability. Team Zoe."

Paula and I are on Team Kyle. We all exchange quizzical looks and call out to Mr. Morello to explain what's going on. He tells us to be patient. He takes a bunch of short lengths of rope from his bag and hands one to each of the students on Team Zoe. He then instructs them to quickly work together so that each of them has their hands tied in front of their bodies.

Terrence is already mouthing off as Fred ties his hands together. "Hey, sir, not all of us are into kinky, you know."

Mr. Morello growls at him to keep a lid on it.

Michael and I are on the same team. I catch him looking at me and roll my eyes in Terrence's direction. He feigns a suffering smile and raises his hands in resignation, the gesture reminding me of the way a parent would respond to somebody commenting on their unruly child.

Mr. Morello is helping to tie Cameron's hands, as he's the last person on Team Zoe. He then turns to address us all.

"Your mission is simple. I've planted clothespins in the gardens, café, and quadrangle areas. The team who collects the most wins. Team Kyle, you have ten minutes. Team Zoe, you have five."

There are groans and cheers, and then Mr. Morello shouts out "start" and people instantly disperse and start running in all directions. I spot a clothespin behind a trash can and swoop down on it before Fred, who, hands tied, is hot on my heels. There's laughter all around, but shouts of "That's not fair!" too. I run to the quadrangle area, grab some more clothespins along the way. Michael, Paula, and Jane follow me, calling out excitedly when they pick one up.

"Quick! Over there!" Michael calls out. "Under the chair. There's a whole stack of them! I'll go to the café!"

Jane and I sprint to the bench, reaching it at the same time as Terrence. All three of us are frantically grabbing at the clothespins. With his hands bound, Terrence doesn't stand much of a chance though. I grab a handful. Just as soon as Terrence picks up his first one, he drops it again. Jane and I, giggling, quickly grab at the clothespin that gets away from him before he can try again. Jane's so caught in the moment that she doesn't seem to have noticed that she's competing against the guy who routinely leaves her tongue-tied. That is, until he hisses, "Bitches."

"It's just a game." Jane's voice trembles slightly.

"No shit, Sherlock," he says scornfully. "Sheez, Morello's an idiot. Like we need to do this shit to know that life sucks when you're a retard."

"That's an appalling thing to say!" I cry.

"Yeah, well, deal with it," he replies.

Michael jogs over to us, grinning madly as he holds up a bunch of clothespins. Terrence sees him and groans loudly.

"This is so rigged!"

"That's the point," Michael says.

I grin when Michael counts out thirteen. Jane is standing beside me, deflated now. "I'll go look in the garden," she says to nobody in particular, and walks off.

We hear a whistle, and people start to call out that time's up for Team Zoe.

Terrence rolls his eyes. "This is such bullshit."

"You're such a sore loser," I snap, fed up with his tantrums.

"If I wanted an opinion from somebody who bankrolls terrorists, I'd ask."

I've never been punched in the guts before, but I reckon it might feel like the impact his words have on me. I stare at him, openmouthed, winded.

Michael flinches too.

"That's not cool, man," he tells Terrence. His tone is grave, and while I don't need anybody to come to my rescue, the tameness of his words makes me feel as though I've been punched twice.

Terrence lifts his brows at Michael, as if confused. "It's your dad's organization that broke the story! Didn't you see the bloke from Aussie Values on *News Tonight* last night?"

I stare at Michael but he's refusing to look at me. When our eyes finally meet for a second, he just can't hold my gaze and looks away.

"Aussie Values? Your *dad's* organization?"

"Yeah," Terrence says in a *well duh* voice.

"I can explain," Michael says.

But I don't want to hear another word from him.

"Nope." I shake my head emphatically. "Don't bother. I thought you were confused. Turns out you're just a hypocrite."

I throw my clothespins at their feet and storm off.

# MICHAEL

When Mina walks away, I know I've lost her before I've even had a chance.

The last bell can't come quickly enough. I leave Terrence thinking I've got to rush home to make it for work. I sprint to the front gates and hop onto the bus, grateful I've avoided bumping into anybody I know. I find an empty seat and lean my head against the window. The glass is cold against my skin, and smudged with fingerprints. Right at my eye level somebody's used permanent marker to scrawl a tiny message to the world: *Kylie loves Paul forever.* When things can fuck up in a matter of moments, that kind of long-term optimism seems silly and naive. I feel like getting in touch with this Kylie girl and telling her to step into the real world.

I want somebody to blame for everything that's happened but I don't know who. I want somebody to fix things but I wouldn't know where to start.

Before Mina, my life was like a completed jigsaw puzzle.

Mina's come along and pushed the puzzle upside down onto the floor. I have to start all over again, figuring out where the pieces go. But some of the pieces to the puzzle don't seem to fit the way they used to.

The thought terrifies me.

How can my parents be right, be good, if it means people like Mina end up getting hurt?

It's so much easier to live in a world where everything is black and white.

I've never done gray before, but I suspect it's one of those things that, tried once, you can never go back.

# MINA

Mum drives me to Paula's house on Saturday afternoon. We pull into a boulevard of contemporary architect-designed mansions, Victorian terraces, and old, grand estates. The last are the kinds of houses that aren't content to be identified by street number but have names like Chelsea Manor and Evergreen Hall. Mum clucks her tongue in admiration as she drives under school-zone speed, gazing in awe at each house. Then, to my mortification, she grabs her phone and starts taking photos, arm stretched out of the window.

"Mum!"

She withdraws her arm and puts the phone in her lap. She juts out her chin, dismissive of my reaction. "I want to show Baba."

I groan.

But then my phone navigator instructs us we've arrived at our destination and I become a little bit silly myself.

"Oh. My. God. Whoa!"

Paula's house is like something you see in one of those home decor magazines you only ever flick through in a doctor's waiting room. A masterpiece of glass and steel and bays and roofs at different heights. I take it all in and suddenly I feel like a kid again, playing Lego for the first time after we were released from the detention center and I'd started school. I built crazy, extravagant houses. I still remember the intense longing that came with those houses. How badly I wanted my make-believe world to be real.

"This Paula friend," Mum says in an authoritative tone, "is very high status. Very high status," she repeats for emphasis.

I don't know how to break it to her that status doesn't operate like an airborne virus.

I kiss her good-bye, jump out of the car, and run up the front steps. Before I've had a chance to ring the bell, the door swings open and Paula's there, grinning at me. I start to take off my shoes. She tells me not to. I tell her my mum would have a fit if she found out. She promises she won't tell her. I explain that I'm quite happy to make up stories to extend my curfew, or manipulate library closing times to stay out late, but not taking my shoes off would be the ultimate betrayal. She rolls her eyes and says, "You were made to be loved, not understood."

"Don't Wilde me at this hour. I want a tour."

She laughs. "You've been studying up on famous quotes, haven't you?"

"Obviously. How else will I understand half of what you say?"

I step in, and to my right is an elevator. A freaking glass Willy Wonka type elevator.

"I feel like I'm in a mall," I say. "And not the Parramatta one. The one in the city."

Her house takes my breath away: white marble floors, white walls and furnishings, with modern art pieces and family photos providing splashes of color. A sweeping staircase leads to a gallery area on the second floor with views of a sparkling blue pool in a manicured garden.

"This place is incredible," I whisper, taking it all in as Paula leads me into a kitchen fit for a five-star hotel. There's a television built into one of the walls in the kitchen, and a fish tank in another wall. I feel slightly overwhelmed by it all. Not by Paula's house in particular. I saw mansions in Kabul and Pakistan too. But spending most of my life since then in Western Sydney—happy and contented—I'd forgotten about how truly uneven the world is. Some people get marble and luxury and urban chic; others get slums and open sewage and payday-to-payday.

I hear a sound from the butler's pantry and Paula's mother emerges. I was expecting to see an incarnation of Barbie in the Dreamhouse. Perhaps a cascade of blonde, loose curls, designer outfit hugging an impossibly slim physique, and a matching Tiffany's set. The kind of person whose appearance leaves nothing to chance.

Instead, a woman in a simple knee-length linen dress and slip-on sandals steps out. Her face is bare of makeup, and her hair is piled up onto her head in a messy bun. If there was a TED *Check Your Assumptions* talk, she'd be on the promotional material.

I feel slightly sheepish and hope my face doesn't reveal my surprise.

She sees me and gives me a warm smile. "Hi, Mina! It's so lovely to meet you. Paula talks about you all the time."

I smile at her. "Thanks for having me."

"Are you kidding? It's so good to have somebody over to keep Paula company! I've cooked up some pasta for you both. I made sure it's vegetarian."

"Oh, thanks," I say, touched.

"There's a banoffee pie in the fridge that I picked up from the store."

Paula, who's tapping food into the fish tank, cheers and does a fist pump.

"If you need me, I'm in my study. I've got a fifty-five-page statement of claim to finish by Monday."

We dish up our food and take it to the cinema room. I become a kid in a pet store when I enter. I make myself comfortable on one of the reclining cinema chairs, putting my hands behind my head and stretching my legs out.

"Can I move in? *Please?*"

She laughs, waving away my comment. "They're just things."

"Pretty things. Nice things. Things that make me all warm and fuzzy inside. Being materialistic is seriously underrated. You should try it sometime."

"Meh." She shrugs.

I notice a family portrait in a frame on the wall next to me and I chuckle. "How old were you in that photo?"

She grins. "Awful, hey? Those were my pre-hair-product, pre-GHD days. Thirteen."

"It's really nice," I joke. "I love when hair looks like brown steel wool."

She hits me on the arm. "*Excuse me?* That's mahogany with a touch of sun-kissed highlights steel wool to you."

I grin at her.

"Anyway, we can't all be beauty queens."

"Please," I say, rolling my eyes at her. "At thirteen I had one eyebrow and hair on my upper lip. You discovered hair straighteners. I discovered laser."

After we eat, I follow her through the house, as she wants to introduce me to her personal zoo.

"Sorry, my turtles are so antisocial. Come on! Let me introduce you to K4. He's in my room."

K4 is lying down on a large cushion in the bay window in her bedroom. As soon as he sees Paula he leaps off, ecstatic. She leans down and starts to sweet-talk and baby him.

"This little guy is my soul mate," she says, giving him a kiss on top of his head. "I'd swap all this for him any day."

I watch her fondly. I've seen all kinds of people in my life. As a kid in Kabul. Then en route to Pakistan. In the camps, the boat to Australia, in the detention center. I've known Paula for only a few weeks, but it's enough. She's one of the good ones.

We sit down on her bed and K4 jumps up beside us, hunkers down next to Paula, and closes his eyes.

It doesn't take long before I'm opening up to her about Michael.

"I'm angry that I'm angry." I lean back against the bottle-green suede headboard. "I'm angry that I fell for his *that's not what I meant* excuses. Stupid me. Stupid, stupid, stupid!"

Paula's too sharp and honest to let me off the hook. Like a seagull sweeping down on my big, chunky, crinkle-cut chip of a comment, she says: "Did you fall for his excuses? Or *him*?"

---

Paula grabs her laptop. Her fingers dance across the keyboard and then she whips it around so we can both see the screen. "Okay, cyber-stalking time. I've found him. He's into the same weird music you're into—"

"Paula, I just *can't* do techno."

"Your loss . . . He roots for the Roosters, likes Heidi Klum—disappointing, Michael, I'm a Tyra Banks girl myself—and, here we go, Aussie Values."

I groan and put my face in my hands.

"Okay, let's see what Aussie Values is all about. It's a public page and . . . *Hello,* rednecks!"

We pore over the page. We can't look away no matter how terrible the comments are. *Abos and slit-eyes and Mozlems and curry-munchers. We grew here, you flew here. Fuck Off We're Full. No to tabouli.*

Oddly enough it gets us giggling.

"*Tabouli?*" I shake my head. "Now I'm *really* offended. I can't believe he likes this," I say.

"Well, what does a Facebook *like* mean, really?" Paula asks.

"Don't get philosophical on me now. Facebook doesn't do ambiguity or nuance. You click like, you freaking well better own it."

"I never even knew Aussie Values existed until that program," Paula says. "I still can't believe Michael's dad is the president."

Paula does an Internet search on Aussie Values and finds their website, parts of which are under construction. She reads out their mission statement, because if you're going to be a masochist you might as well be a perfectionist about it.

I peer down at K4, snuggled up next to Paula, feeling envious, the quiet rhythm of his breathing telling the story of his blissful ignorance.

Paula opens the website's gallery page. There's the guy from *News Tonight,* but in this photo he's in a weird gladiator-type getup. He's standing with a bunch of other people at what looks like a protest. Michael's dad is in the middle of the shot, grinning at the camera, an Aussie flag draped around him. And there's Michael, standing beside him. He's grinning too.

I feel like I know exactly who he is now.

And it makes no sense that it should affect me this much.

# MICHAEL

Dad returns home to a hero's welcome. He has an uneven tan and has lost weight. He looks haggard, dark circles under his eyes. He sleeps for twenty hours straight and emerges the next day, weak-legged and dazed, like a newly born foal trying to take its first steps. But after some coffee and puttering in the garden with Nathan, he tells Mum he's up to seeing some of their friends.

Mum cooks up a feast. Andrew, Carolina, Li, and Kahn arrive that evening, bearing gifts of bottles of wine and dessert.

"There are people whose grandchildren have been born in the same refugee camp they were born in," Dad tells us over dinner. "So anything we do will merely be a drop in the ocean. If it's not going to solve anything, it's really a numbers game in the end. Politicians just fighting about how many we can accept. All we're saying is that the numbers should be reasonable and we should be bringing in the right kind of people.

People who will fit in with our values. Surely that will make their transition to our society easier too?"

What he says kind of makes sense.

But Mina's words do too.

"It hit me hard when we were on the plane back to Australia from Jakarta," he continues. "How does every safety demonstration start? No matter which airline you're on?"

"Wear a seat belt," Nathan says instantly.

Dad smiles at him. "That's right, Nathan. Then it says adults—"

Nathan cuts him off. "The first recorded use of a seat belt in an aircraft was in 1913 by Adolphe Pégoud, a French aviator."

"Boy, did I miss your brain while I was away, Nathan," Dad says.

Nathan beams.

"So," Dad says, addressing us all again. "They always advise adults to put the oxygen masks on themselves first, *and then* small children. You have to look after yourself first before you can help others."

"I don't understand," I say.

"It's basic economics, Michael," Dad says. "Refugees take jobs from Australians. They cost a lot in welfare, they compete for our resources, and then they bring over their families so the situation is exacerbated. We have an unemployment crisis in this country and accepting more refugees will make it worse."

"It's simple. The country's going to the dogs, Michael," Li answers gruffly.

"It's not just about the economy," my mum says wistfully. "Cultural compatibility is an issue too."

Dad nods furiously. "Here we have gender equality and yet we're allowing people with degrading attitudes toward women into this country."

"Is that what you mean by cultural compatibility?" I ask, my head beginning to hurt.

"We're letting in people with different values, and that's dangerous," Carolina pipes up.

"Because there's a dominant culture, Michael," Dad explains. "We're an Anglo nation based on Judeo-Christian values. People are free to practice their culture and religion so long as it doesn't undermine the foundational identity of this country."

"That's really the heart of the issue, Michael," Mum says. "Ultimately this is about protecting our core identity from which everything else stems."

---

There's a persistent, nagging feeling that's lodged inside me, like a squatter that's suddenly taken up residence and refuses to budge.

After dinner, I grab my iPad and make myself comfortable in the hammock on our back porch. I drink in the cool, fresh breeze as I trawl through different websites on refugees and asylum seekers. There are masses of fact files and myth busters from all sides of the debate. Words flash at me: sovereignty. Border protection. Floodgates. People smugglers. Deaths at sea.

Things are only going to get worse. If Mina hates me now, what will she think when *Don't Jump the Queue* airs? What will she think when she sees me on the screen with my parents and Nathan, one big happy Aussie Values family?

I feel sick to my stomach, like I'm on a roller coaster that's slowly climbing the hill but is about to drop me down a vertical fall at high speed. And no matter how loudly I scream, there will be nothing I can do to stop it.

I allow the hammock to gently sway as I navigate through one of the pro-refugee websites. I must be there for some time because Dad comes looking for me, telling me the guests have left.

Passing me a can of Coke, he sinks into an outdoor chair and lets out a contented sigh.

"God, it's good to be under an Aussie sky again."

I raise my drink. "Cheers."

"Cheers." He takes a swig of his beer, and then looks at me and chuckles. "Andrew sure can chew the fat. Thought he'd never leave. So, how are things with you?"

"Good." We haven't had a chance to talk one-on-one yet. "How was it, Dad?"

"Where to start?" He smiles. "There were some truly awful moments. Terrifying. It was tougher than I expected, especially roughing it in Iraq and Indonesia."

"Was it as bad as they say?"

"Worse, Michael," he says soberly. He closes his eyes and shakes his head.

His response takes me by surprise. "Really?"

"Human misery on a scale I've never seen before."

"So where does that leave the organization now?"

He looks at me, confused. "What do you mean?"

"Have things changed for you now that you've, you know, seen that stuff?"

"Once you see the sheer size of the crisis you realize this isn't a problem for us to fix, Michael."

I think about the things I've just read. "But, Dad, don't we have to help them? Legally, I mean."

"It's not that simple, Michael. Everybody's always focusing on our legal obligations toward people who are coming from countries that have no respect for international law. Do you see the irony?"

I shrug. "But isn't that the point of law? That you can't bow out?"

"Sometimes laws are used as blunt instruments and become oppressive and unjust. People are suffering, Michael.

No doubt about it. But it's all relative. Like I said, we can take in some of them, provided the numbers make sense. But not the ones who come here by boat. If they're wealthy enough to pay people smugglers then they're not genuinely in need. The laws and conventions are there for people fleeing persecution, not those just seeking a better life." He studies my face closely and smiles gently. "You're not convinced?"

"Throwing every last cent to a people smuggler and risking your life at sea seems pretty desperate and needy to me," I say. "But what you're saying is that if your life's in danger, and you can afford to get out of the camp and try to reach us, then you don't deserve to be helped. I thought we judged people as refugees based on whether their life is in danger, not their financial status?"

"We should be taking a tough stance so that we stop the people smuggler industry. They're the real scumbags."

"So we punish people desperate for our protection? Anyway, aren't a lot of the people coming from countries where there's war?"

He nods. "Hmm."

"Like, for example, Iraq and Afghanistan and Syria?"

"They're killing each other. Tribal cultures, Michael. And some will try and leave because their lives are in danger. And like I said, we can take in some, but only a small number because we have our own to look after. But others exploit refugee laws. They want to escape these war zones not because their lives are in particular danger but because their countries are in a state of war and there are no jobs, no school, little food. They're not technically fleeing persecution, but a state of war. So how do you solve that? The Middle East should stop its bloodlust and focus on peace, not conflict. That's not our problem to fix."

"But all the countries these people want to go to, like ours, or America, or in Europe, haven't they all been part of those wars?"

Something still doesn't sit right. I wish I'd paid more attention to what was happening in the world.

"Yes."

"So . . ." I pause, trying to articulate my thoughts. "I don't know. Isn't it like starting a fire in a building, walking away, and then being surprised when people try to escape the flames?"

Dad gives me a questioning look. Then he smiles broadly. "I'm proud of you, Michael."

"Huh?"

"You've changed since I left."

I don't answer.

"I'm glad you're taking an interest, doing your own research. Look, Michael, we didn't *start* the fire. When we went into Iraq and Afghanistan we were there to help put the fire *out*. People twist the truth all the time, Michael. They want to paint us as the monsters. We're not torturing and murdering people, Michael. If soldiers step out of line, we're civilized and have inquiries. But when Muslims kill they think they're doing God's will!" He shakes his head angrily.

Again, I don't know what to think or feel. I don't have the words or knowledge to respond, but something deep within me doesn't feel right.

"So you're saying the trip hasn't changed your mind at all?" I eventually ask.

"No, I didn't say that. In fact, it's made me even more determined to make this organization a success."

———————————

I stay up late surfing the net. I read articles and blogs. I watch YouTube documentaries. My mind is buzzing with information overload. September 11. Bombing Iraq. No weapons of mass destruction. *With us or against us*. Guantánamo Bay. Abu Ghraib. Chemical weapons. Arming the rebels. Backing dictators. Overthrowing dictators. Revolutions. Arab Spring. CIA torture. Beheadings.

I go to bed confused and overwhelmed. But I'm also angry with myself. I've never had a problem standing up to my parents and questioning them on trivial things. But when it comes to things that really matter, I just went along with what they told me.

# MINA

Paula texts me at five-thirty on Monday morning.

> There's a poetry slam in Bankstown next Tuesday night. Want to come with me?

Is she kidding? 5:30 a.m.? I'm half-dead and manage one letter.

> K.

I switch my phone to silent and go back to sleep. When I wake up an hour later there are heaps more messages:

> I can come to ur place and we could go together. We can take a cab. I'll pay no prob.

> It starts at 6. We can register to perform or just watch.

Let's just watch for now.

Unless u want to perform?

OMG I'm so excited.

Hey are you awake?

Okay, I guess not. See you in a bit!

---

"You're not normal. Texting me before the sun's up?"

She flashes me a winning smile. "Sorry!"

"Broken sleep *and* you're cheerful."

"So we're all good to go?!"

"My mum's super strict about going out at night so I'd need to be back by nine at the latest—library closing hours, obviously."

"Well, if you need to get back by nine that doesn't leave us enough time." Her face falls, and I nudge her gently.

"Sorry."

She smiles. "It's fine. I'll keep my eye out for something on a weekend, or closer to home instead. Does it feel weird? Having a strict mum who's so young?"

"Trust me, she doesn't let me forget who's boss."

---

My solo free period? Seriously? How does he have the guts to show his face?

I ignore him. He's standing on the other side of the table and clears his throat.

"I had nothing to do with what happened at your restaurant," he says.

I continue typing.

"I'm really sorry you all had to go through that," he adds hastily.

My mouth is dry.

"My dad was overseas," he continues. "Even he didn't know about it. One of the organization's members was behind it."

"The organization your dad founded," I snap.

That shuts him up pretty quickly. I lean back in my chair, fold my arms across my chest, and stare at him. My heart's hammering away.

"So tell me all about Aussie Values, Michael. I'm fascinated. Is it *all* immigration, or just Muslim immigrants? You all seem to be pretty big on assimilation for migrants too. So help me to understand because I'm struggling. Is there some kind of scale? What about a woman who wears a sari and speaks the queen's English, compared to, say, a guy in jeans and a T-shirt with an accent? How would you rate them?"

I go on and on and he just stands there and takes it. It pisses me off even more.

"Oh, so you're too gutless to defend yourself? Happy to hide behind your dad and his stooges? Offer fake apologies?"

"That's not fair," he finally manages. "It's messy."

I search his face. He looks so uncomfortable, conflicted even. I refuse to make excuses for him though.

I shake my head, tired. "Just leave me alone, please. We've got nothing to say to each other."

But he doesn't move. He takes a deep breath. "Okay. But first I need to warn you about something."

I snap my head up. "What now?"

"My dad's part of a new series." A pregnant pause. "*Don't Jump the Queue.*" He winces. "That's why he was overseas. The promos will start running soon. It'll be on in about a month."

"Wonderful. I can't wait."

He runs his fingers through his hair. "I had to go along with the family interview. You can make up your own mind about me. I just wanted you to know . . . it's more complicated than you think."

"It was my *stepfather* that you saw on TV, by the way. Not my dad."

He doesn't know what to make of this, and fumbles, "Oh, okay."

No. It's not *okay.*

"Let's do complicated for a second, shall we? My stepfather refused to fight for a Talib warlord. He was held captive for a week and tortured. He escaped and went into hiding. Eventually he managed to leave Afghanistan and ended up in Australia after paying off some people smugglers. As for my dad, well, he's *dead*. Do you want all the gory details, or are you so cold it wouldn't even make a difference?"

Michael stands there, staring at me, a horrified look on his face.

I can't say any more. It's just not worth it. It's too sad to say out loud. That I was seven when some young guys trying to make a name for themselves in the Taliban knocked on our door and shot my dad point-blank in the head. A couple of months later my dad's brother, our only male relative, was killed by some trigger-happy US troops. We had no protection, but enough savings to get us out. We left my aunt behind, who was later killed too. My mum had the guts to risk everything for the chance at a half life of freedom outside our homeland. She was just twenty-four when she fled with me and Hasan. And then to Australia, with just me.

"I could go on," I say, "but I wouldn't want to *complicate* your already complicated world."

"Shit," he says, and sinks into the chair.

"Yeah," I say. I shove my books into my bag and walk out.

---

When I first arrived in Australia I was just a child. The nightmares visited me every night I was in detention. My mum was broken from the journey and the loss of Hasan. We were like two injured animals caught in a trap, cowering in the lights, unable to comfort each other. When we were eventually processed and released into the community, we slowly rebuilt our lives and the nightmares faded. It took longer for the bed-wetting to stop. When my stepfather came into the picture, his tenderness and devotion to us both was a soothing balm. Slowly we healed.

Tonight is the first time in a long time that I have a night-mare about my father. I'm walking along a deserted street in Kabul. I'm alone. As I walk past each house, the front door opens, revealing the barrel of a gun pointed at me. Then the gun is withdrawn, the door slams shut, and I walk on. House after house, pointed gun after pointed gun. I don't stop. I don't scream. I just keep on walking. It's only when I see my father standing at the end of the street, half submerged in a grave, that I start to scream.

My mum comes running into my bedroom and wakes me. Eventually she calms me down. She asks me about my dream, and I make up something silly. She laughs it off, chides me for having eaten too much before I slept.

I get up and have a shower, hoping to wash the images from my mind. And then I sit in the floral chair and place my head against the armrest. My memories of my life in Afghanistan aren't vivid. I worry sometimes that my memory bank is running on battery power and that the further I *move on*, the faster the battery fades. Will I wake up one day to find the battery dead? And then will it all be like Hasan, that I remember only the form of everything, but not the substance? I can remember how my father would peel my orange in one move and make me a curly snake . . . or was it a curly worm?

Once, somebody on Facebook was ranting about boat people pretending to be refugees when they were just "economic migrants." Her evidence was that she'd seen a group of *them* laughing and taking photos at the Opera House. *They didn't look traumatized,* she'd said. Maha had gone all keyboard warrior on the Facebook thread and ripped through the person who'd posted the comment: *I bet you're the type of person who feels better if a homeless person begging for money looks really starved and miserable. Because then you can congratulate yourself on your charity, hey?*

Unlike Maha, the post hadn't angered me. Instead it had hit me with the force of a semitrailer. Was part of our contract here in this country that we should be walking around depressed and broken? Wearing our trauma on the outside? And what about everybody we'd left dead or living in fear back home? Didn't we owe them? How could I just lead this ordinary life?

Tonight the questions hurl themselves back at me. It's been such a long time since I've had a nightmare about my father. In Auburn I'd settled into an *ordinary* life; into a comfort zone that buried the bad thoughts and memories deep down, away from the surface of the mundane rhythms of my life. Maybe we were naive to think that we could go on like that forever. Were organizations like Aussie Values punishment for our naiveté? A reminder that for some people in this world, freedom and *ordinary* aren't basic rights. They're luxuries you should never take for granted.

# MICHAEL

It's the night of Sienna's party. Terrence and Fred have already had too much to drink.

"You look like shit," Terrence says when he sees me. "Cheer up, will you." He flings an arm around me. "What's got into you these days? You're PMSing. We don't do that, remember?"

"It's not Zara, is it?" Fred asks, passing me a drink. "You missing her?"

"Nope." I look around and take a swig of my drink. Terrence launches into a funny story and it gets us laughing hard. For a while I'm able to rewind my life back to a time when I hadn't met Mina, when my life made sense.

We check out the crowd and complain to each other about the music. Sienna's hired a DJ and has set up a dance space in the open-plan lounge area. The bifolding doors open up onto a courtyard decorated with fairy lights and Chinese lanterns.

Terrence soon starts chatting up one of Sienna's friends from outside school. There's nothing more boring than watching your friend try to hit it off with a girl, so Fred and I leave them at the backyard pergola and head back inside, meeting Jane and Leica on the way.

"Hi, guys," Jane says cheerily. Her eyes are darting around, surveying the backyard. It's obvious she's searching for Terrence. I feel sorry for her.

"Hey, Jane," I say. "Hey, Leica. Is Cameron here?"

"On his way," Leica says.

We make small talk for a bit. Jane's clearly fishing, the way you do when the only thing on offer is the excitement of just hearing somebody's name. But there's an art to this kind of fishing and Jane's still an amateur.

"So did you two arrive by yourselves?" Her eyes are still all over the place, and she's clearly trying to keep it together, but I can sense her agony.

Fred, trying to compensate for his general awkwardness around the opposite sex, launches into a terrifically random and irrelevant story about screaming goats as a YouTube sensation. Jane is listening politely, while Leica is clearly entertained.

Jane soon catches sight of Terrence. He's emerged from a hidden corner of the backyard with Sienna's friend. Jane's face falls and she mumbles a hasty "See you" to us and heads inside. The transformation in Leica is instant. A fierce look of loyalty and protectiveness flashes across her face and she runs after Jane.

"Why she's hooked on Terrence is a mystery," Fred says.

"Tell me about it," I say, shaking my head. "Come on, let's eat."

The house is packed by now. Awful techno music pumps loudly throughout, and people are moving around in what they might claim is dancing but looks more like low-impact step aerobics. The main action is at the large photo booth that's been set up near the dance floor.

Fred and I sort through the retro costumes and props. I decide on a rainbow clown's wig, oversized orange sunglasses, and a mustache. Fred goes for a neon-yellow braided wig, top hat, and beard.

Something about being in that photo booth brings out the idiot in us. We pull faces and strike as many silly poses as we can think of. When our turn's over, we wait outside as the booth prints our photo strip.

And then, to my surprise, *while still in costume*, I turn around and see Mina, Paula, Jane, and Leica together in the queue.

It's quite funny actually.

Because they're all in costume too: crazy wigs and masquerade eye masks.

Mina looks me up and down. She's trying to look coolly amused but it's difficult to pull off when you're wearing a pink feathered masquerade mask and 1980s punk rock wig.

It's too awkward not to say something.

I offer a "Hi."

Mina glares at me. She doesn't respond and turns to the girls and throws herself back into the conversation.

Rejected by a masquerade punk. The night can only go downhill from here.

I throw my costume into the box. Fred, who has been uselessly standing beside me and perving at the girls, follows me to the food table. Terrence and some of the other guys are there, in intense discussion over *League of Legends*. I try to feign interest but I'm too distracted, and my contribution is limited to an occasional grunt.

I can't get Mina out of my head. I make an excuse to leave the guys. Put it down to alcohol, or a sudden surge of impulsiveness, but I find myself approaching the DJ. He has his eyes closed, head bopping to the techno beats. Interrupting his spiritual moment, I ask him to play a track by The xx. He pulls a face like I've stabbed him (freaking techno heads kill my life), but promises me he'll play it soon.

On my way back to the guys, I steal a glance at Mina and Paula. They're outside the photo booth, examining their photo strips and laughing. The guys are still talking about *League of Legends*. Eventually, after what feels like an age of techno, my song request finally plays.

I watch Mina out of the corner of my eye. It takes a few moments for her to realize what song is playing. And when she does, she turns her attention away from her friends and looks around the room. She seems to be searching for me. Her eyes eventually fall on me.

Her gaze lingers long enough for me to hope.

But then she turns away.

# MINA

I beg God for forgiveness and then inform my parents that:

> Paula and I have a joint project so important to my
> overall high school performance that it requires no
> less than seven consecutive hours of work on it;

> Paula can offer exceptional IT resources, whereas the
> Internet at our apartment is slow and the printer
> regularly jams; and—

There's no need for a (c).

Baba agrees to drop me off at Paula's at five and pick me
up at midnight.

As soon as we arrive I feel a rush of nerves. Sienna's older
cousin introduces herself ("I'm Janette, babysitting you lot

tonight") and asks me for a letter from my parents authorizing me to be served alcohol. I can't help but laugh in her face.

"No note, no drink."

Paula nudges me in the side and grins. "Here's my note," she says, passing a piece of paper to Janette.

Back at Auburn Grove Girls High, Maha was the party animal, not me. She came complete with fake ID and a repertoire of stories to use on her unsuspecting parents, who, honest to God, thought that Maha was about as innocent a girl as Our Lady of Lebanon had ever seen (the statue of Virgin Mary excepting). Most of the girls I went to school with celebrated their birthdays with a trip to the movies, dinner at a restaurant, or a party at home with friends and family. It was a school population where girls spent recess swapping how-to-get-around-your-curfew ideas; where most of the tattoos you saw were henna ones; and where it became an annual competition to see who had attended the most weddings in the year.

Drinking alcohol or mucking around with guys was something you got away with, not something you did out in the open. I'd never been interested in sneaking into clubs, getting it on with a guy in the parking lot at Parramatta McDonald's, or drinking.

Paula grabs a Red Bull with vodka, I grab a Coke, and we make our way through the crowd. The music is awful, but

Paula's into techno and swaying slightly as she walks, bobbing her head in tune to the music.

I lean in closer to her. "What if I see Michael?"

"So what?" she says firmly.

"I really don't have the energy to fight with him again."

"Then don't," she says flatly. "The only fights worth having are with people who mean something to you." She grabs me by the shoulders and turns me around to face her. "Does he mean something to you?"

"Of course not," I splutter.

She rolls her eyes at me and chuckles. "Hopeless liar."

Suddenly the music volume gets cranked up a notch and conversation inside becomes impossible.

We go to the backyard and bump into Zoe and Clara.

To my surprise, Zoe grabs my hand and leads me to the back fence. She pulls me down to sit beside her on the retaining wall. Paula and Clara make their way over to us. But all Zoe wants to do is talk about how I did on the *Emma* essay.

"I can do non-schoolwork conversations as well," I tell her.

For the first time since I've met her, she smiles with her eyes. Then she giggles, and I think she's proof that some people really do need alcohol in order to seem human.

"I know," she says cheerfully, her words slightly slurred. "But you're so smart! You've beaten me on every quiz and essay since you started. I know you have. I sneak a peek all the time." She giggles again. "I have some major"—she pats me on the arm—"*major* competition with you. That makes me angry." She puts on an exaggerated pout. "Because I've always, *always* been top of the class. That's *my* thing." She points to her chest with her thumb. "Go back home, Mina. Just go. Please?" She bats her eyelashes at me.

I stare at her. "Okay, I get it," I say, but I'm not angry. Hearing her expose herself like this, and knowing how badly she's going to regret it when she realizes, only makes me feel sorry for her.

Clara hovers over us, cradling her glass as she surveys the crowd in the yard.

I stand up and offer her my seat.

"Do her a favor and keep her away from her phone," I tell her. "They obviously wrote the don't-drink-and-text rule for her."

---

In the next hour, Paula and I try to help Leica coax Jane out of an en suite bathroom in a spare bedroom upstairs. Terrence has apparently been seen with a leggy girl wearing an impossibly small white dress. Jane is beside herself because, like anybody with half an imagination and a crazy unrequited crush, she'd built up a fantasy about what would happen between her and Terrence tonight, which had all the realism of a Tolkien trilogy.

We finally succeed in getting her to wash her face, blow her nose, and clean herself up.

Paula paces the bedroom and then claps her hands together, faces us all, and proceeds to have a meltdown at us.

"We're here to enjoy ourselves, okay? We can be sad and pathetic and make the night about boys, or"—suddenly she's excitable and a little wild—"we can actually have fun and make it about *us!*"

Leica, Jane, and I instinctively lean back, but can't help smiling at her.

"We're going downstairs to take crazy photos of ourselves in costume," she says, firmly and seriously. "And then we're going to dance—and we're not going to give a SHIT if people think we can't dance because, *hello,* people, we are at a party in the North Shore. Nobody can dance in this zip code. That's a racial fact. And then, Mina, you and I are going to go home. And that's that. Got it?"

None of us dares argue with her.

We dress up.

We laugh.

We are very much in the *I Am Woman* zone.

And then Michael and Fred are suddenly before us.

Crazy wigs and fake facial hair.

I try to offer Michael nonchalance. Instead, he gets angry death stare.

---

After we take photos, we just sit back and hang out for a while, because even Paula is prepared to admit that the music is awful.

We talk and laugh, and pretend that we're feminist role models, even though I can tell Jane is thinking about Terrence, and I'm secretly analyzing my encounter with Michael. Then suddenly "Gangnam Style" switches to "Together" by The xx and I know, without a shadow of doubt, that it's Michael's doing.

I see him. And he sees me.

But I quickly look away, because it will take more than sharing the same taste in music for me to be impressed.

———

I spend most of the Easter vacation with my head stuck in my books, trying to get on top of my assignments. Mum fusses around me, bringing me snacks and drinks so that the only things I need to focus on are unavoidable bodily functions and being the top of my class.

Today's a big day, and a welcome break from studying. Paula has tracked down a late-afternoon poetry slam event at the Bankstown Arts Center, an eerily spacious room with rows of bleachers and chairs, and blankets laid out just in front of the stage area, where mics have been set up for the performances. The room is crowded. Girls kiss each other on the cheeks, squealing, hugging, and complimenting each other.

Guys greet each other with big bear hugs and high fives. It's a flurry of activity. Paula and I walk past a long queue of poets who are waiting to put their name on the registration list so they can perform during the open mic. It's Paula's first time with this group so she doesn't know anybody.

We find seats up at the back. Eventually there is complete silence as the hosts, Ahmad and Sara, take the stage and the show starts. Witty and sharp, they bounce off each other. Sara, in a funky turban-style hijab, is confident. Ahmad is a poster boy for tall, dark, and handsome. He has the crowd wrapped around his finger. People take turns performing on all kinds of topics from the heavy (politics, gender, war, sex) to the frivolous (duck-face selfies and food pics on Instagram). The audience snaps their fingers to show their delight. The atmosphere is electric.

Sara and Ahmad return to the stage and inform us that the last person to perform in the open mic section has had to leave. They invite somebody else to come up and have a go.

Paula's suddenly out of her seat and heading toward the stage. She looks back at me and flashes me a grin. I go a little crazy and cheer loudly for her. I'm in utter awe of her courage.

Sara asks Paula to introduce herself.

"I've never done this before," she says, clutching the microphone closely and braving a smile. "Well, not in *public*. At home in front of the mirror I'm a *natural*." The audience vibe is warm and friendly, boosting her confidence as she looks out at us all, a grin spreading on her face.

"Good luck!" Ahmad says, and they step aside.

Paula closes her eyes for a moment as she loosens up her shoulders and draws in a deep breath. The audience is quiet and she begins.

*See, I never asked for the white mansion*

*With the manicured gardens and heated swimming pool*

*See, I never asked for the New Zealand skiing trip and the European summer holidays*

*With you on laptops click, click, clicking and me on the guided tours*

*I would have been happy pitching a tent, listening to stories of where you went*

*See, I never asked for the nanny and the cash you used to silence my tears, placate my fears*

*Fears that I would become a shadow, somebody to pass by in the house sometime*

See, I long to collide with you

Crash into you

Give me a chance to woo you

Remind you of how I feel, smell, and sound

See, you spend days and nights in your offices with the harbor views and the delivered dinners and the text messages you don't respond to and the leave a message voice mail that you ignore because I'm not your client

Tell yourself you're doing it for me, you're doing it for us, you're doing it because we must give our lives up to something bigger

But see, the bigger that something gets, the smaller I become

Until pretty soon I'm invisible

Alone

With a voice so large that it wakes up the world

Except for you

*You who have forgotten the sound my voice makes,*
*the love it takes*

*To actually be a parent.*

Paula takes a bow, grinning out at an audience who have been snapping throughout. They offer her a big round of applause. My chest is bursting with pride but there's a massive lump in my throat as Paula's words reverberate in my head.

"I'm so sorry, Paula," I tell her on our train ride home. "I didn't realize you were hurting so badly." I fix my eyes on her. "You're not invisible. And you're *not* alone. I'm here for you."

She returns my gaze and mulls over my words. Then her lips curl into a bright smile. "Thanks."

We sit in silence for a moment. The couple sitting behind us are in an intense discussion about a new reality TV show.

"Your mum has your photo as her phone screen saver, you know," I say casually.

"Huh?"

"It was next to me on the kitchen bench when we were eating lunch. I caught a glimpse of it."

Paula raises an eyebrow at me. "Is that supposed to make me feel better?"

I let out a small laugh. "Yeah. Sometimes the little things are just as important."

Paula smiles, but it's a charitable gesture. "She works all the time. So does Dad. You know my favorite Wilde quote? *To lose one parent may be regarded as a misfortune; to lose both looks like carelessness.* Isn't that brilliant?"

She goes on before I can answer. "See, he has a point," she says breathlessly. "Maybe I'm just not enough for them."

"I don't believe that for a second."

She smiles at me again but doesn't look convinced. My heart aches for her, but I'm confused too. I can't imagine what it must be like to feel like you need to fight for your parents' attention; compete with their work. But a part of me sympathizes with them. Maybe they're passionate about what they do. Things wouldn't change for Paula if that were taken away from them. They'd probably just start to slowly wither inside, like my mum.

I don't know what to tell Paula. I've seen a lot in my life but there's nothing as complicated as family.

"I still can't believe you stood up there and laid yourself bare like that," I say eventually.

She suddenly breaks out into a goofy smile. "I can't believe it either. Thanks for coming today. I've been dying to try it out but wasn't brave enough to do it by myself."

I nudge her with my elbow, glad to see the full smile on her face. "Don't mention it. Any time—well, let me amend that. Any time it fits within my mother's curfew laws."

She chuckles.

The driver announces the next stop: "*Get excited, people, because next stop is Campsie.*"

We look at each other and the other passengers on the train and burst out laughing.

The driver continues his cheerful commentary with each stop, making us all chuckle. "*Welcome aboard, Dulwich Hill peeps, thanks for bringing along the cool breeze . . . Next stop Sydenham. For those of you who are leaving, I'm sad to see you go but I understand your reasons.*"

When we say good-bye it's as though we both know we've crossed a threshold into that wonderful, intense, and slightly terrifying place only true friends can enter. Some things in life you have to work hard to find. But my friendship with Paula has fallen into place.

There is no nightmare for me tonight. Only sleep hugging me like a friend.

# MICHAEL

The promo ad for *Don't Jump the Queue* starts in the last week of vacation. Mum and Dad are thrilled, shouting out at Nathan and me whenever it comes on TV.

The shots of Dad made me cringe. Lots of arms folded across the chest, staring down the camera with an I-mean-business look on his face. He's described as *the man who wouldn't mind a return of the White Australia Policy*. My parents are unhappy about that. Andrew sends Dad a text to congratulate him.

I ask Dad if he really wants the White Australia Policy again and he's appalled by the suggestion.

"Of course not, Michael. I celebrate our diversity—so long as people assimilate to our values. I don't have a problem with different foods and festivals. That enriches our country. But people need to fit in with the majority instead of trying to mark themselves as different. That's why multiculturalism as a policy has been such a disaster. It sends a message that all cultures and religions are equal so you don't have to assimilate into our society. Well, I disagree. You're welcome into this wonderful country so long as you respect Judeo-Christian values. And believe me, Michael, blending in makes life easier for migrants and their children too."

Mum's stirring a pot on the stove as we speak. She interrupts. "Michael, it's like this soup I'm cooking. The dominant flavor is asparagus. I've got other spices and flavors in here too because that's what makes the soup so rich and flavorsome. But they *complement* the asparagus, rather than take over."

I lie awake in bed tonight trying to make sense of the uneasy feeling in the pit of my stomach. Not only do I not want to follow in Dad's career footsteps, but I'm starting to think that maybe my parents have things drastically wrong.

It makes me realize that I need to tell Dad about my university plans. But if I'm going to crush him, I'll have to do it in stages.

———————

Dad's taken Nathan to see the latest kids' movie at the cinema. Mum's getting ready to go out for a walk. I tell her I'm going to speak to Dad.

She sighs. "Not yet, Michael. Wait for the right moment. It's been very busy since he got back."

I'm not buying it. Pursing my lips together, I watch her pulling her shoes on.

"It's never going to be the right moment, Mum."

"Are you still . . ." She stalls and then meets my eye. "Are you still adamant you won't at least consider—"

"Mum," I say softly. "Please don't."

———————

I retreat to my room.

I read the latest updates on the Oculus VR Forum.

But I can't stop thinking about Mina.

I finish my Design and Technology essay on the pros and cons of self-driving robotic cars.

But I can't stop thinking about Mina.

I do a mind map for my Visual Arts essay on the influence of modernity on the practice of artists.

But I can't stop thinking about Mina.

———————

I spend some days at Dee Why Beach, listening to music, watching the water, sketching in my Visual Arts diary. I let Nathan tag along with me. He sits beside me quietly, reading, only occasionally saying something. The silence between us is comfortable and pure. Other days I go to the basketball court at the park around the corner from our house to shoot some hoops. Terrence joins me a couple of times but I don't make much effort to see him or Fred.

On the last Friday of the vacation I decide to detour to

Auburn on my way back from Dee Why. Nathan, who's with me, notices as soon as we take a different route home.

"Where are we going?"

"Nowhere."

"Impossible. We're somewhere now and we're heading somewhere else and when we get there you'll say we're *here* which is *not* nowhere. So where are we going?"

"Auburn."

"Okay."

I crank up the volume on my stereo.

"Why?"

"Because."

"Does it have anything to do with your angry music?"

"Yes."

"Okay."

"Any more questions?"

"Yes. Can you get me a Big Mac with the pickles and lettuce in a separate bag?"

"Sure. I always do, don't I?"

"Yes."

---

"There are a lot of women wearing hijab at this McDonald's," Nathan says as we sit in the outdoor area. We're at McDonald's on Parramatta Road in Auburn.

"Yep."

He looks around, a hungry, curious, we're-not-in-Kansas-anymore expression on his face.

"I think they look nice," he says. "Actually, that's not true," he says, dissatisfied with the apparent imprecision of his statement. "Some—*most*—look nice. But not *all* of them." He takes a bite of his burger, chews slowly, and swallows. "See that woman over there? She shouldn't be here. She's inviting an obesity condition."

I raise an eyebrow at him, but I can't help but laugh.

"Lower your voice, mate," I say softly.

When we're done, we follow the GPS's instructions and approach a large intersection. I see the minarets of a big white mosque nearby. When the lights change, I take a sharp left and find myself on a leafy residential street. The mosque is on the corner, in front of the railway tracks. I park in front of it.

It's the first time I've seen a mosque up close.

"The minaret and dome isn't a Muslim invention, you know," Nathan says casually.

I look at him. "What's that?"

"I watched a BBC documentary on the rise of the Ottoman Empire."

"Oh."

"Only it was on the ABC, not the BBC."

"Yep, that happens."

"I'm watching a documentary on ancient Greece now. I'm thinking I might become a historian one day. Work on plane engines on weekends."

I nod. "Good choice. You be what you want to be."

"Dad said the Ottoman documentary was *verging on propaganda*."

"Mmm."

There's a stillness to the place, a tranquility I can sense even from my car. The only person around is a gardener tending to the front flower beds.

"I need the bathroom," Nathan suddenly says.

"Oh, man. Why didn't you go at McDonald's?"

"I didn't need to then," he says matter-of-factly.

"Fine, I'll drive us back there."

"I need to go *now*." And then he opens the passenger door, jumps out, and enters the mosque gates. "Come on," he yells out at me, not even bothering to look back.

"Christ," I mutter (probably inappropriately in hindsight). I park the car and run after him, into a quiet courtyard. We search for a toilet sign. I hope we can slip in without being noticed. Nathan is holding his crotch at this point, a look of desperation on his face.

I run through some doors and find myself in the mosque. I'm taken aback by its simplicity. It's just a huge expanse of carpet. Then I look up to a beautiful stained-glass dome. There are some men up front, bobbing up and down in prayer, and some women in the back rows, praying or sitting down, quietly reading. I wave to a man who's doing neither. He hurries over to me.

"Please take off your shoes," he says gently but firmly.

"Oh, sorry. Um, my little brother needs the bathroom. Where are they?"

He shows me the way outside the mosque to the restroom and then leaves us there. Nathan soon emerges, giving me a thumbs-up.

"Let's take a look inside the mosque," he says.

"No," I say, feeling like we've already intruded enough.

But Nathan has already thrown off his shoes and walks into the mosque like he owns the place. I'm mortified and quickly follow after him, hoping to catch him before he speaks to anybody, but it's too late. He's gone right up to the front and is in conversation with a man wearing a suit and one brown and one black sock.

I approach cautiously. "This man's name is Ahmet," Nathan says to me. "He's going to give us a tour. I've explained that we have no interest in conversion." He turns to face the man again. "Andrew says that all Muslims want to convert people, and that being friendly is just a cover."

I moan softly. "I'm sorry," I quickly say to the man.

He looks slightly bewildered. "It is no problem."

"We better get going." I grab Nathan's hand firmly. "Come on."

"But I want a tour," he complains.

"It is no problem," the man says. "I'll give you a tour."

"We really need to get going," I insist. "Some other time. Thanks very much."

I drag Nathan out of the mosque. He mopes behind me to the car.

"I don't understand you," he says when we are back in the car. The ignition is running but I haven't moved yet. "Why did you want to leave?"

I can't explain myself. I feel like a fraud. What am I hoping to achieve, being here in Auburn? Do I really think that being in a mosque will help me understand Mina more?

I drive to Auburn Road, hustle my way for a parking space on the main road. We get out, walk up and down. Mina's right. There's a different kind of life pulse here. It's vibrant, chaotic, and run-down in places, thick with people, colors, smells. There are way more kids around too. That's really obvious. Mums and dads walking surrounded by three, four, five kids or more. There are discount shops selling different kinds of cheap shit, next to tacky clothing stores, run-down barbershops, and all sorts of restaurants and cafés. God is available for everyone here too. We pass a Chinese church just up the road from an Islamic school. There are mixed business stores selling toilet paper, frames with hologram pictures of Jesus at the Last Supper, phone cards, and kitsch dinnerware. There are coffee shops filled with old men wearing tweed suits. Women wearing long colorful headscarves that come down to their knees walk in front of pubs displaying happy hour signs. There are travel agencies, foreign exchange kiosks, signs in different languages.

Some of the food smells incredible. Toasting spices, roasting meat, fresh bread. It's like every part of the world is here, dressed up in all their garb. Long white robes and black sandals, saris, turbans, tight jeans and muscle shirts, girls in headscarves and Havaiana flip-flops.

I even see a woman all dressed up in black, only her eyes showing. It makes me uncomfortable, pisses me off a little too. There's a man with her, holding her hand. They're deep in conversation. He's in a T-shirt and shorts. Yeah, that annoys me.

We walk by a group of guys my age. They have an imposing presence about them. Their hair is shaved in different zigzag patterns. Some of them have thick, bushy beards. They wear tight muscle tops and track pants. I catch snatches of Arabic in their conversation.

I feel myself tense up a little, unconsciously inch Nathan closer to my side. It's not as though I actually think they're undercover terrorist operatives or part of some gang. It's like my body reacts before my brain. Because as soon as I realize, I feel like an idiot.

I feel like a tourist. Which is just so stupid and inexcusable, really. But to the people I've known all my life, Western

Sydney is tacky and unsophisticated. It's gangland and ghetto, underclass and trouble.

I look above at all the flats in the high-density apartment blocks that overlook us and I wonder whether Mina lived in one of them.

That's when it hits me that I've crossed the line from thinking about Mina to crushing hard. I'm in that tragic stage where I'll take any scraps on offer: the sound of her name; a visit to a suburb she once lived in, and misses.

Jesus. I've become Jane.

The thought sobers me.

"I'm hungry," Nathan whines.

"We just had McDonald's."

"So?"

We end up going to a restaurant on the main street for a mixed plate. We can eat all day long, no problem.

# MINA

I sleep restlessly, fading in and out of dreams and wakefulness. It's past two when I hear footsteps shuffling in the kitchen. I get up and find Baba boiling a pot of tea on the stove.

"What's wrong?" I ask him.

"I can't sleep," he says. "Tea?"

"Sure. Here, I'll do it. Go sit down."

He thanks me and walks slowly over to the couch. He's only thirty-nine but he walks like an old man. Like a man hurting. A man trying to live with a body that has been broken and never quite healed properly.

"Did you take medicine?" I ask when we're sitting across from each other, drinking our sweet tea.

"Yeah," he says. I detect shame in his voice. He's always been like this, exuded a sense of guilt at having been a victim, at feeling pain. "I'll see the doctor tomorrow for something stronger."

"What can I do?"

"Not tell your mother."

"Okay."

"I don't want her to worry. Not with the baby."

It's kind of cute, him wanting to protect Mum given all she's been through.

"Are you happy here, Baba?" I ask after some moments of silence.

He continues smoking, takes a little while to answer. Eventually he speaks up: "When you don't have what you want, you have to want what you have."

"What do you want that you don't have?"

"A peaceful Afghanistan I can return to, of course."

"Isn't this home now?"

He sucks on his cigarette. "When I die I want to be buried here," he says suddenly. "That surprises me but, well, look, I suppose that is something."

We get lost in our own thoughts. At one point I notice his face twist into a grimace. I know he is riding a wave of pain.

"Why is it worse all of a sudden? Because of this stupid business with the media?"

He nods slowly. "The pain's always there," he says matter-of-factly. "But yes, I'm worried this media business will affect the restaurant."

"I wouldn't worry," I say cheerfully. "Most people don't take that show seriously." Paula's advice comes back to me and I marvel at how easily I put on an act. "It's all over now.

Attention will turn to the next *bad guy* and things will go back to normal."

"Normal? I gave up on normal many years ago, Mina."

We sip our tea in silence, both of us burdened by memories that continue to haunt us, no matter how much we pretend.

———————————

Paula's over and we're stalking the public profiles of some of the guys and girls in school as we bake cupcakes. Mum's sprawled on the couch, having a power nap.

"Let's check out Michael's page," I suggest as we stand in front of the laptop, polishing off the chocolate left in the mixing bowl.

She eyes me, a mischievous smile on her face. "That's kind of random. Missing him over vacation, are we?"

"Why would I miss him? He's a jerk."

She takes another swipe of batter out of the bowl.

"I'm just morbidly curious," I explain. "It's like when people are fascinated with the lives of serial killers. You want to know more."

She smiles briefly. "Michael may be a racist jerk, but as far as I know, he's not hiding dismembered bodies in his locker."

We look up his page. We can't see much, but from what I can tell from our last visit to his page, it's had a major makeover.

His likes have been cleaned up, leaving only bands, books, and movies. No more Aussie Values; no more offensive memes. I search down the thread of public conversations too, but there's nothing there.

"Wow," I say. "He went from being a white supremacist to a *Hunger Games* fan."

"Aren't you the drama queen today?" Paula chuckles.

*I wouldn't go that far*, I think to myself, but he's definitely changed his online persona. And something about that intrigues me.

---

**Public service announcement from Bus Route 419:**

Two male senior citizens on the bus here today. I spoke to them and they've been friends for sixty years. I hope we're still friends in sixty years, when we're sitting in our hover-wheelchairs.

---

It's the first time I've seen Michael since the party. I walk into homeroom on our first day back from vacation. Mr. Morello hasn't arrived yet. Michael is talking to Terrence and Fred. He notices me walk in and I can practically see the muscles in his neck stiffen. The awkwardness and tension between us is thick and heavy. I hold my head high, don't acknowledge him, and walk straight past his desk.

Terrence, who's sitting beside him, stops me. "Hey, Mina," he says cheerfully.

I pause and consider him.

"How was your vacation?"

I roll my eyes at him.

He pretends to look wounded. "What did I say wrong? It was a polite question."

"Yeah, you're *really* interested in how I spent my vacation."

"I don't get it. I'm just trying to be friendly." He looks back and forth between Michael and Fred for support. Fred isn't really interested, too busy sorting through his bag.

"Okay, let *me* ask," Michael says, meeting my eye. "How was your vacation?"

My eyes narrow. "Fabulous," I say in an exaggerated tone.

"Why are girls *so* sensitive?" Terrence asks, all wide-eyed and innocent.

"I don't know what that is stuck between your teeth, Terrence, but I assume you're saving it for later."

He quickly cleans between his teeth with his finger. I laugh at him and, realizing the joke, he looks momentarily duped. "Yeah, okay, good one," he admits begrudgingly.

I flash him a triumphant look and walk to my desk. But not before I notice the hint of a smile on Michael's face.

Paula and I are goofing around in the café, both of us in a laughing mood. Paula shows me a ridiculous dance move, sending me into a fit of giggles. I love these moments. The laughter takes over your body; you don't know why but you're having too much of a good time to care.

We spot Jane and Leica and wave them over.

"Too much red cordial?" Leica says, laughing.

We shrug and then start giggling again.

Jane sits down next to us and takes out her lunch. Five cherry tomatoes and a green apple.

"You serious?" I ask.

"I need to lose some weight," she says, mournfully popping a tomato into her mouth.

"Please don't do this, Jane," Paula says quietly.

"You don't need to lose weight!" I wail.

"She thinks Terrence thinks she's fat," Leica says, rolling her eyes.

Paula and I groan.

"No, it's not that," she says defensively. "He's never said that."

"But I know exactly what you're thinking," Leica says. "You're thinking, *Maybe if I shrink, he'll notice me more.* Do you not see the irony?"

"Come on," Paula says, standing and grabbing Jane's hand. "Dance with me."

"Are you mental?" Jane says. "Terrence and his group are over there. They can see you, you know." She pauses. "You know he won't let you live it down."

"Oh well, we better stop then," Paula says, but she just keeps on dancing.

Jane looks embarrassed, picks up another cherry tomato, and pops it into her mouth.

# MICHAEL

Andrew, Carolina, Li, and Kahn have been visiting more frequently since Dad's return from overseas. I've been coming home to find them sitting around the dining table that's been converted into "organization headquarters," discussing strategies, media campaigns, and policies with my parents. They're all convinced that *Don't Jump the Queue* will deliver them a national profile, which could transform them from an obscure organization from the suburbs to a movement that people could take seriously—maybe even, with enough members, transform them into a political party.

Nathan responded to their presence the way you might react to a sudden infestation of ants in your home. Unsettled and put out, he tried to get rid of the invasion with his own version of Raid. That is to say, he threw a terrific tantrum at dinner and told them all to go home.

When they all left, Mum and Dad had a long and patient chat with Nathan. My help was enlisted. Nathan eventually came around to the idea that the house will be a flurry of activity as Aussie Values gets bigger. The compromise was that the ants would be contained to certain days of the week. And the rules around Xbox time would be relaxed. I'm pretty sure that was the clincher.

I arrive home from work tonight and find Andrew and Carolina in the family room with Mum and Dad. I'd forgotten it was a designated Aussie Values evening. Andrew sees me walk in and asks me to help them update the organization's Facebook page.

"Michael's *brilliant* with technology," Dad boasts. "He's always had a unique way of being creative and seeing things from new angles."

Genuinely pleased, I grin at him. "Thanks, Dad."

I give Mum a look as if to say, *See, it might not be so bad*, but she just shakes her head and signals with her eyes not to open the topic.

I show Andrew a few tricks with the Facebook page. He wants me to upload some memes he's taken from the English Defence League website, but as one big collage so he can use it as the background picture. I play around with one of my programs and start to insert the memes into a single image. I start to read them as I transfer them across. A sick feeling lodges in the pit of my stomach. I realize that I'm seeing the memes from the point of view of somebody like Mina.

I feel conflicted and dirty, helping Andrew out. I fiddle around a bit more but the feeling gnaws at me. I pretend that the program crashes and lie and tell him I'll work on it overnight.

―――――――――――

"As in Q for queen—sorry?" I say at work, leaning back in my chair to look up at the ceiling. "Huh? Q for *cube*. But cube is with a C. Yeah, it is. I'm pretty sure I know how to spell cube. Okay, right. Next. A for apple."

Finally. Progress.

"Next. N for *what*? N for envelope?" I want to pull out my hair. "Okay, you know what, this phonetic spelling thing isn't working. Just tell me your surname and I'll figure it out myself."

I get through the call quickly. All that torment for a thirty-dollar donation.

Anh, who's always pacing around the call center hoping to catch one of us out, hovers near me, eavesdropping. He doesn't even make an attempt to be discreet.

"Yes, we're collecting money for guide dogs. No, the money goes toward training. Oh, are you okay? Excuse me, sorry . . ." The woman is crying on the other end of the phone. "Sorry, have I struck a raw nerve or something? Are you blind? Oh, sorry, I didn't mean . . . Yep, sure, I'll put him on."

Reluctantly, I wave Anh over. "She wants to speak to my supervisor."

I've been forewarned that this is the most annoying out-come of a call. Anh's impressive death stare confirms it.

He takes the call.

He calms her down *and* manages to get a fifty-dollar dona-tion out of her.

I don't understand. He has zero people skills with his staff.

"She wasn't blind," he says, giving me a cold stare. "Her dog died recently. Notice I finished the call within time. That's because I pretended to care about her dog dying but didn't give her a chance to tell me all the sorry-ass details. Toughen up or they'll have you by the balls."

He walks off.

I figure I'm sounding too young on the phone and that's why nobody's taking me seriously. So I fake a British accent (because who doesn't take a British accent seriously?) and sure enough the money starts rolling in.

---

The house buzzes with a frenetic energy. There's some-thing in the mood that I can't quite put my finger on, until it hits me one night as I listen to them deep in conversa-tion over a dinner of Thai takeout. This one time Dad took me to a house auction up the road from our place. It feels like that now. Like they're all bidding furiously, except it's not to buy a house but to stake a claim as the *most worried citizen*.

Andrew raises his worries about the economy and Carolina bids with her worries about multiculturalism gone too far. Li jumps in, worried about border protection and too many Asians buying real estate, and Kahn meets him with "Australia's turning into an Islamic state" and "the government's given up on the 'battler.'" Mum's worried that Australia is being bullied by the UN, and it all swings back to Andrew, who's worried about Africans on welfare. As for Dad, he's worried about recruitment numbers. In other words, I think, they want more members to worry with them.

I can feel their anxiety, the way it travels through the room, like some kind of mobile energy, touching one person and then moving on to the next.

I watch them, fascinated and enthralled, as I slowly eat my pad thai.

Kahn suddenly sits up straight in his chair, drops his spring roll onto his plate, and beams out at us all. "I forgot to tell you, there's been some gossip about a new Islamic school opening out in Jordan Springs."

Dad considers him carefully. "Really? Jordan Springs?" He looks surprised. "They've reached as far as there?" He shakes his head.

"I'll look into it," Mum says.

Andrew's livid. "If we can get enough grassroots resistance, we might be able to wake people out of their multiculturalism coma," he says gruffly.

"Medically impossible," Nathan declares in a bored tone. "You can *induce* a coma, but you can't *wake* somebody from one."

The way I feel now, I'm beginning to think that maybe, just for once, he's wrong.

# MINA

Irfan's brother, who lives in Pakistan, is losing his battle with cancer, and so Irfan catches the first flight out. Baba hires a temporary chef in the meantime but I step in to help out too. The *News Tonight* program hasn't affected business. We're just as busy as usual. Paula was right. The program ran, talk radio picked over the scraps like vultures over a carcass, and then everybody shifted their hysterical what-is-Australia-coming-to? panic to the next target.

Last night we finished up late at the restaurant. Baba tried to persuade me to go home early but I insisted on staying back to help out. I wake up early to finish an assignment, and go to school on three hours' sleep. I'm paying for it now, dozing off in class, doing that embarrassing head-bopping maneuver that you better hope nobody catches on their phone. Paula nudges me in the side during first period.

"Oi, wake up," she hisses. "Ms. Hamish is on the move."

My eyelids are heavy. I yawn and shake my head to try to wake myself up. I get through class thanks to Paula, who prods and pokes me whenever I start to fade out again.

"Don't forget *Don't Jump the Queue* tonight," Paula tells me when the bell has rung and we're walking to our lockers.

I grimace. "Sadomasochism on a weekday. Just. Great."

---

I'm in a good mood when the last bell rings. Ms. Parkinson was impressed with my work in English and read it out to the class. There's a spring in my step as I head toward the school bus zone.

As I turn the corner of the main gates I almost collide with Michael.

"Oh, sorry," we automatically say at the same time.

I continue walking in the direction of the bus stop. I can hear his steps close behind me.

It's painfully awkward.

He must sense it too. "This an okay distance for you?" he calls out cheekily.

"Yep," I call back.

His persistence amazes me. I remember his Facebook wall. He's out of his mind if he thinks I can ignore it all.

"Just a warning," he says from behind. "I'm gaining on you, but it's only because I've got longer legs."

"Oh, this is just ridiculous!" I stop in my tracks and face him angrily. "Do you seriously think we can be friends again? If that's even what we were before?"

"I'm curious. What's your apology quota? Is there a certain number of apologies before you accept?"

"So how's Aussie Values coming along?" is my response. "Gaining more *comrades*?"

"Yeah, great, we'll be taking over the country soon. All fifty of us."

"Oh, too bad," I say. "You need to vamp up the campaign, Michael. Go picket a halal kebab van or reclaim Vegemite or something. Oh, maybe *Don't Jump the Queue* will boost your numbers! Exploit refugees for votes. Impressive."

Chastised, he stares at me.

"What do you want from me?" I say, wearily. "I don't get you. Why are you even talking to me? I represent everything and everyone you and your parents stand against."

"My parents aren't bad people, Mina. There are all kinds of people in the organization. They're not responsible for every member."

"Maybe not. But they're on the ugly side of a debate. That's enough for me."

"I'm not exactly the best person to explain their policies, but they're not racists, Mina. They're not white supremacists like some of the mob you hear about." I stare at him blankly as he blusters on. "Just the other day they were telling me about how they believe in diversity." He then tells me a story about asparagus soup. I don't know whether to scream or fall over in hysterical laughter.

"So let me get this clear, Michael. Australia is a big bowl of soup and Aussie Values is about protecting the asparagus from an overzealous pepper or cardamom pod?"

He shifts from foot to foot, practically writhing in agony under the weight of my gaze. "Look, I'm beginning to realize I don't necessarily feel comfortable, even agree, with everything they say." His voice falters and he looks away. I'm about to respond but then he flashes an angry look at me. "You know, I get you've been through hell and back, but you could stop being so goddamn pigheaded and actually appreciate that we don't have a choice about who we're born to, or where. This is me, okay? I'm white and my parents started Aussie Values. I'm sorting through that, and it's not easy, thank you very much, so it would be helpful if you quit acting so bloody condescending and superior."

I see red. "You want *me* to make it easier for *you* to confront your privilege because God knows even antiracism has to be done in a way that makes the majority comfortable? Sorry, Michael, I don't have time to babysit you through your enlightenment. The first step would be for you to realize that you need to figure it out on your own!"

I storm off and just make it to my bus, a rising pressure building in my chest. I blink back hot tears, determined not to let anybody see me like this. I feel ashamed of myself, allowing somebody like Michael to affect me so strongly.

———————————————

The nightmares return tonight. I'm trying to save Hasan from sinking in the boat. I swim toward him and make it in time. I grab him, and suddenly we're sitting on the shore and I'm cradling him in my arms. My chest explodes with happiness and I look down at his face. But the baby I'm holding is faceless. I scream and scream.

# MICHAEL

I play hard at our game tonight. I'm unstoppable out on the court, raging at myself and the world. Mina's words are like blades that keep on slashing through me every time I recall them.

I arrive home that night to a full house. Jazz music is playing from our sound system, and the usual Aussie Values devotees are over, sipping wine, nibbling on a spread of fancy appetizers.

Mum notices me first and grins at me. "Jump into the shower quickly, honey, and then come down to watch! It starts in half an hour."

A wave of nausea rushes through me.

I can't even enjoy the escapism a long shower offers. Nathan has been sent to bang on the bathroom door and demand I hurry up and join everybody.

"Okay!" I holler.

I get out of the shower, dry myself off, and throw on some boxers. I stand in front of the bathroom mirror, stare at my reflection. I'm fit and strong. I study hard, get good grades, can code, draw, and game with the best of them. I'm a dutiful son, a good big brother. But suddenly it all feels like a character profile of somebody else. I feel shallow. Because I have no idea who I am or what I believe in anymore.

I get dressed and trudge downstairs. Everybody's gathered in the living room, waiting. Terrence calls my phone, but I ignore him. So he sends me a text message:

> **Cheering you on loser.**

I don't bother replying.

Carolina pats the space next to her on the couch and smiles at me.

"Come on, Michael, sit down!"

"It's okay, thanks. I'm just going to heat up dinner. I'll be back."

I heat some leftovers and return, cradling the bowl in my hands. I stand at the back of the room. Mum and Dad are cuddled up on an armchair. Andrew, looking intense as usual, has a notebook in his hands, ready to record his notes so he can write a review on the organization's website. Nathan is sitting beside Carolina and they're in deep conversation. The others are spread across the rest of the furniture, or on the floor, sipping their wine, munching on their miniquiches and pastry puffs, laughing among themselves. Everybody's relaxed and happy.

Finally the program starts. I cringe as I see a shot of myself with Mum, Dad, and Nathan in the opening credits. It will have to be ripped off like a Band-Aid. I'll only be on there in the beginning, when they're building the family drama element to it all, before Dad takes off.

When I appear back on the screen, it feels like the Band-Aid is ripping off skin. I can't stand it, but I can't look away either. *"Just because we want to protect our borders doesn't mean we're heartless. There are wars all over the world. More and more refugees. There has to be a limit, or we'll be flooded . . . yep . . ."* The camera zooms in on my face then. I look nervous and self-conscious. Then the camera cuts to a shot of Dad in Iraq, surrounded by a group of malnourished kids, some of them grinning up at him, some of them staring blankly at the camera. They're grabbing at his shirt, pressed up close to him. He's smiling down at them, trying to look cool and composed. At one point another group of kids rushes over to him and Dad looks like he's about to lose his balance.

"See that juxtaposition!" Andrew cries. "That's what you call good TV." He looks at us all, triumphant. "Just that shot alone on the back of Michael's excellent point"—he looks over at me and nods proudly—"gives me confidence the producers aren't bleeding hearts."

It's perfect reality TV. Dramatic, shocking, raw, intense. My phone is filled with text messages from friends: *You looked good! Good point you made, mate! Your dad's awesome!* My

Facebook wall has more mixed responses. Some of the more random people I've added over the years aren't impressed. *What about Australia's international legal obligations? Bet your dad would change his mind if he actually had to stay back with those refugees in Iraq, hey? I'm unfriending you, you dickhead.*

I watch with bated breath as Dad and the rest of the group are quickly bundled into an armored personnel carrier and driven away from one of the camps after they've been alerted to a possible ambush. It feels surreal, watching Dad on screen. Watching him try to contain his emotions, deal with exhaustion and fear. One of the other people in the group, Gary, is opposed to Dad's politics, and they get into fierce arguments on camera, the others in the group either joining in, or holding back to watch on. No matter how hard Gary comes at him, Dad responds calmly and coolly, even while he's sitting in a leaky boat, or huddled on a desert floor eating scraps of bread with a bunch of Iraqi refugees. A part of me is proud of the way he handles himself, even if I'm not proud of his politics.

I can't point to where Iraq or Indonesia or Afghanistan are on the world map. Politics here bore me, let alone keeping up with other countries. But something's shifted in me. This must be what living in gray feels like.

As I watch the images unfold on the TV screen and listen to the arguments among the participants, I realize that I know so little.

And that knowledge gives me hope.

# MINA

*Don't Jump the Queue.*

It sounds so quaint, like a queue at a shopping center or a bus stop.

Michael and his family appear on the screen. They seem like a happy family, warm and generous to one another. When the camera focuses on Michael, he offers an almost half-hearted we'll-be-flooded opinion, and his eyes instantly dart to his father, Alan, as though he's seeking his approval. But I don't get a sense that Michael's father is an overbearing patri-arch. There's genuine admiration in the way Michael looks at his dad.

Alan is pleasant, funny, and exudes charm. He's calm and measured and manages to smile his way through an argument about "economic refugees" and "cultural incompatibility." He's not an angry ranter, an unsophisticated, easy-to-mock red-neck. That role is filled by Jeff from Adelaide. Alan plays it smart. He's quick to build an alliance with Jeff, while still distinguishing himself as the reasonable, rational conservative. His main combatants are Julianne, who works in radio, and Gary, a teacher from Melbourne.

There are moments when, to my surprise, I find myself liking Alan, and I realize why Michael is so quick to defend his father. It's hard to accept that nice people can be racist too.

The episode ends with the participants arriving in a camp in Indonesia. The final episode will air on Monday. I close the screen on my laptop.

I'm numb.

I ignore all the messages that have flooded my phone and Facebook wall. I curl up in the armchair that reminds me of my father and remember being a kid, curled up on his lap as he sat in his chair.

I close my eyes and see Hasan's tiny blank face . . . the open sea . . . people vomiting over the side of the boat . . . the dazed look on Mum's face as she cradled me . . . Each memory is a nail inside my head. It sits there, suspended, and I don't notice it until suddenly something or somebody acts as a trigger and a hammer starts to hit each nail until my whole head is pounding.

# MICHAEL

Mina walks straight past my desk in English. I keep my head down, focusing on my laptop screen, but I can hear her laughing with Paula. I ache inside, wanting desperately to fix things, to wipe the slate clean, to be a different person, somebody she'd choose to laugh with too.

Ms. Parkinson hasn't arrived yet and people hang around talking. Somebody mentions *Don't Jump the Queue*. I'm mortified.

"No offense or anything, Michael," says Adrian, "but I can't believe your dad wasn't affected by what he went through."

"Oh, get stuffed, Adrian," I lash out. "How the hell would you know what he went through?"

"What do you mean?" Adrian yells back. "He went on a boat and stayed in the camps and he still thinks they've got no right to ask us for help."

Leica joins in. "And you were talking about floodgates and stuff too. Do you actually agree with your dad and that organization he started?"

"I'm my own person," I snap.

"It's a free country," somebody calls out.

Out of the corner of my eye I notice Mina looking at me.

"Yeah, well, we have the right to say it's bullshit," somebody else says.

"Where's your humanity?" Adrian says. "They've got no choice."

"Yeah, but they don't fit in," Fred says. "They don't learn English, and they treat women like they're second-class citizens."

"Fred the feminist," Paula says with a snort. "I think I've heard everything now."

"The point is, they come here and try to change things," Terrence says. "Like Michael's dad said. There's a big culture clash."

I want to disappear. Just evaporate into thin air.

"Fred, you're forgetting that they want to turn Australia into an Islamic state." Mina's eyes flash at Fred. Her voice drips with sarcasm. "We all know that's *exactly* what's on the minds of asylum seekers and the Muslim *two point five* percent of the Australian population."

I look up sharply. She has a look of pure defiance on her face. A fierceness and courage that takes my breath away.

"Speaking of political parties, there's a sex organization, you know?" Terrence says. "I'll join that."

That gets people laughing.

"Anyway, listen to Fred," Terrence continues, a big grin on his face. "He's Asian. Even *he* thinks it's all bullshit. You can't call him *racist*."

Terrence slaps Fred on the back, like he's scored a point. Fred tells him to shut up, but he's laughing too.

"Another intelligent contribution from Terrence," Paula moans.

"Anyway, Michael," Adrian says, "all I'm saying is it's weird your dad wouldn't—"

"He can think what he wants," I snap, cutting him off. "It's got nothing to do with me." I continue to focus my eyes on my laptop, signaling that the topic is closed as far as I'm concerned.

"Oh, stop giving Michael and his dad a hard time everybody, will you?" Terrence cries. It's only drawing more attention to me but he thinks he's sticking up for me. "It's a free country, remember?"

"Why is it that whenever somebody uses the 'it's a free country' defense they're basically defending the right to act like a bigot?" Mina says to nobody in particular.

I almost laugh. Because strange as it may seem, I'm beginning to wonder the same thing.

---

I'm like one of those stupid birds that keeps on launching itself at the same window. I walk over to the library hoping to catch Mina during our free period, bracing myself for the impact.

She's alone, bent over her work, deep in concentration. I want her to know that I'm not my father. That I only said those things on the program because I hadn't thought much about my parents' arguments before, had always just gone along without questioning them.

I want so bad to be able to talk to Mina. But she's made it clear that she wants nothing to do with me. I have to accept that. I need to man up. I'm being a complete idiot.

Changing my mind, I turn around, but the librarian is walking past at that moment and calls out, "Hi, Michael! How's it going?"

Shit.

Mina turns around sharply and sees me standing there. Oh God, it's awkward. I must look like a creepy stalker.

I mumble something back to the librarian about looking for a book and she smiles and walks off. Meanwhile, I'm frozen in position, like a kangaroo caught in the headlights. Mina's looking at me.

"I'm just looking for a book," I say quickly.

"I watched *Don't Jump the Queue*," she says in an icy tone.

"Mmm." I meet her gaze.

"Did you really mean what you said?" Her eyes search mine.

I sigh. "I don't know."

"You don't know if you meant what you said?" She raises her eyebrows.

"Just don't know," I say, and walk away.

———————————

I'm getting better at my job, but still not reaching my targets, although I have a nagging suspicion they are designed to be impossible to reach. Anh is constantly on my back, monitoring my call times and timing my toilet breaks. It makes me think that call centers would make good training grounds for anybody interested in a career as a fascist dictator.

It's bone marrow research today. I figure out that I could be asking for donations to save children from a burning building and people would still think *telemarketer* and want to reach through the phone and throttle me. Today's call is a first though.

"You could go to university, educate yourself, and get a proper job. You don't have to waste your life in a call center."

"So I can't persuade you to make a donation toward bone marrow medical research?"

"Sure, why not."

And he scores!

"Two dollars is as high as I can go though."

I lean back in my chair and raise my eyes to the ceiling.

# MINA

If I stared at a plant for days I would never notice it growing. I've seen Michael almost every weekday since the start of school, and it's not until today, in the library, that I notice a change in his eyes. When I first met him in class he struck me as the kind of guy who, despite being only vaguely committed to his opinion, wasn't embarrassed to share it. It's only now in the library that I see he's changed. There's a vulnerability in his eyes that I never noticed before. A conflict that tells me he's going through a private battle. And I don't know what's happened, or what caused it, but something in my gut tells me I have something to do with it.

And call me crazy, but it makes me a little less angry.

———————————

Mum's got all her friends coming over for lunch tomorrow and is making me help her clean the apartment. I'm a sucker for pain so I turn the TV on to watch the final episode of *Don't Jump the Queue* as I dust the furniture.

"Mariam's bringing her sister-in-law, Fariha," Mum tells me as she works away in the kitchen. "I can't stand her."

"Why?" I ask distractedly. The credits have started and Michael's face briefly appears on the TV screen. Incomprehensibly, my stomach kind of goes all funny.

"She's a backstabbing, arrogant, judgmental witch, that's why."

"So I take it you don't like her then." I slow down with the dusting as the episode starts. I balance on the armrest of the couch, watching the TV.

"She told Irfan's wife that I've become stuck-up since we moved here because I rarely visit. Can you imagine? We've only been here a few months. Can't I settle in first? Did she even pick up the phone once?"

I block out the sound of my mum's voice as she rants on about Fariha.

Michael's dad is hugging a child, his face a mixture of horror and sadness as he surveys the squalor in a room where a bunch of kids live. I can't reconcile the image with what he preaches.

"But of course I'll have to act all polite tomorrow when she's in my home—come on, Mina, hurry up, there's still the bathroom to clean—and of course she'll be looking every corner up and down . . ."

Michael's dad is arguing with some of the other participants. I can't finish the show.

"Jerk," I yell at the TV, switching it off and throwing the
remote on the couch.

"What's the problem?" Mum asks, looking at me in
surprise.

"That man!"

"Okay. No need to get all worked up. He's on TV. Nobody
to us. Don't forget the cup marks on the TV cabinet."

I refuse to watch the rest. I don't need to see a bunch of
people crying over refugee camps and struggling in a leaky
boat so I can get some *perspective*. I've lived through it. They'll
all return home after the show and eventually life will go back
to normal. Even if the ones affected put up a fight, they'll be
ignored and the government will do what it wants. And the
kids in the camp will keep on starving and the mothers will
give up crying and the fathers will wither away with helpless-
ness and life will go on, even for me, because I'm one of the
lucky ones. I'm grateful that I made it to a country that offers
peace, but what upsets me is that it offers peace to some and
not others. That's the way the world works, isn't it? A lottery
of winners and losers.

---

I call Maha. It's been a while. She can always make me laugh. I
tell her about Michael and, in her typically understated style,

she suggests I find a photo of him online, Photoshop a burka over it, and then wreak social media havoc.

As tempting as it is, I tell her I'll have to think about it.

She promises to watch *Don't Jump the Queue* as soon as the episode is uploaded online.

"At least then I can see if he's a *good-looking* douchebag," she says. "Never, ever trust the accuracy of a person's Facebook profile."

"What difference does it make anyway?"

"Oh, Mina. Isn't it obvious? It'll make stalking him online so much more tolerable if he's at least hot."

# MICHAEL

We don't have much to do with each other for the rest of the term. Things have shifted for me at school in a small way. I'm spending more time in the tech lab, or the art room, trying to get on top of all the assignments the teachers have piled on us. Terrence and Fred notice that we aren't hanging out as often as we used to, but they just assume it's because I've become a nerd.

---

It's Saturday morning and the premier has called a state election earlier than expected. My parents are ecstatic.

"Why is it exciting?" Nathan asks.

"Because it's game on!" Mum says, grinning, as she takes a bite of her toast.

"What kind of game?"

"It's just a phrase, Nathan," she says.

Nathan keeps looking at Mum. "What kind of game?"

But my parents are distracted, talking about leaflet drop-ping in Jordan Springs and helping certain sympathetic candidates in their electorate.

"It's a game where you hunt down people, line them up against a wall, and then chuck trash at them," I tell Nathan.

Mum gives me a look. "Cut it out, Michael. What an awful thing to say."

I grin at her. "Selective hearing."

"Nathan, darling," Mum says, "I just meant now that there's an election, we need to work really hard. It's kind of like a game. Somebody wins and somebody loses."

Nathan leans in closer toward me and whispers: "So nobody's hunted down?"

"Er . . ." Awkward. "Nah, I was just mucking around. Sorry. Bad joke."

"Well, I hope Dad wins," he says.

It takes me by surprise that now I hope he doesn't.

——————————————

I park my car on a side street, grab my sketchpad from under the passenger seat, and walk to Auburn Road. There are roadworks blocking all traffic. I cross the road and see a group of men hanging out together, using the fluorescent-orange traffic cones as seats.

I go to a nearby café and order some lunch. The guy who serves me is built like a tank, muscles squeezing out of his too-small T-shirt, a tattoo sleeve on one arm and even a shaved head that looks muscular.

There's an outdoor table available, giving me a clear view of the street. My eyes follow the men hanging around the cones. I feel animated all of a sudden and pick up my pencil and start sketching.

Lost in my work I don't realize that the guy from behind the counter is talking to me. He places my drink on the table and, glancing at my open sketchbook, says, "You're good."

Embarrassed, I instinctively cover the page with my arm. "Nah, not really."

"You are. Can I have another look?"

He peers closely at the page and then nods, impressed. "You study art at university or something?"

"I'm in eleventh grade. This is for an assignment."

He looks at my page again and then looks over at the men. He fixes his eyes on me, his lips curled into a half smile.

"You live around here?"

I shake my head. "Nope."

"I didn't think so. So why those men?" He jerks his thumb in their direction.

I shrug. I'm not sure myself.

"Do you know them?"

"No."

"They're refugees from Sudan."

"Okay."

His tone is pleasant enough, but I feel I'm being repri-manded. That in his eyes I've done something wrong.

"Imagine I came to your side of Sydney and started sketch-ing the natives there."

"What do you mean?" I say, a little defensively.

"A group of white women wearing matching Lululemon outfits and sipping soy quinoa protein shakes. In watercolor."

I feel my neck burn.

He smiles. "It's cool. I'm only mucking around with you. Enjoy your lunch."

I slowly pick at my food. I look at the sketch and close the book. When eventually I've finished eating I get up to pay the bill.

"Hey, sorry if I came across a little aggressive," he says cheerfully as he hands me my change.

"I didn't mean to offend anybody," I say.

"People usually don't," he replies, still smiling.

When I get home, I hunker down in my room and start my assignment all over again.

# MINA

**Me:**
Want to come to a *Lord of the Rings* movie marathon?

**Maha:**
Where?

**Me:**
Paula's place. Didn't u get my FB invite?

**Maha:**
Haven't seen it yet.

**Me:**
It's dress up. U have to dress like a hobbit. Or elf. Or somebody from Middle-earth. A onesie will also do. Or anything really, so long as u dress up. See FB.

**Maha:**
As if.

**Me:**

I'm serious.

**Maha:**

It's the first time I meet ur North Shore friends and u want me to represent Westies in a onesie? Why can't I dress up like I'm going clubbing? That's legit. I don't wear that in the day.

**Me:**

Yeah. u do.

**Maha:**

I'll do it on one condition. No proof. I'm the door bitch. Anybody brings in a phone or camera gets a broken limb.

**Me:**

Deal.

**Maha:**

I'm nervous. Will they u know, like, need a Western Sydney interpreter?

**Me:**

LOL. U speak ur own language, Maha.

**Maha:**

I know. I'm original like that.

Irfan has returned from Pakistan and is over for Sunday lunch with his wife and their two young daughters, Zahra and Shakira. I'm braiding the girls' hair as we watch *Frozen*. They know the entire movie by heart and take the singing scenes seriously. Our apartment is tiny and the men are sitting with us, trying to talk over the sound of Disney. Mum needs some fresh air and is sitting with Aunty on the balcony.

"Mohammed was telling me at Friday prayer that there are some new brothers on bridging visas, living in Auburn," Irfan says to Baba. "How are they supposed to live with no work? The others are helping them settle in. Apparently they're good cooks. Ehssan wants to offer them some work at the money-exchange place but there just isn't enough work to justify it. We could help them."

"We should," Baba says firmly. "It's a long way for them though."

"They're sharing a car. It could work. We hire them Thursday to Sunday, see if that suits them."

Baba nods. "Okay, talk to them."

The midyear break passes by in a flash. I spend most of my time doing assignments either at home or with Paula at her house.

At senior assembly on the first day back at school, the coordinator, Ms. Ham, announces that there's a gallery of art-work by eleventh- and twelfth-grade Visual Arts students on display in the seniors' common room.

Paula and I go to have a look at lunchtime.

I'm stunned by some of the work. We walk around the room, trying to make our own sense of the different paint-ings and installations and what they might mean. We don't have much of a clue really, but it's fun pretending we're art critics. We go through different reactions: "Ew, creepy"; "Wow, that's amazing"; "Oh my God, I had no idea Adrian could draw like that"; "Oh come on, Mrs. Darwin's nose is not that big."

And then I see it.

It's a series of five sketches, starting with a sketch of a closed wire birdcage, a key dangling on a piece of string out-side the cage and down to the bottom of the canvas. Inside the cage, there's a man running, a small satchel on his back, a trail of identity papers behind him. In the next sketch, the man is in a room behind bars, still within the cage. The key to the cage dangles slightly higher up though. In the third sketch, the man is pressed up against other bodies in a dilapi-dated boat on the sea, still trapped within the cage. The key is dangling even higher now, almost at the height of the cage door. In the fourth image, the man is lying down in the cage beside a small Australian flag pitched next to him. He's extending his arm through the bars, trying to reach the key, which is just past his grasp. In the final sketch, a hand holding a pencil appears out of the corner of the canvas. The tip of the pencil twirls the string upward, so that the man is able to clasp the key in his hands.

I'm speechless, as much because of the images as the name attached to them.

Michael Blainey.

———————————

I look for Michael after school and find him before he leaves to catch the school bus home. I spot him ahead of me and quicken my pace to catch up.

"Hey," I call out.

He turns around.

"I saw your artwork. What's that about?" It comes across as an accusation but I can't help the sharpness in my tone.

He blinks at me. "You didn't like it?"

"That's not what I said."

He smiles broadly. Something about the way he's carrying himself seems different. There's a spark in him, something almost joyful about his manner, as though he's just excavated some insight that's been buried for some time.

Which makes my irrational anger impossible to understand but too strong to suppress.

"What?" I say. "You've suddenly changed?"

He lets out a short laugh, looks at me with disbelief. "Why are you angry?"

"I'm not . . ." I pause, confused by my reaction. I feel like there's cotton wool in my head.

"So what's your problem?"

I throw my hands in the air. "I don't get it. One minute you're all *don't jump the queue*, you're the poster boy for Aussie Values, liking all kinds of racist crap on Facebook, and the next minute your Facebook is cleaned up, you go and do this incredible art—"

"You've been stalking me on Facebook?" He grins.

So awkward.

I shuffle my feet. "What's interesting," I say, hoping really badly that my deflection will work, "is your backflip."

"You're so confusing," he says, suddenly frustrated. "Are you saying you resent what I drew?"

"Of course not! It's beautiful." My voice stalls.

"Then what?"

I stare into his eyes for a moment. "What you drew con-tradicts everything Aussie Values stands for. I don't get it."

"I'm just trying to figure out what I stand for."

"That's . . ." I pause, and then smile at him. I don't bother saying anything. I don't need to.

Paula bounds over to us, a massive grin on her face.

"Michael, that was *amazing*!"

"Is that the best you can do? I would have thought it deserved one of your quotes."

She grins. "Fine. *One does not simply grow a conscience without being invited to a movie marathon.*"

I laugh.

Michael looks at me. "You're doing the *Lord of the Rings* movie marathon?"

"This weekend!"

"We're having it at my place," Paula says. "Given I'm not in the running for any popularity or coolness contests, attending is completely at your own risk."

"That doesn't worry me," he says casually.

"So you're basically admitting that hanging out with me might ruin your reputation but it doesn't worry you?"

Michael grins.

"So you'll come?" Paula asks.

"Sure," he says, throwing a glance my way. Then, smiling, he says, "Unless of course Mina holds grudges?"

"I don't hold grudges!"

He grins again.

"You can bring a friend, but Terrence and Fred aren't welcome," Paula says.

He shrugs. "Okay, I get it. Who else from school is coming?"

"There's a small geek contingent," Paula says. "Plus Adrian, Leica, Cameron, and Jane."

"Okay. Send me the details then. See you later."

He starts to walk away when Paula calls him back.

"Yeah?"

"It's a costume party, by the way. Preferably a *Lord of the Rings* character, but if you can't manage that, any other costume will do. But no tights. I don't care how you're built."

I can't help but laugh.

He looks worried. "Do you seriously think that with my height I can dress up as a hobbit?"

"That's okay," I find myself saying. "We won't judge you if you come as an orc."

"A Hallmark card writer if ever there was one." His eyes linger for a moment, and then he walks to the bus.

# MICHAEL

I receive Paula's Facebook invitation to the movie marathon and accept. As a mark of respect to an occasion of this magnitude, I decide that a generic Facebook invitation with a mere cut-and-paste picture of Frodo Baggins simply will not do.

So I play around with some programs and design an interactive e-card invitation using *LOTR* movie clips and . . .

And then, at 11:45 p.m., I upload it to Paula's Facebook Event.

___

11:50 p.m.

Facebook notification alerting me to a comment from Mina about the *LOTR* event.

> **Not all those who wander are lost. ☺**

A smiley face emoji.

From Mina.

If we're going to do emoji, we might as well have fun with it.

So I send her a friend request.

Within less than a minute she accepts.

I send her an emoji narrative. She sends one back.

This is going to be fun.

---

"It's kidneys this afternoon, Michael," Anh says when I arrive at work.

"Right. Got it."

"I've emailed you the details. Your last shift was an improvement but you're still not reaching target. You have to lift your game. Be ruthless. What do you do if they hang up on you?"

"Move on to the next person on the list?"

"Fail. Hanging up, cursing you, telling you they're not interested means nothing. Just call them on your next shift or pass their name on to one of us to chase up the next day when you're not here."

"But isn't that harassment?"

Anh gives me a look that leaves me in no doubt that he thinks I'm an idiot.

"This job is purely about harassment. Would have thought that was obvious. If they register their number off the call list, fine. If they're too lazy to do that, bad luck, we're coming after them."

"Wow, and I thought working for charities would be about goodwill."

Anh shakes his head at me. "Michael. You're killing me."

---

Terrence texts me while I'm at work, asking if I want to catch up tonight or play a game online. I make up an excuse to get out of both. If Terrence and Fred find out that I'm going to Paula's party, I'll never live it down. I'll have to deal with them later.

I go shopping after work and mix and match a few things to put together a Gandalf outfit. If somebody had told me at the start of the year that I would be going as a cross-dressing geriatric magician to a movie marathon at Paula's house, I would never have believed it.

---

"You need to pull your weight around here, Michael," Mum says as she chops onions.

"Are you crying because I forgot to empty the dishwasher, or because of the onions?" I sneak a carrot from the corner of the chopping board and she hits me on the hand.

"You know," I say, "one day there will be robotic machines for all this domestic drudgery. Probably invented at UTS Design School ..." I grin at her.

She groans. "Can you make yourself useful and pick up

Nathan from after-school care? I don't have a robotic machine just yet and this dinner needs finishing."

Nathan's school is only a short walk from home. We take our time walking back. Nathan likes to avoid stepping on cracks in the concrete.

"What does it feel like to punch somebody?" he asks me.

"Well, to be honest, for a split second it feels good. You feel powerful. And then it feels horrible and it goes on feeling horrible."

"I wanted to punch a kid today. Ray Cooper's brother. His name is Jason Cooper. Ray Cooper is in my class. He called me a spastic."

"Ray did?"

"No. Jason Cooper. The brother. After school."

I feel a heat rise in my chest. "I want to punch him for you."

"That would be futile," he says dryly. "You'd be arrested for hitting a child. It wouldn't solve anything."

I shake my head. "Of course, I won't be punching anybody. I was just being silly. Was there a teacher around?"

"Yes. Ms. Lee. That's Ms., not Miss or Mrs. because she said her marital status is nobody's business. But she is married and he is from China like Ms. Lee and he came here by plane not a boat and she was born in Sydney in 1982."

I balk a little. "How do you know that? I mean, why do you know that?"

He shrugs and then takes a wide step to avoid a crack. "I

asked her if she was an illegal and she said that is a hurtful thing to say and showed us a book called *The Arrival*. It has beautiful pictures but yours are better, except you can't do eyes the way that illustrator does them and his family were boat people too, I think. But a long time ago."

"Jesus," I mutter under my breath.

"Ms. Lee is *Buddhist*."

We turn the corner into our street. There's a man leaning against a car parked in front of our neighbor's house. He walks toward us, blocking our path.

"Michael Blainey?"

"Yeah?" I answer without thinking.

"I'm a journalist with *Vice* newspaper. What's it like being the son of the founder of a racist organization like Aussie Values?"

I instinctively put my arm around Nathan. "Piss off," I say, and try to hurry Nathan up, but with the concrete crack thing, there's no chance.

"Do you agree with your father's policies?"

"Come on, Nathan," I hiss, trying to drag him along, but he refuses to be hurried and continues concentrating on not stepping on the cracks.

"Is that your brother?" The man is walking right alongside us. "How do you feel, kid?" he asks Nathan.

"Leave him alone!" I say, trying to shield Nathan.

"Feel about what?" he asks cheerfully, not looking at him, his eyes focused on the ground.

"Do you think we should stop Muslim immigration to this country?"

"I don't know."

"Do you agree with your dad?"

"I said leave us alone," I yell.

"Muslims are trying to take over," Nathan cries cheerfully. "I like the bathrooms in their mosques. There are hoses inside."

I carry Nathan and run with him to the house, trying to block out his screaming at me to put him down, to not touch the cracks. I rush into the house and slam the door behind us.

I've freaked him out and he's crying his lungs out. I crouch down to his level and try to calm him down. "I'm really sorry, Nathan. I didn't mean to scare you. But that guy wasn't nice."

Mum rushes into the hallway.

"What's wrong?" she cries in a panic.

Nathan's sobbing uncontrollably. Mum holds him close to her and yells at me to grab his plane model from the lounge. I run and get it. She gives it to him and gently lowers him to the hallway floor. She sits next to him until eventually, after a very long time, he stops crying.

---

Mum and Dad talk to me after Nathan's gone to bed. They expect that the media attention will fluctuate in intensity, but reassure me that a repeat of this afternoon is unlikely.

I think about Mina and her parents' restaurant. The Protect Australia rally that Aussie Values is organizing with other like-minded organizations is in the next few weeks. The upcoming protest at a council meeting regarding the Islamic school application out in Jordan Springs.

"Is it all worth it?" I ask them.

"We've been pushed into this corner," Dad says with a heavy sigh. "I don't relish being one of the few who are actually concerned enough about the state our country is in to do something about it."

"It's a burden actually," my mother says faintly, stretching her arms up and yawning. "Oh boy, what a day."

"It's harder for you to see how much things have changed, Michael," Dad says. "So many migrants have come to this country and assimilated to our culture, and we're richer for it. This isn't a racist country. It offends me when people say that. But there are groups who refuse to assimilate."

Mum picks at an invisible piece of lint on her trousers and heaves a sigh. "What frustrates me most is the arrogance. The ones who walk around puffed up with this . . . I don't even know how to describe it. It's like they don't even care that we have a problem with their way of life clashing with ours."

"But what I don't get is how you can tell if somebody's assimilated enough. Who decides?"

Mum stands up, yawning again. "I've got an early start. Let's talk about this another time."

Dad gets up to make a coffee and offers to make me one. I've got a pile of work ahead of me so I say yes and follow him to the kitchen.

"Studying hard?" he asks. "Or am I not allowed to ask?"

"Yeah, better not." I smile.

He grins. "I'm proud of you. I can see you're putting in the effort, Michael. You always have. Well, except for eighth grade." He shudders. "Still trying to forget dealing with you that year. Your generation doesn't do puberty blues like we used to."

I chuckle.

"I appreciate that you're opening up to us with your doubts, Michael," he says. "I want you to feel that you can tell us anything."

I eye him, a lump forming in my throat. "Hmm."

I want so badly to blurt it out. *I don't want to be an architect. Two sugars in my coffee, thanks, Dad.*

# MINA

I go as Aragorn.

Jane comes as Galadriel, Leica as Arwen, and Cameron as a dwarf. Paula's dressed up as Frodo Baggins. There are a couple of Gandalfs, someone in a Gollum mask, an Elizabeth Bennett, a Professor Snape, and, inevitably, someone shows up in a Star Wars costume.

The doorbell rings and I answer it.

"Another Gandalf," I say, smiling at Michael.

"Really?" he says, disappointed. "I thought I was being original."

I cock an eyebrow at him. "Well, your beard's the best so far."

Jaxon is standing beside Michael. He's in eleventh grade as well but I don't share any classes with him. I've seen him on the basketball courts with Michael at recess a lot of times though. I look him up and down and laugh. He's all in black spandex. He's got a big orange, red, and yellow oval over his head with a slit down the front, covered with a black stocking that he can see and breathe out of. His head is like a big ball of flame.

"I give you the Eye of Sauron," Michael says in a dramatic voice, ushering Jaxon in.

"That is awesome!" we all cry.

"He won't answer," Michael tells us. "He's sworn to stay in character all day. He takes his *Lord of the Rings* nerdiness seriously. A man can only respect that."

Jaxon surveys the gathering, doesn't say a word, steps into the cinema room on our right, and sits down, hands folded in his lap, facing the TV screen, patiently waiting for the movie to begin. It's hysterical and we all burst out laughing, but Jaxon doesn't so much as flinch.

*"Aragorn?"* Michael whispers to me when we're standing at the buffet spread Paula's laid out, getting a tub of popcorn before the first movie starts. She's really worked wonders with the emotional blackmail; thanks to her parents' credit card there's a Bilbo cake, loads of food, a popcorn machine, and enough junk food to turn us all into diabetics.

Michael looks me up and down, amused. "I was hoping you'd come as Arwen."

I can feel my cheeks burning. Is he flirting with me?

"Aragorn's hot," I declare.

"Right. *Okay,* but that doesn't really explain why you'd dress up as him."

"No, it doesn't," I say, grinning. "But I didn't feel like doing the whole pretty elf thing."

"See, I think Arwen's gorgeous but I'm not going to come dressed in a white dress and crown, now am I?"

"You'd be fetching in a dress, Michael," Paula says as she walks past us with some soft drinks.

"And what's that badge say?" he asks, pointing to me.

"Mrs. Ryan Gosling," I say seriously.

He bursts out laughing.

We all mingle around the food for a bit, getting all the introductions over with.

I go to the bathroom and find Jane standing outside waiting for me when I've finished.

"Hey, do you know if Paula invited Terrence?" she asks shyly.

"She didn't," I say.

Her face crumples. "Oh, okay. I thought she must have because Michael's here."

"Nope. Neither of us have a good history with Terrence, do we?"

She looks uncomfortable. "I think he just does it to show off. I don't think he means it. We were paired up together in math the other week and he was really nice."

"It's not my problem if he has multiple personality disorder. I get the racist, angry personality and Paula gets the juvenile bully. Don't blame us if we can't see his good side."

"Hmm," she murmurs.

I take pity on her. It's not her fault she's fallen hard for him.

"Come on, let's go inside now. Forget about him for the next few hours at least."

I drag her along by the arm.

---

My phone beeps. It's Maha telling me she's about to ring the doorbell and she wants me to answer so I can assess the suitability of her outfit. I text her back and run to the door. She's standing with another one of our friends from Auburn Grove Girls High, Tammy Xiang. Maha looks slightly nervous. I burst out laughing. I should have known she wouldn't be caught dead wearing a *Lord of the Rings* costume. She's come as Marilyn Monroe: white dress, high heels, blonde wig, fake eyelashes. Tammy's dressed as Galadriel.

I throw my arms around them and we jump up and down squealing.

"Do I look okay?" Maha asks, self-consciously tugging at her dress. She looks down and her blonde wig tilts slightly to the left. She fixes it, grinning widely at me.

Tammy looks equally nervous. "You're *sure* everybody's dressed up?"

I grab them by the arms. "You both look fabulous."

Tammy leans in close to me. "Are they snobs?"

"No!" I laugh. "Not this group. And certainly not Paula."

"Paula's the one who owns this mansion though?" Maha

looks at me quizzically. "I thought it was an apartment complex at first."

I giggle. "So did I. Wait until you see inside."

"So Paula's cool with us being here?" Tammy asks as she adjusts her pixie ears. "Man, these are itchy."

I laugh and throw myself at them again. "God, I've missed you guys!" They hug me back.

"What's with the street?" Maha asks in an urgent whisper, as I lead them inside. "I swear to God it felt like we were driving in a national park."

Tammy rolls her eyes but laughs affectionately.

"I bet you they have millions of redback spiders and funnel web spiders here," Maha says. "Guaranteed. So introduce us to your friends. Any cute guys? Actually, hold that thought. We're at a costume party for a trilogy about hobbits. It would never work."

Paula, Leica, Michael, and Cameron are huddled together by the food table. As I lead Maha and Tammy toward the table I feel nervous. What if they don't get along? What if Maha thinks Paula's geeky and uncool—especially if she drops an Oscar Wilde quote? And what will Paula think if Maha says "youse"? I close my eyes for a moment and inhale sharply.

Paula catches my eye. She breaks from the group and quickly comes over to welcome Maha and Tammy. When Paula introduces Michael, my body tenses with the fear that Maha might throw me a knowing glance. But to my relief she doesn't so much as flinch. It's only when Michael's looking the other way that she furtively winks at me. I smile into my drink.

"So, *Lord of the Rings*," Maha says, facing Michael and Paula. "Is it some kind of religious wedding rom com?"

Maha is deadpan and I lock eyes with Tammy and snort.

"I'm joking," Maha says with a grin. "It's all about power and temptation, death and courage, and is based on Tolkien's iconic fantasy series."

"Wikipedia's awesome, isn't it?" Tammy says, grinning at Maha.

Leica is trying to use a straw to collect a piece of strawberry out of the bottom of her glass. "I'm not a fan either," she says casually. "I just came along to see who'd have the guts to show up in elf tights."

"Um, excuse me, your boyfriend," Michael says, motioning to Cameron, who's pulling his fake beard down so he can scratch his chin.

It's like this for the next fifteen minutes. Everybody cracking jokes and telling funny stories. Tom, one of Paula's poetry slam friends, is especially animated and bounces off Maha's self-deprecation and bubbly personality. When we eventually make our way back to the cinema room, I catch myself feeling a wave of anxiety about who Michael will sit next to. It turns my stomach to think he might not choose to sit next to me.

We file into the large room and Maha leans in close enough

so only I can hear her. "You've got a good group here, Mina," she says in a hushed tone. "I was expecting some alphas but they seem really nice. As for *you*: I was expecting to find you curled into the fetal position, confused and disoriented. But you're part of the designer overpriced furniture around here now."

I chuckle. "I miss Auburn badly. But I'm starting to settle in here too."

Maha glances at Michael and then nudges me and grins. "Yep. I can see why."

I roll my eyes at her. "I owe it to *Paula*, not Michael."

The gleam in Maha's eyes tells me she's thoroughly unconvinced. "I'm grabbing a beanbag with Tammy. Sit here and I'll bet he'll be beside you before the opening credits are done."

She's right and I want to shout for joy. Before I know it, Michael plops down next to me as if it's the most natural thing in the world. My heart is hammering away so fast that I'm worried he's going to hear. But as the movie unfolds, I relax. We end up sharing popcorn, and when he gets up to get himself a drink he brings back one for me too.

It's nighttime when we make it to the end of the three movies. Surprisingly, people generally remain quiet as we watch. We take breaks in between, manage to stretch our bodies. Some of the hardcore fans get up and recite lines during dramatic scenes, which makes us all laugh. Tom throws a plastic spider on Paula in the spider scene toward the end of the third film and she screams, sending us into hysterics.

For the first time since the beginning of the year I feel I've found a new corner in the world that I can also call home.

———————————

I'm waiting in front of the house for Mum to pick me up. I'm one of the last to leave. She called to say she's five minutes away. Michael comes outside and leans against the rails of the wraparound veranda to face me.

"So what's so special about Ryan Gosling?" he jokes.

"He's not just special. He's perfect."

"Oh, well, if you say so." He watches me, a playful look in his eyes.

"You do realize you're questioning Gosling's looks while dressed as a wizard, don't you?"

"I bet Gosling couldn't pull off Gandalf the way I can."

"You started okay. But once you took your beard off to eat, you kind of just looked like a badly dressed, sexually confused busker."

He points to his robe. "This could be the next big look."

We laugh.

"So, did you have fun?" I ask.

He stretches his arms up overhead. "Yep. It was great! I feel like I need a run though after sitting down all day. I'll probably go for a jog when I get home. Do you want to have coffee next Saturday?"

"Huh?"

"Yeah, sorry, that came out quicker than I planned." He looks at me sheepishly.

"You think?"

"So how about it? To celebrate The xx album drop. Have you preordered?"

"Obviously. You?"

"Obviously."

I drum my fingers against the front porch rail. "Coffee where?"

"Wherever you want."

I think for a moment. It's surreal. Michael is asking me out for coffee and I'm about to say—

"Okay," I blurt out.

I cringe wondering if I've come across as too eager.

But he smiles. "So, do you want to suggest a place?"

"The library."

"You know, one day parents will realize that most books are online and it will be RIP to the library excuse."

"Hopefully not while I'm a teenager."

We agree to meet at the Chatswood food court at one and he asks me for my number.

I give it to him, and he gives me his. He smiles again. I smile back. There's a lot of smiling going on.

Who would ever have thought: Michael Blainey is in my contacts list now.

# MICHAEL

I try not to get too excited, to read too much into Mina saying yes, but who am I kidding? I go home buzzing. I feel slightly tragic asking her out the way I did. Luckily she said yes so maybe the Gandalf costume saved me.

The next night Mum, Dad, Nathan, and I are in front of the TV watching one of those reality talent shows I can never keep up with but have to pretend to enjoy for Nathan's sake as he is fascinated by them. I'm finishing off a sketch for an art assignment, Dad's multitasking, watching and working on his laptop, and Mum's putting leaflets in envelopes for the next Jordan Springs mailbox drop-off.

Nathan takes the competition seriously and is on the edge of his seat as one of the judges rips into one of the performers. I get up to grab a snack.

When I return, Mum's flipping through the pages of my notepad.

"You're so talented, Michael," she says.

"What's that?" my dad says, looking up from the laptop screen.

"Michael's sketches. They're lovely. Here, look at this one. It's of Nathan at the beach." She holds it up and Dad takes it from her.

"The effect of your shading and outlining is really impressive, Michael," he says as he studies the picture, nodding with approval. He goes to turn the page. "Can I have a look?"

"Sure." I nod.

He turns the pages slowly, attentively. "What's this one of?" he asks, holding up the book to show me.

"A group of men out in Auburn."

"Auburn?"

"Yeah. I went out there during break."

Dad looks surprised but just shrugs, inspecting the picture more closely. "Good, strong lines here. Are they using the traffic cones as seats?" he asks, amused.

"Yeah."

He lets out a faint laugh.

"Who are the men?" Mum asks, peering at the picture.

"Refugees from Sudan."

"There's something so wretched about them," Dad says. "Sad and pathetic and unfortunate. It's not their fault really."

I look at him in surprise. "Do you really mean that?"

"I mean the whole refugee situation is the government's fault. They bring them in here when they shouldn't and then they squeeze them all into one suburb, create these ethnic enclaves, and look at the result: These men probably never mix with Australians, they seek out the company of people from their own country only, and they never assimilate.

"I saw one of them working as a trolley boy at Coles the other day," he says. "I wanted to be friendly. I said g'day, asked him how he was. He didn't even return my smile."

"Maybe his English wasn't so good," I suggest.

"Hmm, maybe," Dad says. "That's kind of the point though, isn't it?"

# MINA

Coffee with Michael.

Outside of school.

On the weekend.

Not because of an assignment.

Voluntarily.

I'm just going to put it out there once and for all. This will be my first date.

Except is it a date?

And even before I waste brain cells contemplating that one, I have to think of the minor matter of my parents' dying from self-immolation if they discover me alone with a guy on something that maybe isn't a date but looks like a date. And even if, for argument's sake, I manage to see Michael behind their back—something I can manage easily enough based on Maha's expert advice given she's positively perfected the *I'm going to the library/study group/charity raffle* excuse—how can I ignore the fact that Michael's family resents *people like me*?

This is what's going through my brain as I go for a walk around the block on Sunday morning. As I'm walking, thinking myself into a frenzy, it hits me that I'm being a complete moron.

It's two people meeting for coffee.

He hasn't actually asked me out.

Do people actually get asked out officially or do you just go with the flow?

Can you actually die of a brain aneurysm through over-analyzing whether your date is, in fact, a date?

———————————————

Baba comes home from the restaurant in a good mood tonight.

"Adnan and Mustafa are excellent," he says, grinning at Mum and me as we sit down for dinner. "I put them onto Ehssan—"

"Ehssan who runs the money-exchange shop?" Mum asks.

"Yes. He knows a guy who's good friends with Saaleh— you know, he has the mixed goods shop on Alan Street—and he's the one to go to if you want to find shared accommodations. So he's helping them until they can stand on their own two feet and find their own place."

"That's great," Mum says. Then, her tone stoic and quiet, she says: "So the after-school-care job hunting is officially over. I applied to all the local schools. A lot of them are after temp workers so it would suit me before the baby arrives. But nothing. Don't say I didn't try. So I am embracing being a stay-at-home mum before the baby is due, and I've joined that women's gym in the mall."

"That's great," I say with affected cheeriness. Having seen her in action at the school where she worked in Auburn, I try to hide my disappointment for her.

I see a flicker of sadness in Baba's eyes. He seems to be weighing how to respond but he's saved when Mum speaks up first.

"I met two lovely women at the gym too. We're going to have coffee this week."

This makes Baba smile. "New friends? That's really good to hear."

"And I tried out the yoga class."

Baba suddenly looks concerned but Mum interrupts him before he can say anything.

"Don't fuss, Farshad," she says. "It's the best thing for pregnant women. Wait until you see me. Nine months pregnant and doing a handstand."

"You're joking?"

Mum and I laugh.

Baba shakes his head. "God help me if we have a girl. I'm already outnumbered."

"Girl, boy, they'll always take my side anyway," Mum teases.

"So who'd you meet at the gym?" I say.

"A woman called Emily. Would you believe she lives here too? In the block closer to the park. She used to work in IT but had twins so she's home now. Poor thing. She put on so much weight, so she's trying to lose it. I told her to eat nothing but chicken for three months. And I met a Muslim lady too. Rojin. She's Saudi, here on a working visa for two years. She's a gynecologist working part-time at Westmead. Her husband's in the ER there."

"If you become a yoga junkie and get a better body than me I'll die of embarrassment," I say.

# MICHAEL

Saturday can't come soon enough. I won't receive the CD until Monday but there's no way I can wait. I'm ready to buy it online as soon as possible. I wake early to see if The xx has dropped their album. It hasn't happened yet, so I distract myself getting ready and head out a little early.

Terrence texts to join him and some other guys for a game of basketball in the park. I text him back and tell him I have to work. The album drops when I'm at the shops, checking iTunes as I walk up the escalator to the food court. I buy it, connect my earphones, find a table, and do some people-watching as I wait for Mina.

I spot her from afar, walking slowly, looking around.

It's as though the shopping center suddenly empties of every-body. It's not like the first time I saw her. Now it's different.

Maybe you only get one chance at meeting somebody who really gets inside you, wakes corners of your mind and heart that you didn't know were asleep.

Eventually she spots me.

"Did you listen to it?" she cries, her eyes beaming at me.

"Incredible! Well, the first two songs anyway. I haven't heard all of it yet though. I only just managed to get it. You?"

"Three songs. I just got it too. Oh my God, I love them!"

I laugh. "Have you watched *The Great Gatsby*? The soundtrack is unbelievable."

"I missed it at the movies and I never got round to seeing it."

We grab some lunch and frappes and sit down. It feels like we sit there for hours, talking about music and movies and school and whether Carlos has a crush on eleventh-grade Zoe not twelfth-grade Zoe, which would be weird given she freakishly looks like his sister, and whether Ms. Chalmers, the chemistry teacher, who can be heard having psychotic episodes in the lab at least twice a day, is sexually frustrated or just born angry, and what's on our bucket list and whether we believe in life after death.

When we eventually say good-bye it feels like we're actually at the start of something, not the end. There's so much promise in her good-bye that it makes my insides feel all funny.

Yeah, it's kind of the best day that I've had in a long time.

# MINA

I can't stop thinking about Michael. He's like handprints in wet cement. One moment there's nothing; the next moment, a lasting imprint. He's stamped his way into my mind and, dare I even admit it to myself, my heart. I've seen girls fall for a guy before. The guy becomes their "complete me"; their *other half*. But I've never wanted a guy who would make me feel like a fraction. I just want a guy who can talk the small stuff and the big stuff. Who can make me laugh. Who can make my body tingle and my day feel like it's playing to a good soundtrack.

Somebody, it turns out, like Michael.

---

Mum's cooking dinner, talking a million miles an hour on the phone with Rojin and then, later, with Emily. She invites them for lunch at our place.

When she hangs up she turns to face me. She's glowing but it's more than the baby.

"Emily and I went for a walk today," she tells me as we prepare for dinner.

"That's great, Mum."

"We see each other at the gym most mornings." Mum turns off the tap, cracks her neck to the side, and arches her back. "It's a good thing I'm doing yoga. This baby is killing my back."

I laugh. "I can't believe you're doing yoga. Next thing you'll be drinking kale protein shakes."

"Kale? What on earth is that?"

"Hopefully something that never enters this apartment."

She waves vaguely at me. "You're talking in riddles." She rubs her lower back.

"Does it feel different this time?"

"Oh yes. I was a skinny teenager when I had you. At nine months I looked like I'd eaten a bit too much dinner, that's all. When I went for checkups my sister would come with me and they would mistake her for the pregnant one."

"Were you skinny or was she fat?"

"Both," she says with a fond smile.

There's silence. Then she gives a forlorn sort of sigh. "God have mercy on her soul."

My aunt wasn't able to get out. One more person in our family buried in Afghanistan's soil. My memories of her are scratchy. I remember sitting in her lap as she peeled the white off my orange. I remember how her breasts would suffocate me whenever she embraced me. I remember her holding me tight throughout the night Dad died because Mum had collapsed, her eyes blank holes that had stared at me without recognition. My throat tightens and I force myself to banish the memories from my mind.

"Here, pass me the gloves," I order her, my voice a slight tremble. "I'll finish up here. You rest."

"Really?" But she's already peeled off the gloves and hands them to me. She grins at me and falls onto the couch, stretching her legs out and looking up at the ceiling. She looks so beautiful it makes me ache.

"Emily is in a bad way," she says. "She's depressed about her weight, about looking after the twins alone all day. Her parents live in Queensland, her in-laws are in England, and her husband works long hours. I offered to help her with the twins during the day."

"That's nice. It'll get harder once you get bigger though."

"She cried."

"Why?"

"Looking after a baby alone is hard enough. Imagine doing it alone with twins! Her husband's not very supportive either. He comes home from work and wants to rest."

I stack the plates and carry them over to the table. "That's not fair."

"Do you know what's funny, Mina? *She* feels isolated."

"There you go," I say, smiling. "You have your own project now."

"I wouldn't call it a project," Mum says as she sits up, inspecting her nails. A smile spreads slowly up to her eyes. "But, well, it's nice to feel needed."

---

For the next two weeks at school Michael and I fall into a rhythm of hanging out during our free study period, when we're alone and can talk like the music geeks that we are without boring other people to death.

I wake up for school every day and feel a surge of energy and excitement at the thought of seeing him. When our eyes meet, or he grins at me across the classroom, I feel my skin tingle.

Paula, Jane, Leica, and I are sitting in the café when Terrence and Fred walk in. Michael isn't with them because he's got an extra art class today.

Leica's having a bit of a moment because she didn't get the grade she was expecting on a math quiz and we're trying to calm her down. We're failing miserably though because the three of us are also major stress heads about our work and have had moments like this ourselves. Hence our attempts to make her see reason don't exactly ring true when Leica's witnessed our own individual I-can't-do-this-anymore meltdowns.

"It's not the end of the world," Jane says meekly, rubbing Leica's back.

"I told you that when you got your grade on that Studies of Religion assignment and it made you cry harder!" Leica says.

Jane doesn't bother defending herself.

"And it *is* the end of the world," Leica says dramatically. "If I can't do well on a mid-semester quiz, how am I going to do well on the final exams? I might as well give up on getting into medicine and focus on a hairdressing career."

We all try to say something to make her feel better but Leica's determined to beat herself up.

"What's wrong with you?" Terrence and Fred are standing over us at the end of the table. Terrence is looking at Leica like she's an interesting science experiment. "Have you been crying?" he asks tactlessly.

"No!" she says, and sniffs.

"You know it's better to blow the boogies out than sniff them back up," he says authoritatively. "Here's a napkin." He throws one across to her and then, because there are no free tables left in the café, the two of them sit down, just like that.

"Who invited you?" Paula asks.

"No free tables," Fred explains.

"Free country," Terrence adds, and they start to eat.

They've ordered the same amount of food we'd eat in three days. There's a bit of grunting and loud chewing and smacking of lips. And Fred drinks with food in his mouth, which makes me want to gag. They clearly have no interest in defying teenage male stereotypes. It's all-out Neanderthal behavior. And it's exactly what Leica needs to put her quiz grade into perspective.

"So who made you cry?" Fred asks, his mouth full.

"Nobody made me *cry*," Leica says defensively. "I just got a bad grade on the math quiz."

"I got thirty-eight out of forty," Terrence says.

We all glower at him.

"Mr. Sensitive," I say.

"What?" He shakes his head. "Can't a guy outperform you girls in a subject without you going all feminist on us? If it makes you feel better, I failed that English essay."

"Yeah, but you deserved it," Fred says, laughing.

"I almost got away with it," Terrence chuckles.

"With what?" Jane asks.

"I couldn't reach the word count so I wrote the word *and* one hundred times in white font so you can't see it on the screen but it comes up in the word count."

We roll our eyes at him, although I'm secretly impressed by his ingenuity.

He grins. "Oh well, she gave me a fail and a warning, big deal. They're not going to raise the roof over it. With our fees? Our backs are covered."

"You poor thing," Jane coos, batting her eyelashes at Terrence. It has little effect.

"I like her," Fred says. "She gave me a B."

"On an essay about gender representations in *Emma*?" Paula is just as incredulous as the rest of us.

He shrugs. "Yeah. I spun some stuff."

Terrence grins at Fred, nudging him playfully in the side. "That's Fred's secret talent. Don't be fooled. He's a whiz in English. But he sucks at math even though he's Asian. Figure that one out."

Paula and I groan loudly.

# MICHAEL

Tonight Mina and I are messaging each other on Snapchat as we do our homework. She tells me she's considering journalism, and I tell her she'd be the perfect news anchor: argumentative and unrelenting. Then, with a smile, I send her another message. *And not just SBS material either.* She sends me a funny photo, eyebrows raised, mouth gaping open in shock.

Mum calls me a short while later. She's forgotten a bunch of important paperwork at home and asks me to drop it off to the local veterans' club, where Aussie Values is having a meeting.

Reluctantly, I drag Nathan away from the iPad and head to the veterans' club. I walk into the room and to my surprise I see that the numbers have almost doubled. Nathan points out Mum and Dad, who are at the front of the room addressing the audience.

Dad's updating everybody about the Jordan Springs campaign and some of the alliances that are being built with grassroots groups in the area who also oppose the opening of the school. There's furious nodding of heads, a couple of small cheers from the audience as he speaks.

Mum notices me and gives me a small wave. I gesture that I'm leaving the folder on the table next to me, and she nods and gives me a thumbs-up. Nathan and I turn to walk out, but Andrew's suddenly before us, a big smile on his face.

"Michael! Nathan! Where've you been? We've missed you. *Young blood*, mate. We need more young blood spreading the message." He grins at me.

"Yeah, um, I've been busy with schoolwork."

"Oh sure, right. Eleventh grade's a tough year. Home stretch now."

He keeps me standing there listening to his small talk, bragging about all the work he's putting into the campaign, the hits he's getting on his blog. His latest piece has been picked up and shared by some famous activists in France and the US. And then I hear my mum speaking on the microphone. "There's no jobs for them, so they hang around all day and are dependent on welfare." Her voice isn't shrill and hysterical like some of the other members. There's a pleasant and easygoing calmness in her tone. "Why, just the other day my son Michael, who was on his school break, saw a group of African men just hanging around, midweek, in the street, using the traffic cones as seats, if you can imagine that." A few people in the audience laugh. Andrew lets out a loud guffaw.

My mouth is suddenly unbearably dry, like a cracked riverbed after a long drought.

Mum's relaxed in front of the audience, slowly pacing to the right and left, weaving the microphone cord around her hand. "The problem is that our economy isn't producing enough jobs for Aussie citizens," she continues, "let alone all these refugees who come in and obviously can't find work. We end up having to finance their welfare. The government must be held accountable for this mess."

A heat begins to build in my chest, growing, uncontainable. I feel dirty, as though I've stripped those men of their dignity, taken something intimate between them and caused it to be the subject of public ridicule.

I can't bear to stay there a second longer. I tell Nathan we're going and walk out, ignoring Andrew, who calls out to me.

As I drive home it hits me so hard that I have to stop on the side of the road and focus on my breathing, on not breaking down in front of Nathan, who's buying my line about listening for something in the engine.

I feel as though a chasm has opened between my parents and me and that things between us can never be the same again.

To tell them how I feel means attacking the very core of who they are, what gives them meaning and purpose in their lives. I feel stuck, as if the only choice in front of me is keeping silent or breaking their hearts.

I pick Mina up from the local library. We listen to music in the car, not embarrassed to sing along quietly to ourselves. Mina has no idea where I'm taking her. I tell her I've organized a day for us to just hang out.

We haven't so much as held hands, and we haven't spoken about what's going on between us. I think we're too scared to give "us" a name. We've been hanging out together at school, mainly during our free study period. Nobody has guessed anything yet, although obviously Paula knows. We call or message each other in the evenings and sometimes study together over the phone.

"So what are we doing?" Mina asks, looking out the window as we drive. "Where are we going?"

"I'll tell you when we get there. What time are they picking you up from the library?"

"Six. Going straight to the restaurant from there."

My phone beeps. I check the message. It's Mum, and I quickly send a reply.

"She wants me to pick up some food from that Middle Eastern restaurant in the Village on my way home . . . they've got a meeting tonight."

"So they'll eat Middle Eastern cuisine while they talk about keeping Middle Easterners out?"

"Pretty much."

"Wow. I'm speechless."

"Miracle."

Mina hits me playfully on the arm and I feel electricity pass between us.

"I've got to hand it to them," she says, "it's impressive, maintaining that kind of hypocrisy. No offense."

"It's okay. You have the right to be mad at them. Anyway, change the topic. Today's not about them. It's about us."

"Us?" She grins.

"Yeah." I grin back. "And pizza."

I pull up to the curb in front of my favorite pizza shop.

"Vegetarian and seafood?" I ask her.

"Double supreme with extra ham, thanks."

I almost fall for it and she laughs. She waits in the car as I run out and grab the order.

"So, what's the plan?" she whines. "Come on, tell me."

"Nope."

It doesn't take long for us to arrive at the beach. I know that the point I'm taking us to won't be busy. It's winter, always the best time to visit the beach in my opinion.

I park the Jeep, the rear facing the beach. I open the trunk. I tell Mina to wait outside in the front and not sneak a peek.

I set up the cushions in the back and take out the portable DVD player.

"Okay, you can come round now," I call out to her.

She walks slowly toward the rear of the car, eyeing me suspiciously. "What's going on?"

"We've got a view of the sea while we eat pizza for lunch

and watch *The Great Gatsby*. And I've managed to hook up the sound to the car stereo so the background soundtrack will blow your mind."

A smile spreads slowly up to her eyes and she grins broadly. "Not bad, Michael Blainey. Not bad at all."

---

After the movie we're sitting on a bench at the lookout. Mina's sitting close to me, my arm around her shoulders. Her hair smells like shampoo, her breath like the raspberry lollipops we've just eaten. I have my iPod on my lap, the volume on max.

"What was it like, Mina?" I ask her, treading carefully. "Coming out here on the boat?"

She doesn't answer straightaway, just looks out at the sea.

"Every moment I was awake I thought we were going to die," she says quietly. "I couldn't swim. It was just ocean and there we were in a boat made of wood, trusting people who had taken our money on a promise they'd get us here safely. We all knew they couldn't make any promises, not on a boat like that, not with people who'd believe anything because the alternative was too awful."

I feel unworthy of responding. I just let her talk. Eventually, a comfortable silence settles between us as we each get lost in our own thoughts.

"So how old is your brother?" Mina asks me. "I saw him on the show. He looks like you."

"Lucky guy."

She pokes her tongue out at me.

"Nathan's ten."

"Hasan would have been ten this year."

"Oh. I'm sorry." I heave a sigh. "What's a person even supposed to say? It's too awful."

"I can't remember his face." She says it matter-of-factly, but her expression reveals the agony behind the words. She draws her knees up against her chest on the bench and wraps her arms around them.

"We don't have any photos. There was no death certificate. We were in this weird waiting room, trying to get from our homeland to a safe place, and it's like life becomes nothing there. Death literally snatched people away and nobody gave a shit. I feel like . . . like if I don't remember his face then there's nothing left to prove he existed."

"But you and your mum know he existed."

"I can't explain. It's more than that. It's like all these nameless, faceless people getting killed all around the world every day and nobody gives a shit because they're not Aussie or American or French, you know what I mean? It's like dying and getting killed is just something *people like us* do. It doesn't shock anybody. If we live, then people are surprised." She lets out a short laugh. "If I can at least remember Hasan's face then I bring him out of that fog. He becomes real and he matters." She shrugs and then tilts her head to face me.

"What's Nathan like?" she asks, smiling at me.

"He's a great kid. Crazy about planes and gaming. A straight shooter. Remembers everything and has zero problem reminding you of a time you screwed up even if it was two years ago. I worry about him. A lot."

"Why?"

"Because I won't always be around to protect him. When he was younger we'd be at the park and I'd see the way some kids had this sixth sense for picking up his vulnerability. And he had no idea they were after him. They'd be asking him if he's a retard, stuff like that, and he'd have this goofy, innocent grin on his face. I'd tell off the kids. Sometimes their parents too." I laugh.

"My mum's having a baby," she says. "I can't wait to be a big sister again. But it's terrifying too. The job of protecting somebody."

"I went to the Auburn mosque," I suddenly find myself saying. "Hung out in Auburn for a bit."

She puts her feet back down on the ground, gives me a searching look, and then grins. "You stalked my hood?"

I laugh again. "Yeah."

"Should I be worried? Creepy or endearing?"

"Let's leave it at endearingly creepy."

And then, because I can't hold out any longer, I take a chance, lean in, and kiss her. So softly it makes my insides ache.

# MINA

At work that night all I can think about is my first kiss.

I replay it over and over in my mind, a dreamy, goofy expression on my face. I can't think straight. I have to double-check my running of the accounts several times because I keep making mistakes. Every time I think of our lips locking, the feel of our tongues meeting, the tenderness with which he held me close to him, my stomach plunges the same way it does on a roller-coaster ride. A part of me feels guilty. I know I've gone against my faith and culture, betrayed my parents, who would never, ever think to doubt my word. I'm racked with guilt about deceiving them. But the temptation is too great, the excitement too much to resist. I've been strong for so long and Michael's attention to me, the way he makes me feel, is just too powerful to turn away from. And I see the power I have over him when I smile at him, flash him a look, turn my head a certain way. I see his body tense up, the look of anticipation in his eyes. The thrill of knowing I have that kind of effect on someone is intoxicating.

"You're in a very cheerful mood tonight!" Baba exclaims as he files something in the drawer behind the counter.

I don't dare look him in the eye.

"Did you taste the kofta challow?"

I shake my head. "No, I had the lamb korma though. Delicious."

"Those new boys can cook. We should get them on that *Chefmastering* show." He laughs, pleased with his idea.

"*MasterChef*, Baba," I correct him gently with a smile.

Yep, it's all smiles tonight. I feel alive, every cell in my body buzzing in a way I've never felt before.

---

"He came up with the idea all by himself? *The Great Gatsby*? In the back of his Jeep Wrangler? At the beach? With a pizza picnic?"

"Yes." Even though we're sitting in a quiet section of the school lawn, I look around self-consciously, worried somebody might hear.

"Michael Blainey?"

I nod, my eyes shining at her.

Paula clasps her hands together and pretends to swoon. "Enough said. I'm quoteless. The end."

"Well, this is a first."

"Seriously, only a complete idiot wouldn't have been able to see you two were falling for each other." She twirls a strand of her hair around her finger and fixes her clear green eyes on me. "So the next crucial question is this: good kisser?"

I blush. "How did you know we kissed?"

She rolls around the grass, laughing hysterically.

"What?!"

"You're such a dork!" she cries when she's caught her breath.

"Seriously, how did you know?"

"You just told me, dummy. Oldest trick in the book. First time?"

I nod. "Yep."

"Lived up to expectations? Or do you feel cheated out of your foolish daydreams?"

"Neither. Exceeded expectations."

"Nice work, Michael!"

We laugh and I feel giddy with the excitement of it all.

She sits up on her knees. "Oh, hey, I'm organizing a poetry slam festival here at school at the end of term! *Please* say you'll perform! The more people the better, and I know you'll be awesome."

"No way!" I say. "I'll leave the performing to you."

"Oh, come on! Please!"

"I can't do slam poetry!"

"Just tell me you'll think about it." She bats her eyelashes at me, clasps her hands together as though she's praying. "Please? Pretty please?"

I laugh, hit her on the shoulder. "Oh, fine, I'll *think* about it."

"Good girl. I already have some tenth graders who want to sign up."

"Poor kids don't know what they're in for."

"You can perform a love poem to Michael," she teases.

"Don't make me gag," I say. "I don't do corny."

"Okay, then he can perform one for you."

"I can't see that ending in anything but *good-bye, Michael.*"

"Well, he's over there, looking this way, and judging from the expression on his face it's *hello, Mina.*"

I shake my head at her but can't help laughing. "I never thought I'd say this, Paula, but it's getting way too corny here and I actually miss the Oscar Wilde quotes."

"Oh goody. Then take this one: *I can resist everything except temptation.*" She stands up as Michael approaches us. "And on that note, I'll leave you two alone."

She winks at me and walks away, her laugh echoing behind her.

———————————

The sky is angry today, ash and lead, covered in gray cotton wool. The complete opposite of how I feel inside. Inside I'm a kid running through a backyard sprinkler on a stinking hot day.

I dump my bag in my locker and head to homeroom. I spot Michael sitting next to Terrence and Fred at the back and my insides go all funny. I'm trying to keep a straight face, give nothing away. He winks at me when no one's looking and I hide my grin by covering my mouth and pretending to cough. Leica's bent over her desk, head leaning down on her hands, eyes closed. Jane's beside her, biting her nails, nervously throwing glances toward the back of the room. But it's only Michael, Terrence, and Fred in the back row, and they're not looking at her.

I sit down, saving the seat beside me for Paula, who's running late. She walks in as Mr. Morello starts marking the roll.

It takes me less than a second to notice something's wrong. "What happened?"

She slumps low in her chair, fixes her eyes on the desk. "Nancy called last night," she says quietly. "She got a job in New York."

"Oh."

"She was supposed to be back next month. I was counting down the days."

Mr. Morello's collecting the diaries to check that parents have signed his notes. We pass ours up to the front.

"What did your parents say?"

She shrugs. "They're happy for her. Less guilt if she's not around."

"Maybe they're just happy for her getting that kind of opportunity."

She doesn't look convinced.

"They love you, Paula. They just have high-end jobs. It's shitty but has nothing to do with their love for you."

"So what if they love me? I'm their daughter. That's their job."

I don't have an answer to that.

"I should have known Nancy wouldn't come back. I miss her so badly. I feel so lonely at home since she left. I can't remember the last time I had quality time with my parents. Most weeknights I'm in bed before they get home, or else it's a short excuse of a heart-to-heart when I know they're hankering for a shower and bed before it all starts again the next morning."

I listen without saying anything, giving her the space to pour it all out.

"She could have come back, gotten a job here, moved out and gotten a place of her own. I could have at least visited her then. We'd have each other. There's no way she'll return." She groans. "I can't compete with New York. She'll meet some hot guy and they'll spend their time having picnics in Central Park and watching *Law & Order* being filmed on location."

"A couple of years and you can move out too."

Her eyes narrow. "You bet."

Mr. Morello's voice interrupts us. "Joy, Craig, Paula, your parents *still* haven't signed your diaries. There are notes here that are over a month old. I've called and left several messages with your parents."

Paula squirms in her seat. She looks ashamed. Mr. Morello notices. He glances her way, pauses for a moment, puts the diaries aside, and says he'll deal with the matter later.

"My parents don't sign my diary all the time either," I tell her.

"Do they ignore five calls from school? My mum actually complained to me that she feels harassed. It's on her to-do list, she said."

"Below colonic irrigation? Brazilian wax?"

That gets a smile out of her.

Mr. Morello reads out some announcements. We almost make it to the bell but Terrence gets up to throw something in the rubbish and notices Paula as he passes.

"What's with you girls? You're always PMSing. Have you been *crying*, Paula?"

"No," she snaps.

"You sure? Your face is all blotched and puffy." He laughs, shoots the scrunched-up bit of paper in his hand into the trash can.

"Knock it off, Terrence," Michael says, but Terrence is in a goofball mood and having too much fun.

"Relax," Terrence says.

"Sit down, Terrence," Mr. Morello barks at him.

"But, sir, Paula's crying."

"She's not crying, you idiot!" I yell.

Paula stands up. "Screw you, Terrence," she says, and runs out of class.

Mr. Morello gives Terrence a detention. Terrence acts like his human rights have been violated. The bell rings as Paula returns. Mr. Morello asks Paula to skip the next class and meet him in his office. Jane looks upset but her eyes are following Terrence, not her cousin. Michael looks embarrassed on behalf of his dirtbag friend and I'm staring daggers at Terrence.

———————————

I close in on Michael in the hallway on our way to English.

"Your friend is a jerk," I say in a low voice so only he can hear.

"Yeah. I know." He looks guiltily at me. "I'll talk to him."

Terrence is ahead, Jane on one side, Fred and Leica on the other. They're all laughing.

I corner Jane at lunchtime.

"She's your cousin."

She looks guilty for a moment, then flicks her hair and says, "So?"

"So Terrence gives her a hard time and you still act like he's God's gift?"

"He's only mucking around." She rolls her eyes. "That's what he's like. He's always joking. She shouldn't take things so seriously. He was fine at lunch the other day, remember?"

"So he can do normal and jerk. How is that an excuse?"

"There's another side to him. I told you."

"What kind of excuse is that? *Oh, he's not a jerk* all *the time.* I don't know why you insist on defending him."

She blushes. "We're kind of . . . well, we might be going out."

I blink slowly. "What do you mean, *might be?*"

She laughs nervously and runs her fingers through her hair. "Okay, I'm dying to tell somebody. Leica's having a fight with Cameron so she's in her own world at the moment. I feel bad opening up to her when she's feeling so low." She sighs, then takes a step closer to me and leans in. "We hooked up on the weekend." Her eyes flash with excitement. "At Kaleb's party."

I look at her, aghast. "You're dating him now?"

"I mean, I wasn't planning on, you know, going all the way with him. But he made me feel so special . . . And I felt bad leading him on and then, you know, stopping." She sees the look of horror on my face. "No, it's not like *that.* I wanted him to."

I let out a slow breath and she shakes her head. "Maybe it happened quicker than I expected but it's fine . . ." But her tone doesn't inspire confidence. She can tell I'm skeptical.

"You think I'm a slut, don't you?" she says.

"What?"

"Just because you come from a backward culture you think I'm a slut now."

I feel like she's slapped me in the face. I stare at her, stunned and hurt. Just as soon as the words escape her mouth I can tell she regrets them. Her shoulders deflate and she looks at me, ashamed.

"I'm sorry, Mina. I didn't mean to say that. I'm just not so sure of where Terrence and I stand *now*, after the weekend . . ." Her voice trails off and she shrugs. "It hurts so bad, Mina. Not knowing. I thought he'd pay me more attention this morning in homeroom. But he was distant. Then in the hallway he was warm and funny." She's lost in her own thoughts, biting on a nail. "Maybe he's trying to protect me? Like, not let everyone know about us until we've spoken about it?"

"Yeah, probably," I say. A part of me pities her. But there's a part of me too that can't believe she's fallen for somebody so mean.

"Anyway, I'll sort it out." She puts on a brave face and smiles at me. "Don't tell anybody, promise?"

"Yeah, I promise."

"And I'm sorry. Really."

# MICHAEL

"Man, that wasn't cool or funny," I tell Terrence.

He laughs. "Yeah, it was a bit low, hey. But I couldn't help it. I'm so over seeing girls moping around like they're surprised that life sometimes sucks." He rolls his eyes.

I remember when I first got my driver's permit. I accidentally ran over a dog and Terrence fell apart on the side of the road, sobbing uncontrollably. I've seen Terrence pick on kids just because he's bigger, perfect the atomic wedgie in PE. But I remember when Travis Bates came to our school for two terms last year and Terrence caught some ninth graders making fun of him because he has cerebral palsy. The look in Terrence's eye was wild. He would have beaten the shit out of them if we were out of school. Just one word from him and they left Travis alone. He has no problem calling somebody four-eyes, but Travis was hands-off. He never hung out with Travis, but he told him that if anybody messed with him he'd fuck them up. When he's over at my place, he's nothing but patient with Nathan and will sit for ages listening to him drone on about plane engines.

And then he goes and taunts Paula like that, and I wonder who the hell he is.

He's like one of those half-baked cakes. Some parts are hard and overcooked, others soft and gooey. You can never tell which part you'll get.

The scariest thing about people like Terrence and my parents is not that they can be cruel. It's that they can be kind too.

---

Anh is pissed off with my stats and pulls me aside at the beginning of my shift.

"Look, you're not meeting targets. You've got to push harder."

"Honestly, if it was between a crooked politician and us, I reckon people would choose the politician. I can practically feel the hate coming at me through the phone."

"Derek over by the window is a zit-faced frigid who probably hasn't had a single relationship in his life unless he's paid for it. He couldn't strike up a water-cooler conversation to save his life. But put him on the phone and he rakes in the money." I look at Anh, bewildered. "So. If *he* can do it, you've got no excuse."

"Right. Um. Okay. I'll try."

"Now go collect shitloads of money. We've got a contract

from the RSPCA this month. Think of neglected puppies and cats that seemed like a good idea at Christmas only to be kicked out midyear."

The first half of my shift is a disaster. I'm calling when busy stay-at-home mums have just picked up the kids from school. I'm the last call they want to deal with. I glance at Derek, who's busting a pimple as he speaks. He's obviously just scored a donation and is grinning.

The idea hits me and I run with it before I have a chance to talk myself out of it. I decide to make up rare endangered animals to get more money. There's the white kangaroo, western hairy platypus, green-nose frog. It becomes a sort of fun challenge, trying to think up new names. I don't know what it is about endangered species but it gets people's attention. I exceed my target and Anh is ecstatic.

Until somebody calls in to complain that there's no such thing as a western hairy platypus and demands a refund.

I get sacked.

---

Mina and I are huddled up in a café booth. She's in fits of laughter. Not exactly the shoulder to lean on that I was hoping for.

"Tell me again," she says, having way too much fun teasing me to feel an ounce of sympathy for the humiliating way I lost my job. "How much did you get for the white kangaroo?"

"Fifty bucks."

She cackles. I take her hand and softly kiss her palm.

"Where are your morals?" She shakes her head in parody of a disappointed parent. "Honest people's money."

"Going to a good cause. The RSPCA would still get the money. It's not my fault if a cat can't arouse people's sense of charity but a blue mountain bee can."

"A *blue mountain bee?*" She laughs. "How much did that one get?"

"Twenty bucks." I kiss her other palm. "And only because I told him the honey produced by these bees had won some international honey award."

"A *honey* award?"

"Yeah. He was impressed." I lean in to kiss her but she has the giggles and pulls back.

"Speaking of honey," she says, "I feel like a brownie."

"Oh, I can see the connection." I stand up to buy her one.

"Sugar. Duh." She sits up, stretching to see the display of cakes. "As a feminist I don't expect you to buy it for me because I'm a girl. I'm asking you to get it because I'm too lazy to get up."

I laugh and she grins at me, poking her tongue out of the side of her mouth.

Terrence calls me as I'm paying. I don't take the call, and text him that I can't talk and will call him back soon.

"Do you have to go?" she asks me when I return.

"Nah, it was Terrence. I'll call him later."

"I don't get you two. You're so different."

I shrug. "We go way back. It's hard to just end a friendship."

"I can't imagine you having much in common."

I take a long sip from my milk shake. "Basketball. Gaming. That's about it. I know he can be a jerk and a sexist pig. But I know he can be a good guy too."

She frowns. "Just because somebody can be good sometimes doesn't make up for the times they're a jerk."

"Yeah, I know. Look, I'm not making excuses for him."

"Sounds a bit like you are." She takes a bite of her brownie and watches me closely as she chews.

"I'm not, I promise. I hate how he acts at school sometimes. But . . . people are complicated, is what I'm saying. You see one side to him. I see others. He's always been there for me. You need him and he's there, no questions asked. Like I said, we have history. It's hard to turn my back against that."

"He hurts people's feelings. He hurt Paula's feelings."

"I told him off about that. He'll leave her alone now. I'm sure of it."

She picks at her brownie, unconvinced. Eventually she says: "What's the story with him and Jane?"

"He enjoys stringing her along. It's cruel."

"She thinks he's serious about her."

I raise an eyebrow. "Terrence isn't serious about any girl."

"Well, Jane's under the impression she's the one to change all that."

"That's stupid. Terrence is a player. Always has been. Everyone knows that."

Mina's quiet. The mood is suddenly low.

"Look, why are we even talking about Terrence? I'm not even that close with him anymore." I take her hands in mine and pull her closer to me, wrapping my arms around her. "Forget about everybody else for a moment. Jane, Paula— give them some credit. They can look after themselves."

She looks up at me, defiant. "Paula's my friend. She hurts, I hurt. And Jane's got it in her to be strong if only she had the courage to see through Terrence. You don't just leave people to go through things on their own."

I can't help but squeeze her tighter. "If only I had a heart as big as yours."

"You underestimate yourself. Although"—she looks at me with a cheeky smile—"I could never collect fifty bucks off some innocent guy for the sake of a white kangaroo."

# MINA

Jane tracks me down just after lunch and pulls me aside in the corridor.

"Are you and Michael seeing each other?"

Her words are like an allergic reaction and a heat instantly builds up my neck.

"No," I say, as emphatically as I can manage.

She stares at me, studying me closely. "You're always together at lunchtime."

"Not *always*. Anyway, we're not alone. He just hangs out with us sometimes. With me, Paula, whoever's in the library. You've been with us plenty of times. Do we act like a couple?"

"Well, no. I mean, he's obviously into you though. I see the way his face lights up when he looks at you."

I try not to smile.

"Why doesn't Terrence hang out with you guys?"

"Because Terrence is the last person we'd want to hang out with."

"Hmm."

I approach cautiously. "Have you, you know, worked things out?"

"I'm going nuts," she says flatly. "One minute he's texting me, flirting with me, making me feel like I'm the center of his world. The next minute I'm invisible. I just wish I knew where I stand. I wish I knew what would make him like me. *Really* like me. Like, enough for us to be together."

She looks stricken and pathetic and I want to whack her on the head and tell her to chuck him out of her life, but I know as well as she does that the heart and head are like parallel train tracks. I try the *you deserve more, he's not worth it* pep talk; trawl through every cliché on self-love that I can bring myself to utter. But she's fallen hard and I can see my words are like floating bubbles around her, pop, pop, popping before she's even had time to register them.

———————————

In Society and Culture the next day, Jane walks in with Terrence. They're holding hands. I steal a glance at Michael. He looks just as surprised as me and shrugs. Paula takes one look at the couple and shakes her head in disappointment. But Jane, deliberately avoiding our gaze, is unable to wipe the contented smile off her face.

Mr. Morello walks in and promptly reminds Jane and Terrence of the hands-off policy. Jane giggles and sits next to

Leica. Terrence saunters over to his usual spot in the back, next to Michael and Fred.

Paula slips me a note.

> *There are only two tragedies in life: one is not getting what one wants, and the other is getting it.*

Poor Jane.
I slip her a note back.

> *Glad to see you're quoting OW again. I was beginning to worry.*

She chuckles.

Mr. Morello announces that he has our midterm essays ready to hand back. We're all nervous and jittery as we wait to find out our grades.

I get eighteen out of twenty and want to dance on the table. I look back at Michael. He grins at me. A good sign. We worked hard together researching the essay. Zoe is grinning too as she looks at her mark. Instantly, I see her search me out.

Mr. Morello tells Terrence he wants to see him after class. Terrence asks for his essay and Mr. Morello tells him he'll discuss it with him privately. Terrence plays it cocky, but even I can tell he's worried.

News travels fast. Mr. Morello has Terrence suspended for three days for cheating. He's handed in an essay that a student from several years ago submitted. I can't believe his stupidity.

> **Me:**
> Sorry I couldn't talk before, Mum was around. Can you talk now?

> **Michael:**
> Not now. Terrence needs a lift to basketball. His dad's confiscated his car for a month. And cut his allowance. Some major shit going down for him at home because of the suspension. He didn't see that coming.

> **Me:**
> Boo hoo.

> **Michael:**
> Try not to be too happy. He feels persecuted by Morello. Wallowing in self-pity at the moment. And plans for revenge.

> **Me:**
> What's he going to do? Slashing tires is so lame.

> **Michael:**
> If you cross Terrence, slashed tires would be the least of your worries.

It's Friday night. The door to the restaurant opens and a cou-ple enters. One of our waiters, Mariam, approaches them to seat them. After about five minutes I hear what seems to be a heated discussion in the middle of the restaurant. I quickly walk over to investigate.

The couple is arguing with Mariam.

"Is there a problem?" I say calmly as I approach the table. I notice other customers have stopped eating and are staring at the table, trying to listen in.

The man flashes a smarmy smile at me. "Oh, hello there, miss. We were just trying to place our order and your waiter seems to have a problem understanding us."

I look at Mariam, my eyes searching hers for a clue. The man's tone is so condescending that I'm pretty sure the customer-is-always-right rule has no application to this scenario.

"Mariam?"

She tucks her hair behind her ears and seems to be struggling to contain her anger. I feel sorry for her. She's con-stantly making mistakes but Baba and Irfan want to give her a chance. She's another one from community detention they took pity on.

"I came to take their order," she explains to me in Farsi, "and after I wrote it all down they said they wanted the non-halal option." She scrunches up her face. "I explained that all the meat is halal and they're not happy."

"Um, excuse me, English, please?" the man says. "Just common courtesy I would have thought."

"So you're not happy about the meat being halal?" I ask.

"Damn right we're not," the man says, flashing me that patronizing smile again. "Is it too much to ask that a person doesn't have halal food shoved down his throat in Australia?"

I take a deep breath, try to conjure a smile. I need to defuse the situation quickly because we're now providing free entertainment for the busybodies nearby who have swiveled around to get a better view.

"Sorry, I'm not sure I understand. What exactly is the problem?"

"We. Don't. Eat. Halal," the woman says slowly, as though I'm an imbecile. "It's barbaric and inhumane and who knows what halal funds. So we refuse to eat it."

"Maybe you'd like a vegetarian dish instead?"

"But we're not vegetarians," the woman says indignantly, as though I'd accused her of being a devil-worshipper. "If you insist on serving up that barbaric meat, you should at least offer a non-halal option. This *is* Australia, not the Middle East after all."

"Afghanistan isn't in the Middle East," I can't help but snap back. I quickly recalibrate, take a breath to calm myself down. The man demands to speak to the owner and so I tell Mariam she can return to work and let me handle the situation.

"I'll go and get him," I say. "But I normally deal with all the complaints."

The woman smirks. "Oh, really? That's quite a lot of freedom for a Muslim girl, isn't it?"

I walk off quickly, worried I might go down for assault and battery if I stick around another second longer.

Baba is in the back, bent over a delicate dish he's trying to assemble. I fill him in on the situation.

"Can you ask Irfan to deal with it, Mina? He's in the stockroom. His English is better anyway."

I talk to Irfan and he joins me, but not before first smoothing down his clothes, combing his jet-black hair to the side, and spraying on half a bottle of aftershave.

I notice Mariam is back at the table, looking overwhelmed as they talk to her. I quicken my pace to reach her before any more damage is done, although they seem to be quite friendly and chatty with her now.

"It's okay, Mariam, we'll handle this," I tell her hastily, and she gives me a bewildered look and steps away to deal with a new family lined up waiting to be seated.

"Well," the man says triumphantly. "Is this the manager?"

"Yes, sir. Mina has been telling me about your worries about the halal food. It is humane, I promising you. That is what our religion is preaching us."

Good Lord, Irfan's going to make things a million times worse now! I quickly interrupt.

"Look, there's nothing we can do for you, sorry. We're not here to debate halal slaughter practices. We clearly advertise this as a halal restaurant. It's entirely your choice and right not to eat halal and there are plenty of other restaurants you can go to."

Irfan is looking at me with horror but I refuse to meet his gaze and tell him in Farsi that he needs to trust me to do the talking.

"So you don't offer a choice of non-halal?" the woman says.

"No, we don't," I say, losing my temper. "Just like a vegetarian restaurant isn't going to serve up a roast lamb. We've chosen to use halal meat and we know we might lose customers but restaurants make those calls all the time. As you can see from how busy we are, it doesn't seem to bother most people. I'm sorry you wasted your time tonight but the sign is at the front."

I would have thought the conversation would be over by now, but the man folds his arms, seems to have more to say.

"Is it true you're hiring people who are on bridging visas?"

I blink once. I feel like things are spinning out of control.

Irfan stares blankly at them. "Begging pardon?"

"Mariam—sweet girl—has a bridging visa, she told us. And you have two others working here too."

"And so what? Why is this your business?" Irfan says.

I wince. He's just confirmed it to them.

"She says they're all very grateful for the help you've given them. But from what we know, they're not allowed to work. So you've got yourself a bit of a situation there, don't you? Cheap labor, cash wages."

"Work you could give an Australian citizen," the woman snaps.

"I think you should leave the premises now," I say softly but firmly under my breath.

"Sure thing, love," the man says, and they stand up. "But you haven't heard the end of this. We're actually part of a new political organization and we're going to make sure this comes up in the state election agenda. People like you are taking jobs away from honest Aussies."

A wave of fury comes over me, wrenching itself from the pit of my belly.

"You're from Aussie Values?" I demand.

"Yes," the woman says proudly.

"That is the bullshit organization who coming with the TV!" Irfan says angrily. "Get out, please." He's all worked up now. "You getting out now!"

Everyone's eyes are on us as Irfan's voice rises. I try to calm him down but he's too distressed. "You making us terrorists on the TV!" he cries. "Get out!"

The man and woman are calm, smirk at us, and walk out. I'm mortified. Irfan storms to the kitchen, no doubt to consult with Baba. I smile meekly at the people closest to us, offer as many apologies for the disturbance as I can, and quickly follow Irfan.

I try to calm them down but they're both panicking, wondering if they'll be caught. Mariam walks in with an order and I stop her before she leaves.

"What did you tell them?" I ask her urgently.

"They were friendly and asking me where I'm from, how I'm coping here. I explained how kind your baba and Irfan have been to me and the others. They kept asking me questions and I did not know how to get away."

I groan, lean my forehead against the door frame.

"I'm sorry," she says guiltily. "Did I do something wrong?"

"No, nothing, Mariam," I console her. "It's fine. You didn't do anything wrong."

I go out to the front for some fresh air and call Michael. He's our only hope.

He picks up after the first ring.

"Hey," he says brightly.

"Michael, I need your help!" I say quickly. I fill him in on what's happened, ask him to stop the organization from taking it further, talking to immigration or the media.

"They're not allowed to work but how are they supposed to live? We're just helping them out. And the media?! I can't let my parents go through the stress of it all. Why are they picking on us? We're an Afghan restaurant in the lower North Shore. We're hardly going to swing an election for them."

"I don't know," he says with concern. "I'll talk to my parents."

———————————————

Baba comes home that night and heads straight to the balcony. He drinks tea and chain-smokes until past midnight. Mum paces in the family room until eventually she falls asleep on the couch.

She wakes up in the morning and cancels her lunch invitation to Emily and Rojin. It tears me apart to see my parents so distressed.

# MICHAEL

I text Mina.

> **Me:**
> Haven't seen Dad all day, he'll be back later tonight. Tried calling him but he's at some convention on the Central Coast. Better I talk to him face to face.

> **Mina:**
> Okay. What about your mum?

> **Me:**
> She's with him.

> **Mina:**
> Do you think they'll go to the media?

> **Me:**
> They're always looking for a story to get them in the news.

**Me:**

I'm sorry.

**Mina:**

My dad's been up all night. And Mum's stressed because he's stressed, and he's stressed because he thinks Mum's stressed so everybody's stressed. Why can't your organization just back off?

**Me:**

It's not my organization, Mina.

**Mina:**

Yeah, I know. Sorry.

**Me:**

No, I'm sorry you have to go through this. But don't work yourself up. They're all talk, they can't do much damage. They get some attention from trashy media and then it all dies again.

**Mina:**

Meanwhile we just have to toughen up and learn to cope with racism, hey?

**Me:**

There's nothing in the world that kills me more than the fact that you're in this situation because of my parents.

I promise Mina I'll speak to my parents. They're back late from the Central Coast and so I grab the chance the next morning before school. Dad's at the kitchen bench, eating his breakfast and reading the news on his iPad. Mum's packing Nathan's lunch, and Nathan is eating his toast and watching TV in the family room.

I pour myself a bowl of cereal and sit down at the bench across from my dad. I start eating, trying to figure out the best way to bring up the topic. *Stuff it*, I think. I just have to throw myself in.

"Dad?"

"Yep?" He doesn't look up.

"Apparently a couple from Aussie Values was at a local Afghan restaurant on Saturday night. There was a bit of a commotion about—"

He looks up sharply. "Oh, yes! I completely forgot to mention it. Listen to this, Mary. Jeremy and Margaret were at some Afghan restaurant—the same one Andrew busted on *News Tonight*—and there was a scene over the halal food they serve."

"Really? What happened?"

"The usual. Halal or nothing. So we have them on that front. But the best part is that they found out that they're hiring people on bridging visas. They don't have work rights, remember?"

My mum shakes her head in frustration.

"We can really do something with this, Mary. Expose the rot at the core of this system. These people are in breach of their visa conditions. They've been released into the community on *trust*. And these restaurant owners are happy to exploit them as cheap labor."

"Dad," I interrupt. I take a deep breath.

"Yes?"

"Please, could you leave this one alone?" My eyes plead with him.

"What do you mean?" He's genuinely confused. "We have to speak out, Michael. Bad things happen when good people remain silent."

"They're not allowed to work, Dad. Is it so bad if somebody helps them out?"

"They should have thought of that before they decided to break the law," Dad says seriously.

Mum nods as she cuts up Nathan's sandwich.

"How can this possibly make any difference to you? You're getting results in Jordan Springs, you've got some more members. Why can't you show some freaking mercy?"

Dad is taken aback and Mum, raising her eyebrows at me in dismay, says, "What has this restaurant got to do with you?"

"The owner's daughter is in my class."

"I thought they were refugees too."

"Yeah, they came here from Afghanistan. So?"

Mum seems surprised, indignant even. "And they can afford Victoria College?" She shakes her head in disbelief. "That only makes things worse, hiring cheap labor when business is obviously highly profitable."

"For God's sake, Mum, Mina's on a scholarship. Don't worry, they're not going to overtake you on the class ladder."

"What's gotten into you, Michael?" Mum stares at me, clearly stung by my words.

I take a deep breath. "It's one restaurant. I'm asking you to please let it go."

Dad fixes his eyes on me. "If it means that much to you, I'll talk to the others," he says calmly. "But I can't promise you anything. This is bigger than us now, Michael. And the personal shouldn't matter when it comes to what's right and wrong."

"Right and wrong is *always* personal."

# MINA

Emily stops Mum and me in the hall on our way out to the car on Monday morning.

"Is everything okay?" she asks Mum with concern. "You didn't sound like yourself when you called to cancel."

"Everything is fine," Mum says, smiling at her. "Thank you, Emily."

"Are you sure?"

"Yes, I am sure. I must take Mina to school now. I will see you soon, okay?"

"Okay." Emily gives her an uncertain smile.

We rush to the car and I scold Mum.

"She does not need to know about our problems," Mum says firmly. "I am sick of problems. She has her problems and *I* will help *her*. We will deal with this by ourselves. Understood?"

I stare out the window. "Suit yourself," I mutter. I'm sick of everything.

I go to school with my stomach in knots.

I'm opening my locker when Michael grabs me from behind and hugs me.

"*Michael,*" I say under my breath, wriggling my way out of his embrace. I can't help but laugh though. "People will see."

"Relax, there's nobody around. Anyway, so what?"

"I can't. And no, I'm not ashamed of you, so don't even start that up again."

He laughs. "Yeah, yeah, I get it. The Afghan rumor mill that works from Kabul to Auburn to Lane Cove to your mother's cell phone. Got it." He pecks me on the cheek and I giggle and push him away.

"Hey!" I warn him.

"Okay, okay." He holds his hands behind his back in submission. "Happy now?"

"Yes, thank you."

He leans against the locker.

"Did you speak to your parents?" I'm almost too scared to ask.

He nods, but the expression on his face worries me.

"No use?"

"Dad said he'll talk to the others. He's the leader of the organization so that has to mean something . . . But he said he can't promise anything. I know that's not very reassuring. I'm so sorry, Mina."

I bite my lip, too anxious to say anything. He puts his hand on my arm and peers into my face.

"I tried. You believe me, don't you?"

"Of course I do," I say. And I mean it.

"I'll speak to him again tonight to check that he's spoken to them. They're all busy with the Jordan Springs campaign, so this will probably drop off their radar. They've got bigger Muslim fish to fry." He grins at me and I hit him in the arm, a faint smile on my face.

---

I need to vent to Paula. With Michael, I have to hold myself back from swearing about his parents. I mean, as much as I wish they'd drop off the face of this planet, they are the parents of the guy who makes me weak at the knees.

But I don't get a chance to talk to Paula because she arrives at homeroom after the bell. It's our weekly one-hour period with Mr. Morello today. Terrence is back and the color has returned to Jane's face. She was moping for three days and it took all my self-control not to slap her out of her stupid crush.

Paula walks in and says hi to Mr. Morello, who smiles warmly at her and continues talking to us about leadership skills. A few minutes after Paula's taken her seat I hear snickers from behind. I peer backward and see some of the kids looking at Paula with amusement, trying to stifle their laughs.

Terrence is sitting with his arms folded across his chest, a triumphant expression on his face.

Mr. Morello is in no mood for disruptions and we get a two-minute power silence. Clara yells out at Terrence to shut up and respect the fact that some people actually come to school to get an education. That sets him off giggling and so Mr. Morello increases the power silence to four minutes. Mr. Morello asks what the joke is, which only gets Terrence and some others laughing more. They don't say anything though, and Mr. Morello gives us six minutes.

We have early recess today and we spill out of the class when the bell rings. We're walking out into the courtyard and it's like a tiny crack in a windshield has suddenly grown until the glass smashes.

I hear it first. Terrence walks past Paula and says, "So exactly how long have you been in love with Morello for?"

His voice is loud enough for others to hear, sending them into fits of laughter and backslaps. A small crowd has gathered. I see Zoe and Clara slow down, listening in and watching what's happening.

The question practically knocks the wind out of Paula. It's not her fault, but her reaction is just making it worse.

I play it cool. "Morello? Hello, who isn't crushing on him?"

But he's not backing down. "Nice try, Mina."

Then, to my astonishment, Zoe lets out a laugh and says, "Terrence, you're such an idiot. Practically every girl in eleventh grade likes Morello. With guys like you around us, it's pretty obvious why."

I feel like reaching out and giving her a hug. Paula stares at her in surprise. Our eyes meet for a moment, an understanding forming between us, and then, satisfied that they've chipped away at his rumor-mongering, Zoe and Clara walk away.

Terrence glowers at them and then focuses back on Paula. "How many one-on-one sessions have you had with Morello in his office?" he asks, smirking.

Paula is mortified, shaking. I hold tightly on to her hand and try to lead her away but she's frozen to the spot.

I can't understand how Terrence knows. Paula had confided only in me. But then I see Jane standing nearby, watching Terrence laughing with his mates. The guilt in her eyes is unmistakable. She sees me staring openmouthed at her, and I almost sense the shame take her over. She looks away and runs off, which is when Paula notices her. Realization dawns on Paula's face. It's like she's been punched in the stomach.

"Isn't he a bit too old for you?" Terrence taunts her.

He's not teasing like he usually does. There's something malicious about him now. I remember Michael's texts. This is payback to Mr. Morello for the suspension. And Paula? Well, she's just collateral damage.

I get up right in his face. He doesn't scare me. "You know, I keep trying to find something redeeming about you. Some guys are jerks, but they can at least pull off witty and charming too. But you? It's no use. You're a one-talent show. The only trick you've got is first-class pathetic."

The muscles in his neck bulge and he flashes an angry look at me.

"What are you going to do about it? Put an SOS call to your terrorist buddies?"

"Yeah, that's right. I'm from the land of Al-Qaida, remember."

Some of the boys laugh. I stare back defiantly at him.

"Hey, when I want an opinion from a boat person I'll ask," he says smugly.

"Quit it, Terrence," I hear Michael shout from behind as he storms up to us. I'm not one to play the damsel in distress but I have to admit it's quite a turn-on.

"When are you going to stop being such a fucking dickhead?"

Terrence is momentarily too surprised to respond.

"Are you taking their side?" he finally manages.

"Hell yes," Michael cries. "What's Paula ever done to you?"

"Where's your freaking sense of humor?" He looks at the other guys and laughs. "Anyway, Paula doesn't need you. She's got a terrorist defending her."

It happens in an instant. Michael shoves him in the chest and Terrence stumbles backward. The boys start cheering and making noises generally heard in wildlife parks.

"Michael, don't! He's not worth getting suspended for."

Terrence lets out a short, bitter laugh. "Is this how you treat a mate?"

"A mate? If I was really your mate I would have called you out for being an asshole a long time ago."

Terrence looks wounded for a moment, but then his face twists in anger.

"Fuck you," he spits out, and walks away.

———————————

It's then that I notice Paula has slipped away. I lock eyes with Michael and a rush of affection for him floods through every atom of my body.

I run out of the corridor, bumping into Jane outside.

"How could you do that to anyone, let alone your own cousin?" I say furiously.

Jane stammers and fumbles, avoiding my eyes.

"I never thought he'd tell. Honest. It just came up in conversation."

"You think it's okay to betray Paula?"

"No." She makes a face. "I just . . . it's hard to get his attention . . ."

"Oh, I get it. Blabbing your cousin's secrets keeps him close, hey?"

"You wouldn't understand." Her voice trembles slightly.

I sigh, exasperated that I have to explain the bleeding

obvious to her. "Listen to me. If you need to betray friends and family to keep a guy, you need to dump him. He's the *wrong* guy."

She lets out a hard laugh. "We were never going out for me to dump him. He made that clear to me last night. He got what he wanted at the party. After that, the only time he seemed interested in me was when I was . . . you know."

"Feeding him gossip?"

She nods slowly. "I feel like shit, all right? When Terrence made a move on me I couldn't believe it. Not many guys have before, let alone somebody like him." She shrugs. "I learned the hard way."

"No. Paula did."

Her face crumples and with it my anger. She bites down on her lip, her eyes darting everywhere to avoid my gaze.

"I'm sorry," she mumbles.

Pity floods through me. If only she knew that she didn't have to be the kind of girl who only knows how to exist when she's wanted by a guy.

I smile at her and, wearing her shame like a heavy coat, she manages a small smile in return.

———————

I find Paula sobbing in a toilet cubicle in the library.

"Open the door, Paula," I plead with her, leaning my head against the door.

She doesn't open the door and she doesn't speak.

"It stinks in here. And sure, I know you're in a shitty place right now, but you don't have to take it literally. I promise you can cry as much as you like but at least let's go somewhere hygienic."

I hear the slightest movement. A tiny rustle.

"Did you see the graffiti on this door, Paula? They've drawn Ms. Ham, only they've given her a triple D cup. That's not her. Have her boobs seen better days?"

She opens the door and I smile at her.

"My life sucks," she says, her face crumpling again.

"Listen to me. The only people who know the truth about your feelings for Morello are Jane and me. We just deny it. Terrence is known to talk shit all the time. Leave Jane to me."

"It's a bit too late to deny it. I fell apart." She stands in front of the mirror, staring at her face. "Not to mention Morello's going to hear the rumors. I can never face him again."

I rub her back. "Yes, you can. Who's to say it even gets back to him? It'll blow over."

"But what if it doesn't? What if Terrence keeps on spreading it around?"

I lead her out of the bathroom and we take refuge in the privacy of a study cubicle on the second story of the library.

I drum my nails on the desk, deep in thought.

"I could always rent a terrorist."

Paula stares at me. "Huh?"

I smile. "I know some guys in Auburn. Big. Bushy beards. Nike tracksuits. Westie accents. They just need to pay Terrence a visit. Pass him on the street and ask him for the time, maybe, then mutter *Allahu Akbar* or something and he'll crap his pants."

Paula laughs. "You're crazy."

The bell rings.

"I don't want to go to class," she moans.

I lift her up. "Come on. You don't go and he wins."

"I can't face anybody. They'll all be talking about me."

"I just *know* Oscar Wilde has a quote for this moment."

———————

Society and Culture. Paula and I walk in with our heads high. Zoe and Clara catch our eyes and smile at us in solidarity.

Terrence is sitting tight with Fred, trying to affect nonchalance but failing miserably as far as I can tell. I walk past him and flash him a bright, insincere smile that I'm confident successfully conveys the extent of my disdain for him. Jane's next to Leica and is nervously avoiding eye contact with Paula. Michael's sitting alone, his long legs stretched out under his desk, looking as cool and calm as ever I've seen him.

Class goes on normally. Mr. Morello obviously has no clue about what's happened. But something has shifted in the room. Terrence is trying to play it cool, but I can sense his ambivalence about how he's come out of all of this. While

Paula's never been popular; she's always been respected from a distance. As for Mr. Morello, he's well liked, one of the "cool" teachers. If Terrence had hoped to marginalize Paula, or get people talking about Mr. Morello, it hasn't worked.

He's crossed the line and, judging from the look on his face, I'm guessing he realizes it too.

# MICHAEL

It's the semifinals tonight, and as badly as I want to be with Mina, I'm not going to let the team down. I'm not sure what's going to happen, playing alongside Terrence. We haven't spoken all day. Some things you can't come back from. It's taken our fight to make me realize we grew apart a long time ago.

I arrive a little late to practice. He's on the court already, doing drills with the rest of the team.

I throw my bag under the bench, pull off my top, and put on my jersey. I take a swig from my water bottle and jog out to the court. He sees me but doesn't acknowledge me.

Coach trains us hard before the game. By the time the siren sounds for the game to begin, I'm pumped up, ready to play hard.

But Terrence is taking our fight to the court, ignoring me when I call for a pass, dropping comments when I miss a shot. The referee calls the first time-out and our coach storms over to us.

"What the hell is going on, Terrence? Michael was open and you passed to Hamish!"

"Oops."

"Wipe that smirk off your face. Whatever's going on, keep it off the court or I'll bench you for the rest of the game. Got it?"

Terrence mutters a yes.

Coach fixes his eyes on me next. "Michael?"

"Yeah, of course."

We run back onto the court. Terrence scowls at me. I ignore him.

At least he's gotten the message. We play like normal but there's none of the usual backslapping and joking. Things are tense between us, and everyone knows it.

We win by one point. Finally, a high note in the day.

Usually I'd drop Terrence home, but tonight I don't offer. I pull on my top, collect my stuff, say bye to the rest of the team, and walk to the parking lot. He follows me outside.

"What? So that's it?" he demands.

I throw my bag in the front seat and turn to face him. "You think you can treat people like that and get away with it?"

"I'm the same guy. I haven't changed."

"Yeah, well, I have."

I can see a flicker of hurt in his eyes. Then it's gone and the anger returns.

"It never bothered you before."

"Yeah, it did. Only I was too lazy to do anything."

He folds his arms across his chest. "Are you going out with Mina?"

I knew it was only a matter of time before he asked. I want to show Mina off to the world but I respect her too much to betray her.

"We're friends now. I defended her because you crossed a line. With Paula, with Jane, and with her."

"Bullshit. I don't believe you."

"Honestly, Terrence, I couldn't care less what you believe."

"I've known you since seventh grade. You've known her one term. Are you going to shit on our friendship for someone like her?"

I feel the veins in my neck bulge out. I crack it. "What do you mean, *someone like her*?"

"Are you fucking kidding me?" He's incredulous, and throws his hands up in disbelief. "Your dad's leader of Aussie Values, for God's sake. What the hell's happened to you? You suddenly got some wog-chick fetish?"

I almost lunge at him but the thought of Mina stops me. How do I explain to him that I went along with everything my parents said because it never occurred to me that they could be wrong? I never dared to think I could question them until I met Mina. She's turned my life inside out and nothing's been the same since.

"Well?" he presses me.

I shrug. "At some point in your life you have to decide what you believe in. I don't want to be that guy who figures it out when it's too late."

"That's such New Age bullshit, man."

He looks so confused and betrayed that the anger drains out of me, leaving nothing inside me but pity for him.

"We've got nothing to say to each other anymore," I tell him, and get into my car and drive away.

———————————

Dad texts me to say he's with Mum and Nathan at Andrew and Carolina's place. I send a text back asking if he's spoken to the others about backing off. He responds: *Yes. It's under control. Don't worry.*

I breathe a sigh of relief, and let Mina know.

# MINA

Maha texts me.

**Maha:**
It's been ages. Sorry. I've been meaning to ask. What's happening with you and Gandalf? The chemistry in that theater room was science-class worthy.

**Me:**
We are kind of . . . seeing each other.

She calls within seconds.

She's screaming like I just aced my finals. She demands details. It's a long conversation.

---

I find Adnan out back having a cigarette on his break. I empty the rubbish into the garbage bin and sit on an upside-down crate across from him. There's a stench coming from the bin, but I try to ignore it.

He's tall and lanky, thick jet-black hair swept to the side, locked into position with Brylcreem judging from the scent. His face is riddled with acne scars but you hardly notice because when he smiles his face lights up.

"Did I tell you we're getting more people raving about your food?" I say, grinning at him.

He smiles. "Yes."

"Where'd you learn to cook like that? You're only a couple of years older than me. Eighteen, right?"

He nods. "My father was a chef back home. I helped in his restaurant there."

"Ah, that explains it."

He takes a long drag of his cigarette, stares at the ground.

"Dad mentioned you quit school," I say.

He shrugs. "When I turned eighteen, immigration told me I had to leave."

"*Why?*"

"They wouldn't fund it anymore. The people at the school encouraged me to stay. I tried for a while but they didn't realize how short of money I was. I wasn't paying for my train fares to come to school. One day I nearly got caught on the train without a ticket. They would have sent me back to Villawood. So I left school. Not worth the risk in the end."

"I'm so sorry," I say, biting down on my lip with anger. But he just shrugs, stands up, flicks the cigarette onto the ground, and presses down on it with his foot.

"It's okay. I have a job now. Thanks to your father and Irfan. I've got to go back, marinate the chicken. See you inside."

I sit there for a while longer, lost in my thoughts.

We came so close to losing Adnan, Mustafa, and Mariam. It shouldn't be like this.

Soon I realize I've become desensitized to the smell of the garbage bins. That's life, I guess. Stick around shit long enough and pretty soon you can't smell it.

I don't want that to ever happen to me. I want to feel, to be affected, to get angry. Nobody changed the world by being polite. I'm going to fight with all I've got.

---

"Baba? Is that you?"

"Yes, Mina."

He's shuffling around the kitchen, making himself some tea.

"Want some?"

"Thanks."

It's just past one in the morning. We go out to the veranda, careful not to make too much noise as we open the sliding door. Baba sits down slowly, grimacing with pain. He lights up a cigarette, inhales deeply. I see how his body relaxes, how his face loses some of its edge.

I know it's his personal pain relief, his numbing agent, but I hate the fact that he chain-smokes.

"Did you take your pills?"

He nods slowly.

A silence settles between us. It's cold but we're both wearing lots of layers and I've wrapped myself in a shawl. The inky night sky is like a blanket above us. The last quarter moon dazzles me, and I sit staring up at it, cradling the steaming cup of tea in my hands.

"Baba, don't stress," I tell him eventually. "It'll be okay. It's over now. I told you there's a guy in my school who knows someone in the organization. They're leaving it alone."

"I don't worry about them," he says with scorn. "Do they know what I have seen? Do they think they can scare me after what I've been through?"

"No, Baba."

"When we arrived in this country we had to learn the differences of this new place and we had to also learn that for everybody *we* are the difference. I think, Mina, there is something the majority wants us to do in order to be fully accepted, but they never tell us what it is."

# MICHAEL

"Michael?"

Dad's hovering at my door, peering in nervously.

"Hmm?" I'm bent over my desk, working.

"I picked these brochures up for you," he says hesitantly.

I look up from my essay.

"There's a graphic design expo in the city in a couple of months," he says. "Thought you might like to go."

I don't even bother to disguise the shocked expression on my face. "Mum spoke to you?"

He sits on the edge of my bed.

"Yes, your mum spoke to me." He leans forward, resting his elbows on his thighs. "I feel like we've grown apart these past few months, Michael. It hurts that you would feel unable to talk to me about changing your mind about architecture."

"You've had your heart set on me following in your footsteps for as long as I can remember." I soften my voice. "I didn't know how to break it to you."

He nods slowly, and takes a long, calming breath. "To be honest, I tossed and turned all last night. And accepting your decision is not the same as feeling happy about it. You get to my age, Michael, you see the instability around you, and you know that more than half the battle is a good, solid job. And then your straight-As son says he wants to design games. Tell me how I should feel about that."

"I don't just want to design games, Dad."

"Well, then, tell me what you want to do."

So I tell him, and he hears me out without interruption. We look through the UTS Design School website, and he listens to me carefully as I take him through the different subjects and career paths.

"Tell me how your mother and I should feel about this?" Dad eventually asks me.

"How about feeling happy that I know what I want to do with my life?"

Dad's jaw is tense but he doesn't reply. He just nods slowly. It's a start.

———————————

Terrence and Fred ignore me throughout all our classes, which suits me fine. It's not as though I don't have other friends, and I have no problem sitting alone when I feel like it either.

I go to the basketball courts at recess and join the guys who are already shooting hoops. I see Terrence and Fred approach the court, laughing together as they bounce a ball. Terrence notices me and makes a point of turning around and joining the guys assembled at the other end of the court.

When the bell rings, I walk off the court with Cameron and Adrian. I notice Jane walking alone. She looks miserable.

I tell the guys I need to go to the bathroom and they continue on without me. I jog over to Jane, who's clearly in no rush to get to class. I startle her when I say hi and she looks at me quizzically.

"Take it from me," I say to her. "He's not worth it."

I can tell she's trying to figure out if I can be trusted.

"We're not friends anymore," I tell her.

"It's like a drug," she eventually says, her voice shaky. "I feel like I'm going through withdrawal. I was so close to going up to him just to say hi so I'd get a small hit of his attention." Her voice stalls. "I'm pathetic. I hate myself."

"Don't say that. We've all been there before."

Suddenly her eyes flash with anger. "I betrayed my cousin for him. Mina's only known Paula since the start of the year, and yet she stood up for her. Even Zoe spoke up. I'm family and I stabbed her in the back."

"You'll find a way to make up with her. But Terrence you have to quit. Cold turkey. He talks to you and you ignore him. That's the only way to get him out of your system."

"Yeah, but how do I get the strength to do that?"

I grin at her. "You stay angry, that's how. Not because you're not together. But because you nearly were."

# MINA

We're standing at the bus stop outside of school when Paula's voice drops to a whisper. "Oh. My. God."

I look over to where she's staring. Her mum has just parked the car and is getting out. She's wearing a suit and big black sunglasses. She seems to be searching for Paula; she scans the bus queues and groups of students pouring out of the gates, and then takes out her phone.

"She never picks me up," Paula says. "I can't even remember the last time."

Paula's phone rings.

"You better go to her. Text me to let me know everything's okay."

"Yep." She waves at her mum, trying to get her attention, and then runs across the road. Her mum sees her and practically flings herself forward, embracing her in a tight hug. They then get in the car and drive away.

Immediately I send her a text.

> **Please tell me everything's okay?**

I get a response five minutes later.

> **K4's sick.**

---

Paula's away from school the next day. I text her and she says K4 may have cancer. They're at the vet. She'll speak to me at school tomorrow.

Baba is working late tonight and Mum and I make grilled cheese sandwiches and watch an Iranian movie while I summarize an article on the League of Nations for Modern History.

I can't stop thinking about Paula though. I don't want K4 to die, not when he's her anchor at home, her get-out-of-bed reason. I don't want Paula to confront death yet. Grief, especially when it's still raw, is like having a thirst that no amount of water quenches. It can't be consoled; it can't be alleviated. It's unrelenting and constant. I wish I could tell her that it will get easier with time.

But if I told her that I'd also have to tell her that easier doesn't mean it ever goes away.

---

There's no chance to talk during homeroom the next day and I have a double period of Modern History so we aren't in class together. Finally, the bell rings for recess and I meet Paula in a quiet section behind the library.

"We spoke to Nancy last night," she says. "She's a mess."

"I'm so sorry, Paula." I grab her hand. "How bad is it?"

"He's got a skin tumor. He'll need surgery to remove it and to do tests to see if it's spread." Her voice cracks and she starts to cry. "I don't want to lose him, Mina."

I hold her close to me.

———

Nothing happens at the restaurant tonight. Baba advised Adnan, Mustafa, and Mariam not to come to work just in case. But it seems Michael's dad has come through after all. There's no big rejoicing among us though; just a weary sense that we've been saved from a disaster.

It's like we never left the boat. Ten years on and we're still on deck, being rocked and swayed, coming closer to the rocks and then pulling back, smashing against waves.

Mum's phone rings on our way home. I see Emily's name on the screen. Mum lets it ring out.

"I'll call her back," she says.

I press Mum to reschedule her lunch with Emily and Rojin but she makes up an excuse to get me off her back.

I have a feeling that, like me, she falls into bed tonight, exhausted.

———

"K4's booked in for surgery." Paula fiddles with the zip of her pencil case. Her face is racked with grief but I can tell there's something else going on too. "I'm sorry, Mina," she says softly.

"Sorry?" I stare at her, confused.

Paula scrunches her nose. "Here I am falling apart because my dog is going into surgery and you've lost your dad, your baby brother. You've been through war, you've—"

"You've got nothing to apologize for," I say firmly.

She shakes her head. "My pain can't compare with—"

I cut her off again. "It's not a competition." I force her to look me in the eye. "Okay?"

Eventually she gives in and nods.

"Okay," I say matter-of-factly. "Vent."

"I never expected Mum and Dad would take it so badly," she says quietly.

"He's part of your family, Paula. Of course they would."

"What's the point of loving someone if the fact that you do takes them by surprise?"

"At least they love," I offer.

"But isn't that the minimum? It shouldn't be enough. When was the last time they spent time with K4? Why do people always wait for something bad to happen before they show they care?"

"Because that's life, Paula. And your parents aren't alone in that."

"I hope I don't sound ungrateful," she says. "I know I'm

lucky and that from the outside we seem to have it all. And, Mina, honestly, I hope I don't sound like a pretentious snob. Not with all you've been through."

I shake my head at her. "You are a solar system away from pretentious snob, okay? Everyone has the right to grieve. Just let it out. I'm not judging you."

"I know," she says shyly. "From where I'm looking I have a big gorgeous house that's lonely and empty and a best friend that's a dog who might die. I'd live in a shack if it meant I had a full-time family . . ."

I feel terrible that there's no answer that will fix things for her.

"You know, I really respect what Mum and Dad do; I know it doesn't sound that way but I honestly do. I really do get that they've got important jobs. That they're ambitious and smart and doing jobs that can never be nine to five." She groans, puts her head in her hand. "It's so confusing. I get mad at them, but especially my mum, and I feel like I'm shitting all over every feminist principle I believe in."

"Your vent is equal opportunity," I say, playfully nudging her in the side. "You're upset with your mum and dad. Anyway, you're not saying you want them to quit their jobs, make you gourmet dinners, and be here at three-thirty to pick you up."

She bites on a nail. "Not at all. I just want them to get the balance right."

She pauses, thinks for a moment. "Shouldn't parents be able to figure out when they're needed?"

"I think parents make it up as they go along, to be honest."

She smiles. Just a little. "I think you're probably right."

# MICHAEL

We have a free study period at the end of the day. The bell rings and I steal a quick kiss from Mina, between the steampunk display and nineteenth-century poetry. She laughs, and then quickly ducks, her eyes darting around, checking to see if anybody has noticed.

"Relax," I whisper in her ear. "Zoe and Clara are near the graphic novels shelf, their eyeballs glued to their screens. And I happen to know for a fact that this particular aisle, while affording a view of the library, remains—and this is really quite poetic—hidden from view."

"How do you know that?" She looks at me, a mischievous glint in her eye. "I'll puke if I find out you've brought another girl here."

I grin. "This is the PG-rated library aisle, Mina. You're my first PG-rated girlfriend."

"I gave you more credit than that, Michael," she says, rolling her eyes at me. "Rating relationships by movie classifications is so juvenile."

Then she takes me by surprise by giving me a long, hard kiss, says good-bye, and rushes off to catch her bus.

———————————

Dad's home early from work, drinking a coffee at the kitchen bench while Mum prepares dinner. Nathan's in the TV room, finishing his homework so he can earn some iPad time. I'm rummaging in the pantry for an afternoon snack. Dad gets a call and takes it outside; when he comes back he's wearing a look of concern and guilt. Mum notices too.

"Something wrong?"

He throws a quick glance my way and then, clearing his throat, sits back up on the bar stool. But there's something diversionary about his manner, and I ask him what's wrong.

"Jeremy and Margaret called immigration," he says, his tone cautious. "I spoke to Andrew about leaving it all alone. I never thought Jeremy and Margaret would get involved. They've been so busy with the Jordan Springs campaign."

Mum turns her back to the stove and faces us.

"Has something happened?" she asks.

"*Immigration?*" I repeat.

He nods. "The three people they had working at the restaurant were picked up and sent to Villawood."

I'm frozen, momentarily paralyzed as I try to process his

words. It's like cement's running through my veins, choking me from the inside. My throat tightens with every thought of Mina, her parents, the asylum seekers working there.

"I told you, Michael, this is bigger than us," Dad tries to explain. "I'm sorry that you have a connection with the people who own the restaurant. But they're the ones in the wrong." His eyes plead with me to understand, and then his phone rings again. He looks down and takes the call.

"Michael," Mum says gently.

I flash her a silencing look. "Don't," I warn her through clenched teeth.

I don't drop my eyes from Dad for a second. He finishes the call, hangs up, and looks at me. "A reporter's out there," he says slowly. "Jeremy and Margaret too."

"Are you serious?" I yell. "THIS is your idea of *It's under control*? I told Mina you had it sorted out! She trusts me!"

Dad snaps. "I spoke to Andrew, Michael! He was the one who took an interest in the restaurant. I can't control people!"

Mum interrupts, her voice strained and desperate. "Jeremy and Margaret didn't mention they had anything to do with the restaurant, Michael. How was your dad to know?"

"You're actually going to tell me you're surprised that people who spend their time opposing an Islamic school might join Andrew's witch hunt?" I laugh bitterly.

Nathan walks in, looking worried.

"What's going on?" he asks. "Why is everybody screaming?"

"Nothing's wrong, darling," Mum says with affected cheeriness. "Why don't you go and play on your iPad."

"Why are you fighting?"

"We're not fighting," Dad says tensely, running his fingers through his hair.

"I'm going there," I say, and storm out. I can hear Mum urging Dad to follow me; warning that things could get ugly.

Dad calls out to me but I ignore him. He catches up to me as I'm at the door.

"Calm down, Michael," he says. "Just please calm down."

"I don't have the right to be calm," I say coolly. "Not when three people are back in detention. Because of us."

He rubs his eyes tiredly and takes a long, shuddering breath.

"I don't want you driving in this state. We'll go together. Okay?"

———————————

We don't say a word to each other in the car. Dad tries to call Andrew, Jeremy, and Margaret, but nobody's answering. I try calling Mina, but her phone rings out. I text her, asking her to call me urgently.

We pull into the parking lot behind the strip of shops. A reporter is standing on the footpath, talking to Jeremy and Margaret. There's a cameraman too. Mina's nowhere to be seen.

The reporter looks like a rookie. It's probably his first

exposé. He keeps checking his teeth through the reflection in the camera lens. One protein-smoothie-drinking, kale-eating, foundation-junkie cliché.

Jeremy and Margaret grin wildly when they see us approaching. But their smiles dissolve when they see Dad. He steps close to them, a tense expression on his face, and whispers that he needs to speak to them privately for a moment. The reporter's too quick and steps between them, breaking their huddle.

Flashing Dad a wide White Glo smile, he says, "Alan Blainey, leader of Aussie Values?"

Dad nods. "Excuse me," he says politely. "I just need a moment alone with Jeremy and—"

"This is perfect!" the reporter gushes. "Can I interview you instead?" He quickly waves over the cameraman, who's got the camera up on his shoulder and rolling before anybody knows what's happening.

"Look," Dad says, firmly this time, "do you mind if we do this after I've had a chance to speak to my associates?"

The reporter looks disappointed. "Fine, but can you make it quick as I have another story to get to."

Dad takes a confused-looking Jeremy and Margaret to the side. I take a step closer, but Dad motions at me to remain where I am.

The reporter is using the time as an opportunity to practice his face-to-camera piece. A restaurant serving halal food taking over an Aussie fish and chip shop. Steeped in controversy ever since. Asylum seekers working illegally. Being sent back to Villawood because of a concerned citizen's tip-off. Raises questions about halal funding.

A few moments later, Dad, Jeremy, and Margaret return. Dad asks the reporter to adjust his story, focus on the anti-Islamic school campaign the organization is leading, and a more general story about halal food funding terrorism.

"You can talk about asylum seekers gaming the system, but can you leave this particular restaurant out of it?"

He throws a glance my way, expecting me to thank him.

It's like the feeling you get after a swim. Your ears are blocked and then suddenly you're walking along and *pop*, they clear and you can hear again, find your balance. Dad's words pierce the air bubbles trapped inside my head and I can finally hear what he's saying.

And I realize that I don't want any part of it.

The reporter presses Dad, arguing that the restaurant will make the piece stronger. Jeremy and Margaret nod in agreement. Dad seems torn, looking at me and then back at the reporter.

"Michael, talk to your dad," Margaret urges me.

The reporter overhears, jerking his head to face me. "You're Alan's son? It'd be good to get a young person's point of view."

Suddenly the camera starts to roll and the reporter is asking me "as one of the organization's youngest members," for my opinion on asylum seekers and Aussie Values' platform generally. It all happens so quickly. I try to gather my thoughts, ignoring the look of apprehension on Dad's face.

The reporter asks me again. "So what's your opinion about it all?"

"I guess I feel that there's a racist way to be worried about the economy, or people dying at sea, and there's a nonracist way," I start, looking the camera squarely in the lens. I feel myself gaining momentum, as though with each word that I utter I'm throwing off a rock in a backpack that's been weighing me down. "We've signed up to international laws."

I can hear Jeremy and Margaret draw in sharp breaths and whisper my name under their breaths, trying to stop me. Dad's looking at me, his eyebrows knitted in confusion, but I feel an unassailable urge to keep going.

"Legally, we have to help these people. Instead, we lock them up. We abuse them. Then we bring in laws so that we can jail people who report the abuse. I don't get how we can let that happen in a democracy."

"So then you *don't* support your father's organization?"

Dad's eyes plead with me.

"Sorry, Dad," I say. "But Aussie Values is all about being angry, defensive, and paranoid. You said that bad things happen when good people remain silent. So I'm speaking up. I'm against your organization and everything it stands for."

# MINA

Irfan is pacing up and down in front of the counter, running his fingers through his hair, muttering under his breath. Baba's sitting in the ridiculous velvet-cushioned throne, nervously jiggling his leg up and down, smoking in urgent, short drags.

"Mina, we don't have to talk to that reporter, do we?" Mum asks, gently placing her hand on Baba's arm.

"Of course not! They can all wait outside as long as they like. They'll give up eventually."

"I can't live with myself if they're sent back," Baba says, so quietly I almost don't hear him.

"The lawyer will help, Farshad," Mum says brightly. Even I can tell she's trying to put on a brave face.

I walk over to Irfan. "What happened? Is it true? Did they take them to Villawood?"

He nods slowly.

"Who came?"

"Immigration officers. I'll never forget the look on their

faces, Mina." The words catch in his throat. "We're in trouble too," he adds eventually. "Your dad called a lawyer. Hopefully she can fix this mess."

---

I sneak a peek out the window from behind the blinds. To my surprise, Michael's on camera, talking to the reporter. I see his dad too, but he looks devastated as he watches Michael. I don't know what to make of it all.

We're supposed to open in an hour. There are too many reservations to contemplate canceling, so Baba, Irfan, and Mum head back to the kitchen to start preparing. I call in some extra help from our list of part-timers and then start setting tables.

I feel numb. I can't see how Michael and I can pretend as though we exist in a bubble, when every moment we're together his family threatens to burst it.

But the thought of saying good-bye to him hurts so badly that I want to vomit.

I keep checking what's happening outside. Eventually, the sidewalk is clear and they appear to have all left.

I grab my phone from off the charger and switch it on to call Michael. I see that I've missed his calls and texts. I go to a corner of the restaurant where I'm out of hearing and call him.

"Where have you been?" he asks in a panic. "I'm so sorry. Some members went behind Dad's back. Are you all okay?"

"Yeah, we're okay." But then I start to cry silently. I collapse into a chair and try to stop the tears. "They took away Adnan, Mustafa, and Mariam. I thought you said your dad was going to take care of it?"

"I thought so too," he says quietly.

---

We go to bed early. I expect a restless night but I'm out before I know it and wake up in the exact same spot I fell asleep in.

I'm lying awake in bed, trying to buy some time before I have to get ready for school, when Baba receives a telephone call: Tim, from the pizza shop next door.

The next few minutes are chaos. Mum rushes to the bedroom to quickly get dressed, Baba's looking for his keys as he argues with me, insisting that I will not miss school, while I insist that I will. He decides there's no time to draw the fight out and orders me to bring my schoolbag along just in case. He's so distracted that he doesn't realize that I'm wearing jeans. I don't even bother bringing my bag. Mum's ready and the three of us race outside, into the car, and speed off to the restaurant.

---

Visually, the graffiti is quite impressive.

*Fuck Off We're Full* on the front door. *Halal Funds ISIS* on the window. Well, the window that isn't smashed through with a brick.

"Don't you love how they've made halal a noun?" I say dryly to Mum as we survey the damage. "It's like halal's a person. Some bearded, hairy monster in a cave somewhere, counting the money he's making from the labels on Vegemite."

———————

Irfan is on the phone with the insurance company, while Baba and Mum take photos of the tables close to the windows that have been showered with shattered glass. I finish taking photos of the graffiti on the front windows and then go back inside.

We sit down, unsure if we're supposed to clean up or wait for instructions from the insurer. Baba gets up to make some tea as we wait for Irfan to end the call.

Mum's phone rings. She rummages in her bag and takes it out.

"It's Emily," she says. "I'll call her—"

I grab it from Mum's hand, answer the call, and dangle it back in front of her. If looks could kill.

"Hi, Emily. Yes, I am fine. I am good. Yes, we had to come here to the restaurant this morning for something important. No, everything is fine, thank you."

She goes on like that for another minute. When she hangs up, I shake my head at her.

"You could have told her, Mum."

"Why? So she can see that we are nothing but problems? We are on the TV and speaking to police and sitting here in our own restaurant surrounded by broken glass . . ." She takes a deep breath, tries to compose herself. "She has enough to deal with anyway."

She scratches at her stomach and tries to get comfortable.

"Look, don't worry about all of this." She smiles at me, bright and big and reassuring, and it pulls at my heart, the way she's trying for my sake, because my mum doesn't do big smiles, not unless something's wrong. She's always left her big smiles for moments when she thinks I need to be protected.

I want to tell her that I'm grown up now. I'm not that little girl on the boat who can be distracted with a story, or song, or forced big smile.

Baba returns with tea and we clasp the small glasses like they contain the solution to all our problems. We sit in silence until Baba's raspy voice interrupts our thoughts.

"I love this country," he says. "But I don't feel it's mine because I must tell people I love it. That's a fact." He shakes his head angrily. Mum is sitting, not saying a word.

"We refugees are different from immigrants, Mina. The immigrant's heart is caught between the struggle of wanting to stay or return, return or stay. The uncertainty never stops. Every decision is shadowed by what they are missing out on back home. And when they return to their birthplace, they want to come back here. And when they come back here, they wonder if they should have stayed. But us? We have been robbed of those choices. I cannot return to my home-land. And so I must simply stay in somebody else's homeland, as an outsider and a guest. I am the guest who brings a gift of food to their host. Except what I think more and more is that they do not eat the food, they eat *us* here."

I peer into his face, frowning. "What do you mean?"

"When they don't like the taste of us, when we have too much flavor and spice, and do not follow their recipe, we are like indigestion, and they want to vomit us back to where we came from."

"Even if you're right, Farshad," Mum suddenly speaks up, "don't you dare lose hope. Don't you dare hand your power over to these people." She takes his hand, places it on her stomach, and looks him straight in the eye. "Not just because you let them win, but because despair is a luxury people like us cannot afford."

———

I grab Mum's phone when she's in the bathroom. I take down Emily's and Rojin's numbers and then send them a text from my phone, letting them know what's happened but reassuring them that everything is okay.

Irfan emerges and tells us we can start cleaning. Baba insists that Mum remain seated, but she waves him off, grabs the broom, and starts sweeping with such urgent, fierce strokes that we don't dare argue with her. Baba shifts his attention to me and tells me I should go to school, but then he sees the look on my face and doesn't bother continuing.

"Let's hope it's a boy," he mutters to no one in particular, and Mum and I lock eyes and share a brief smile.

"Shocking," I hear coming from a voice near the front door.

We all look up. It's Tim, from the pizza shop.

"Too bad there are no cameras," he says, shaking his head as he surveys the mess.

"Yeah. Too bad," I say quietly.

"The writing outside looks very bad for us," Baba tells him. "Very bad for business."

Tim smiles and holds up a bag. "There's a trick to removing it," he says. "I've brought over the magic tools. If we start now, we should have it done in no time."

# MICHAEL

Dad hasn't spoken a word to me since the interview. I tried to say something in the car on the way home but he asked me to leave it for now. His words didn't cut me. It was the politeness, the civility of his tone that hurt, that told me this was as bad as things had ever been between us. It was just after six, and Nathan and Mum were sitting at the dining table doing a five-hundred-piece puzzle of a fighter jet.

Dad muttered hello to Mum and went straight to the study. He closed the door behind him. Mum stood up and anxiously asked me what had happened. I didn't know where to start. I shook my head and went upstairs. I heard Mum knocking on the study door and Dad telling her he needed some time alone.

I tossed and turned all night. I heard the study door open and footsteps up the stairs. The floorboards outside our bedrooms creaked as Dad walked to his bedroom.

I checked the time. It was three in the morning.

Mina's not at school. I call her and leave messages. Paula does too. But there's no response. I stare at a selfie we took and my insides ache as I wonder if she's okay. I want so badly just to hold her.

I go to the café to get a coffee at lunchtime. Paula, Jane, and Sandra, a girl from twelfth grade, are on café duty. I stand in the queue, watching Paula and Jane try to cooperate as they take orders and make and serve the coffees. The tension between them is like a fourth person in the small space behind the counter, rubbing up close to them, bumping and nudging them whenever they're forced to communicate.

Paula's eyes widen when she sees me. "Did you hear? Mina sent me a text just before lunch. The restaurant was vandalized overnight. She's there cleaning up with her parents."

"No, I didn't hear." I badger her with questions. *Who vandalized it? How bad is the damage? What exactly did they do?*

But there's one question I don't ask her, and that's *Why didn't Mina contact me?*

"I said I'm going after school to help them with the cleaning," Paula says.

"Is that an invitation? Because I can't exactly show up there, can I?" I snap, immediately regretting it. "Sorry."

"No prob," she says brightly.

"What a freaking mess," I mutter.

The guy behind me tells me to hurry up. I order my coffee and wait at the side.

Jane's helping Sandra make the coffees. She's been listening to Paula and me but trying not to make it obvious.

I hear Paula make a correction on one of the orders and Jane says, "Got it. One sugar, not two. I'm coming with you to Mina's, by the way."

Paula stares at her for a moment. It's a stare to run away from. But Jane stands tall and holds her gaze. I can tell she wants to speak but I think just meeting Paula's eyes takes enough out of her for now.

And then Paula shrugs and says casually, "I'll pass by your locker before I leave."

———————————

I check my phone again. Still nothing from Mina.

———————————

The cars are parked in the garage but when I enter the house it's eerily quiet. I throw my bag at the bottom of the stairs, grab a drink from the fridge, and check my phone again. Finally! Mina's sent me a text.

> Sorry. Things are crazy here. Will call you when I get a chance.

I feel a pang as I read her text. There's nothing of her usual warmth. But then I feel stupid. It's not exactly the time for flirtatious messages!

I hear Mum call out to me from the family room. I walk over and she's sitting on the couch beside Dad. Nathan's been dispatched to a friend's house for a playdate. They say, "We need to talk," and it's like accidentally taking a sip of milk that's gone off: An instant feeling of nausea takes hold of me.

I stare blankly at them and then sit down.

"We can't understand why you would betray us," Dad begins. "*Publicly.*"

"Why you would disrespect us like that," Mum adds.

I don't say anything. The look on Dad's face tells me he has something to say. I just know he's been deliberating over every word, preparing his speech. I feel a moment's pity for him.

He clears his throat. "I dealt with my *profound* disappointment at you rejecting architecture, Michael," he says, slowly and calmly. "After all the years we talked about it and planned for it. But I put my feelings aside out of respect for your choices. Then there were your doubts and questions about Aussie Values, which I addressed with patience and understanding. I spoke to Andrew and told him to leave the restaurant story alone for your sake, even though those three workers deserve to face the consequences of breaking the law. I also tried to get the reporter to tone down the story, again for your sake. I did *all* of this for you." Dad's voice breaks at this point, but he pushes on. "You publicly repudiated me, Michael. Made me look like a fool."

His words just sit there, suspended above us. I focus my eyes on a mark in the carpet.

"We're really disappointed, Michael," Mum says.

I sigh, and Dad says, "Well? Don't we deserve a response?"

"Yeah." I sigh again. "You do. This isn't easy, okay? A part of me regrets going against you on TV." I pause, and choose my words carefully. I feel like a bottle brush is stuck in my throat, choking and prickling me. "But only because of how it's made you feel. I *hate* hurting you." I take a deep breath. "But another part of me doesn't regret it. And I'm sorry that hurts you, but it's the truth! You said this is all about something bigger than us. That it's not about the personal."

"You're twisting my words, Michael," Dad says. "I said that in a different context."

Indignation suddenly burns through me, like opening a hot oven and feeling the heat hit you in the face. "We're talking about people here, Dad! The personal's wrapped up with something bigger, for everybody, not just *you*! And it hurts, doesn't it?"

"You humiliated me on national television. What does it say about me and my organization if my own son doesn't support me?"

"I get that, okay. And I said I'm sorry. But instead of thinking about the humiliation, can't you stop to think about the effect of what you're saying and doing? Maybe think about *why* I don't support you?"

"Are we monsters, Michael?!" Mum says with a quivering breath.

"No! But that's the point, isn't it, Mum?" I ignore the pained expression on her face. "Do you know that the restaurant was vandalized overnight? They threw a brick through the window and graffitied the front windows. *Fuck Off We're Full.*"

Mum winces. "What are you talking about, Michael?"

"The restaurant was attacked last night. Who was it? Andrew? Somebody local, or was it *rent-a-racist*?"

Dad's face goes blank. He blinks at me, like he's in some kind of stupor. Nostrils flared slightly, he reaches into his pocket for his phone. He takes it out and dials a number.

"Andrew? What happened last night? Over at that Afghan restaurant?" He questions him, from this angle and that. When he ends the call, he exhales slowly, sinks his back into the couch, and looks up at the ceiling.

"Well?" Mum asks.

He sits up and hunches forward, resting his elbows on his thighs.

"He's denying it," he says, eyes fixed on the floor, "but he sounds a little too satisfied not to be involved somehow." Then he looks at me. "That's not what we stand for, Michael," he says, gently but firmly.

"Of course we don't," Mum hastily adds.

"Can't you see that you've given the people who threw the brick permission to hate?!"

"That's just not true, Michael!" Mum snaps.

"But it is true, Mum! *Fuck Off We're Full* has the same impact, whether it's spray-painted on a window, or hidden in polite language on your website."

"What are you saying, Michael?" Dad asks.

"Your organization is making racist hate speech against Muslims and asylum seekers normal."

"I reject that, Michael," Dad says, sitting upright and furiously shaking his head. "We have never encouraged hate speech, not to mention vandalism! We stand for constructive debate. And it's a bit more complicated than pulling out the race card. Muslims are not a race."

"Go and look at the Aussie Values Facebook page," I say. "Go and read the comments under the articles you post. *Bomb them to the crusades. Shoot the lot. Assimilate or go back to your caves.*"

"Those comments are unacceptable," Mum says.

"There are articles up on that page about Islam being an ideology like Nazism," I continue. "There's one that says that if you don't control Muslim numbers they'll take over and start raping and beheading people."

"I never posted those articles," Dad says tersely. "But I won't deny people their right to free speech."

I think about Mina and her family. "Free for people like us," I mutter. "Because people like *them* pay the price."

My parents don't reply. They stare at me, and a thick, oppressive silence settles between us. We sit like that for a while and then, quietly, deflated of all anger now, I say: "You know what hurts? You guys just think I woke up one day and decided to rebel against you out of some teenage protest . . ."

Mum puts her elbow on the armrest and cups her head in her hand as she hears me out. Dad is leaning forward, elbows on his thighs, hands clasped together. He looks worn out. His eyes are closed, but I know he's listening too.

"I want you to know that's not what happened. I've tried really hard to see your point of view. I've struggled to reject the things you believe in. But I've done my own research because in case you've forgotten, it's the two of you who taught me never to accept things at face value."

Mum nods once, but doesn't respond. Dad opens his eyes, but also remains silent.

"Where do we go from here?" I ask, because sometimes trying to change somebody means having to break them first, and I don't want to be the one to do that to them, no matter how much it hurts to know that the way I'll navigate my life will forever set me on a different path from them.

The mood is somber, the room enveloped in shadows as the sun starts to set. Mum, as if reading my mind, gets up to turn on the light.

"We'll just have to find a way," Dad eventually says, resigned, sad even, but at least not angry enough not to want to try.

# MINA

"Mina, your friends are here!" Mum calls out to me.

"Who?" I call back, walking out of the kitchen carrying a pile of menus and napkins.

Paula and Jane are standing at the door in their school uniforms. I put the menus and napkins on the table next to me and run over to them. We hug each other tightly. Then we step back and I give them a questioning look.

Jane self-consciously tucks a strand of hair behind her ear and starts to stammer. "I came because I wanted to say—"

Paula stops her. "It's in the past. Forgiven."

A smile spreads slowly up to Jane's eyes.

They both take in the scene around us: the damaged furniture Baba and Irfan have stowed in a corner for the insurer to examine. Piles of trash spilling out of bags and waiting to be disposed of.

"What can we do?" Paula asks.

"The cleaning's all done. But can you keep me company while I sort the cutlery?"

"No," Jane says. "We'll keep you company while we *help* you sort the cutlery."

I grin at her.

---

I glance at the clock. It's almost five. A sudden feeling of fatigue courses through my body.

"How's Michael?" Paula asks as I walk her to the door. Jane is ahead of us, on the phone to her mum.

"I haven't had a chance to talk to him," I say. "I'm confused."

"Confused about what?"

"Not about my feelings for him . . ." I feel scared to say what's been running through my head all day.

"Then what?"

I motion around me. "*This* is because of Michael's family, Paula." I shake my head. "I just can't see how things can work between us. They're not going to stop. And we'll be caught in the middle."

Paula smiles. "Maybe. But sometimes you have to get in the trenches. Some people are worth the risk."

"Wilde?"

"No. Me."

We laugh.

I close the door behind me and sink into the throne, my legs aching. I close my eyes. Before I can stop myself, I fall asleep.

I wake up to the sensation of Mum gently shaking me by the shoulder.

"We've decided to close for tonight," she says, pulling me up. "Come on, let's go home."

The last of the daylight slowly fades away as we drive home. I send Michael a text.

> I miss you.

I smile to myself when he replies within seconds.

> I miss you too.

I lean my head against the glass as I type another text.

> Are we worth all of this? The fight ahead?

His reply is instant.

> Yes, Mina. Absolutely.

Baba pulls into our parking spot and Emily sends me a text message, letting me know she's made us dinner. She's been checking for us from her window. She doesn't want to impose and knows Mum needs her rest now that she's closer to her due date. She asks me to pick the food up from her apartment.

I show Mum the text, which means explaining my earlier text. Mum's furious with me, but I don't give her a chance. I snap at her—something corny about friendships and honesty—and storm off to collect the food.

The three of us collapse onto the couch and tuck into Emily's chicken noodles and fried pastries. Mum finishes eating, goes to her room, and closes the door. I sneak up and listen at the door. She's talking to Emily. When it sounds like the conversation's drawing to a close, I run back to the couch and jump next to Baba.

Mum emerges, her eyes brighter, a lightness in her step. She shakes her head at me, giving me a half smile that tells me she might forgive me.

Baba turns on the TV, muttering under his breath as he flicks through the channels.

"What's wrong, Baba?"

"Irfan saw the ad. It's on *News Tonight*. Now."

I sit up straight and alert. He flicks the channel again and there's the reporter, introducing the story, under the caption *Refugee Scammers*.

I'm expecting the worst. Instead, there's Michael's father and two Aussie Values members watching with horror as Michael denounces Aussie Values on national television.

I'm overwhelmed with emotion but don't want my parents to see. I jump up, mutter something about needing fresh air, and go outside, onto the veranda. I lean against the rail and look up at the inky sky. I can hear the hooting of an owl in the distance. Hot tears fall down my cheeks, but I welcome them.

There's a lot of ugliness under this sky. But there's plenty of beauty here too. I want to find it, spread it around, all over the cruelty and injustice. I want to shake this world like a can of soda, pop the lid, and watch the bubbles explode. Join a revolution to do nothing less than change the world. I want to get angry and be passionate. But the best part is that I have Michael beside me, and it looks like he wants to do the same thing.

# MICHAEL

Dad is fielding call after concerned call following the *News Tonight* program. I'm doing my homework at the dinner table and can hear him in the next room. *"It doesn't change anything. Well, that's his right . . . Yes, it could just be some kind of adolescent rebellion. I hope people will make up their own minds."*

Mum is sitting at the kitchen bench, dunking a cookie into her cup of coffee as she completes a field-trip form for Nathan. I can tell she's listening to Dad too, and she throws the occasional glance my way.

"Is there a girl, Michael?" she asks out of the blue. She clears her throat, speaks gently. "Is that why you've suddenly changed?"

I groan softly. "If you're asking because you think I said those things to impress a girl, then the answer is no."

She taps her fingers faintly on the bench. "But there's a girl?"

I sigh. "Yes, there's a girl. But not how you think."

She treads carefully. "Well, tell me about her," she says cautiously. "She's obviously changed you."

"Actually, no, she didn't, Mum," I say. "As corny as this will sound, she made me realize I didn't need to change, I just needed to figure out what I stand for."

She purses her lips and murmurs something to herself.

Dad emerges then, his face solemn and weary. He turns on the kettle and stands in front of it, staring at the countertop as the water boils.

"Are they calling for my head?" I ask Dad in a droll tone.

He raises his eyebrows. "Don't flatter yourself. We can survive without you."

I stare at him, slightly shocked. But then I see the beginnings of a faint smile on his face and I can't help but let out a laugh.

"Glad you can both see the humor in this," Mum says.

"We're not the first family to divide on politics," Dad says matter-of-factly. "It shouldn't split us apart."

"Well, obviously I won't let *that* happen," Mum says tersely. "We wouldn't be much of a family otherwise, would we?"

# MINA

It's almost ten at night when I remember. Guilt stabs me and I reach for my phone and call her.

"Paula! K4! What happened? I'm *so* sorry for not asking."

It doesn't surprise me that she's quick to forgive me. "Oh, come on, I totally understand. Nothing's happened yet anyway. Surgery's actually tomorrow."

―――――――――

"Mina! Wake up! It's time!"

I open one eye, half asleep as I peer at Baba in confusion. His eyes are wild. He's trying to tuck his shirt into his pants, smooth down his hair, and put his shoes on all at the same time.

"Keep your phone charged and close to you! I'll call you."

I hear a sound coming from inside. A loud moan.

"Is she okay?"

"No!" He half laughs, half chokes. "Oh my God, Mina, it's happening! Get dressed, quick!"

Mum moans again, only louder this time.

---

We arrive at the hospital, and Baba and I help walk Mum inside. She's quickly taken to the delivery ward and I'm left alone in the waiting room.

It's just past eight in the morning and I lean back against the wall, close my eyes, and try to block out the infomercial break in the morning breakfast program.

A midwife comes past an hour later and tells me Mum's making good progress. I go downstairs to grab a coffee and a muffin. I text Mum's friends to let them know. Rojin calls me on the spot, asking if Mum would mind if she visited her in the hospital, and if I could let her know as soon as the baby is born so she can bring a gift.

By midday I've read every pregnancy-related magazine in the waiting room and consider myself an expert in all things prenatal. I text Paula to check up on K4 and she calls me instantly, laughing and crying as she tells me that the lump was detected and removed before it had the chance to spread.

"Oh, Mina, I'm so excited! And guess what? Just guess? Go on, try! You won't guess. But try! Okay, fine, I'll just tell you. Dad's applied for long service leave! And Mum spoke to Nancy and guess what? Nancy's going to cancel her Europe trip at the end of the year and come here instead! FOR A MONTH."

We go a bit silly over the phone. She invites me to her place for celebratory cake, and I tell her I'd love to but I have a prior engagement otherwise known as *I'm going to be a sister again*!

It's all-round squealing.

---

Three hours later and Baba emerges, his face wet with tears.

"It's a boy!"

I scream out with joy and he hugs me so strongly I feel as though my ribs might pop.

"How's Mum?" I ask anxiously.

"Exhausted! But she's okay. Come on, she's in a room now. He's beautiful, Mina. Looks like a hairy monkey. A perfect hairy monkey."

Mum's lying back in the hospital bed, pale, eyes droopy with exhaustion, but smiling. I kiss her and she points to the bassinet beside her. I approach cautiously. Inside is a tiny thing with a shock of black hair. He's fast asleep, mouth pouted and eyes shut tight. I love him already.

"What did you name him?"

"Nabil."

I pick him up and sit down on one of the visitors' chairs. Nabil is sound asleep. I stare into his perfect tiny face.

"Hello, Nabil," I whisper.

I study his face. I don't want to break my gaze for a moment. He's cast a spell over me. I raise him up closer to hear him breathing. The sound of a baby's breath seems like a miracle to me. The more I stare at my baby brother the more I am reminded of Hasan's face. These eyes are almond; Hasan's eyes were more rounded. These eyelashes are long and straight; Hasan's curled. This nose is small with nostrils that flare slightly, like Hasan's. These lips are thick on the bottom, thinner at the top; Hasan's were thick and pouted. This baby's skin is the color of honey. Hasan's skin was pale.

My chest is fit to burst. I feel complete again. For Nabil has returned my brother to me.

# MICHAEL

Mina and I arrive at school early, when it's easier to meet in private, in a secluded section of the oval. I see her approaching me and feel like she's hooked a lasso around my heart. She plants herself in front of me and grins.

"Come here, you," I say, and open my arms. She throws herself against me and I wrap my arms around her.

Dropping my hands around her waist, I lean back slightly and she tilts her chin up to meet my eyes.

"So you're a big sister again, hey?"

She smiles. "He's beautiful."

She touches my right cheek with the palm of her hand. "I saw you on TV. Michael, you were incredible. That took guts. But how are you coping at home? It's not fair on you."

"They're devastated and upset, but making an effort." I laugh faintly. "I'm trying to get them to appreciate the funny side of the situation. You know, get them to see that things could be far worse. I could have come out and told them I was converting. Or dating a Muslim. That's for another day."

Mina smiles.

"That put things in perspective for them," I say brightly. "So, anyway, enough about them. Did you miss me?"

She looks at me coyly. "A little."

"Well then, prove it."

And I bend down and kiss her.

# MINA

"The poetry slam is on at school tomorrow," Paula tells me during last period.

"Nice."

"Come watch?"

"Yeah, of course."

Butterflies erupt in my stomach. Because there's a poem in my head. It moved in weeks ago, just like that, unannounced, big and bold, daring me to evict it. It's been playing on repeat, settling in and getting comfy, like when you try to make your own dent in a new couch. It's there, like a challenge. And no matter what I do I can't sweep it away, or drown out the voice inside that keeps reciting it.

---

Baba calls me during recess, talking so fast I can barely make out what he's saying. I tell him to slow down and he laughs.

"Mina, Mina, Mina!" he says in a singsong voice. "The

lawyer says Adnan, Mustafa, and Mariam will be released on Saturday! Thank God their visas weren't canceled!"

I race through the school grounds in search of Michael. He's at the basketball courts. I wave at him and he jogs over. My heart is pounding wildly and I'm grinning like a maniac. I tell him the news and he picks me up and spins me around.

---

It's lunchtime. The poetry slam is being held in the school hall. Several people have performed so far and the audience is really getting into it, clapping and snapping their fingers at their favorite lines. Paula's arranged for one of the slam artists from Bankstown to visit. Sara performs a piece that manages to cover her first love, body image, and working out. From the moment she speaks, she sucks us all in. She's fast-paced, angry, funny, tender, and totally uncensored. When she drops the F-word the audience cheers. I can see the teachers nervously looking at each other, but one of them shrugs as if to say *let it go*.

I'm sitting in the front row, alongside Michael, Cameron, Leica, and Jane. My stomach is churning. Poor Brian's got an impossible act to follow. Not to mention he's slamming about his cat.

Terrence and Fred start to make meowing sounds.

Brian finishes and Paula calls my name. The others look at me, eyes widening as I slowly stand up.

"You're going up there?" Michael asks in shock.

"Are you nuts?" Jane says helpfully.

I laugh. "Yep. Talk me out of it, please."

"No chance," Michael says, grinning.

I don't realize how large the hall is until I'm standing up on stage in front of endless rows. People are chatting among themselves, laughing and mucking around. Paula introduces me and the teachers start their shushing and pacing, flashing menacing looks at the ones slower to realize I'm ready to start.

I look out at the audience and an unexpected wave of confidence rushes through me. I have something to say and it matters. I'm not embarrassed and I don't care what people will say about me.

I recite a little prayer to myself, take a deep breath, clasp my fingers tightly around the microphone, and begin.

*I've come from the place of go back to where you came from*

*From unmarked graves and stinking camps*

*From seas that wanted to swallow me*

*And prisons that wanted to disappear me*

*From places other people will travel to*

With travel blogs, and itineraries highlighted in
fluorescent Sharpies,

and Instagram accounts that show how they
"found themselves"

In places some people are allowed to visit

While others are never allowed to leave.

The exotic are a short drive up the road

Zip codes vending an experience of elsewhere

But without the frequent flyer points and itinerary

They are just ghettos.

When you feel like a dandelion

Just a wish from being blown away

When you feel like a spice

Just a sprinkle of flavor to your taste

When you feel like a souvenir

In a bazaar of identity that peddles fear

You feel

That you must carve yourself out of resistance

But then some people showed me:

That anger is good

But with action it is better.

That remembering is good

But with hope it is better.

That change is good

But with discovery it is better.

That questioning is good

But with trust it is better.

*That resisting is good*

*But sometimes those you resist do not matter.*

*And that standing up is good*

*But standing up alongside others is better.*

Thunderous applause, like a storm has erupted, the sound of rain crashing down onto the top of a tin roof. It washes over me like a midday rainstorm. It's pure and beautiful and I've never felt so alive.

I search the audience for Paula and Michael. They're grinning, clapping wildly.

Michael's eyes meet mine.

He thinks he's learned from me. He's wrong. It's me who's learned from him.

He's taught me to never give up on anybody.

# ACKNOWLEDGMENTS

Thank you, Mobinah Ahmed, Asme and May Fahmi, Annarose Zayied, and Sara Saleh for Facebook-status-inspired hilarities, geekiness, and anecdotes. Like the Eye of Sauron, I am watching (and yes, sometimes using) you all. And I think you love it.

Thank you to the Bankstown Poetry Slam for inspiring parts of Paula and Mina's journey.

Thank you to Mariam Veiszadeh for clarifying Afghan words and customs for me. Any errors are my own.

Thank you to Zeinab and Sumaia El-Kadomi for the music. What a difference it made.

Thank you to Peter Gould for advice on general tech and gaming geekiness and for almost getting me hooked on AR blogs.

I am so incredibly lucky and honored to be publishing this book with Scholastic US. Thank you, Lisa Sandell, for believing in my work after all these years.

Last but not least, thank you to my family for your constant support and encouragement, without which nothing would be possible.

# ABOUT THE AUTHOR

Randa Abdel-Fattah is an award-winning author, former attorney, and an expert on Islamophobia in Australia. She is the author of the critically acclaimed novels *Does My Head Look Big In This?* and *Ten Things I Hate About Me*, as well as the middle-grade novel *Where the Streets Had a Name*. Ms. Abdel-Fattah lives in Sydney, Australia, with her husband and their children.

Discover these remarkable novels from critically acclaimed author

# Randa Abdel-Fattah!

SCHOLASTIC
scholastic.com

SCHOLASTIC and associated logos are trademarks and/or registered trademarks of Scholastic Inc.

ABDEL-FATTAH